# SOLAR WINDS

## CROSSROADS
### APPENDICES

BRYAN G. SHEWMAKER

Printed in the United States of America
Editing and typesetting by Kingsman Editing Services
Cover art design by Antelmo Aguirre

ISBN: 978-0-9989606-4-7

# CONTENTS

# APPENDIX 5
# HISTORY OF THE INTERSTELLAR COMBINE

## PREFACE

WHEN COMPARED TO THE Solar Empire, the Interstellar Combine was a far younger civilization. It was also perhaps one of the few great civilizations that had less knowledge of its origins than did humanity. The Combine may not have as much history as the Empire, but it remains a civilization that was many thousands of years old. To detail all major events would be an arduous task requiring many volumes. The history presented here was the most accurate depiction that can be given, but it remains a simple summary. Only those events which had had a major influence on the culture of the Vaar, or that were particularly relevant in the modern day were included here.

The majority of Vaar were unaware that their species was engineered, and believe that it evolved naturally on Prithone. The fact that evidence of evolutionary precursors was incredibly scant does little to change this belief. For Vaar have iron bones, prone to rust and other chemical reactions that will rapidly degrade it after death. The jungle environs that dominate most of Prithone's surface further were less conducive to helping preserve historic artifacts over millennia.

The Combine government went to *far* greater lengths than the Solar Empire to control its historical narrative. Within the Combine, it was illegal to teach any course on history in an academic setting if that course has not met state approval. This approval was based almost entirely on politics with concerns such as academic accuracy rarely cracking the top ten list of priorities. He who controls the historical narrative controls the present, and he who controls the present shapes the future. The Combine state would not allow any challenge to its priorities on this issue.

Though one can say what they will about the Combine, and the Vaar, it cannot be said that the Vaar did not have a long and distinguished history. As a species they successfully colonized numerous star systems before ever developing faster-than-light travel. As a species they have visited more galaxies than any other sapient race known to exist, humanity included. Part of this was a simple matter of proximity. The Deep Sea was located deep in what humans would call the Virgo Cluster and was home to far more galaxies than the Local Group from which humanity hailed. But it was an insult to the Vaar not to acknowledge that the spirit of exploration resided within them and that it played a large role in motivating their travels.

The Combine expanded at an irregular pace. Upon colonizing the Vortex Sea, the Vaar were forced to rein in their lust for expansion at any cost. This led the nation to focus more heavily on developing the galaxies it had to the best extent while moving outward in a careful and organized fashion, though on occasion the Vaar briefly picked up the pace. Despite their lust for expansion, the Vaar expanded at a fraction of the pace they could have. There were two simple reasons for this. The first was a fear of overextending and having territory taken from them by another great power because they could not adequately defend it. The second and more important reason was control. Vaar governments have often been deathly afraid of investing great effort in colonizing a region, only to then have that region break away from them.

The Combine exerts total control over five galaxies but maintains outposts in over a thousand more. One should be careful not to allow this number to lead them to overestimate the Vaar or the Combine. The Deep Sea, Proximity Sea, Vortex Sea, Disorder Sea, and Ink Sea together accounted for over 95 percent of the Combine's population. They still had a presence in other galaxies. These were seed galaxies, with claims preemptively staked for the day the Vaar intend to invest more in them, be that day in a year, or in ten thousand years. The Vaar meanwhile had an easier time reaching many galaxies when compared to the Empire. The more galaxies that were concentrated in one place, the easier it was to hop from one to the next on a transpatial drive. And there were a lot of galaxies in the Virgo Cluster.

The calendar and dating system used by the Solar Empire was based on the year, day, and hour measurements that originated on Earth. The Combine used a date system based on the metrics of Prithone. A Prithone year was made up of four hundred, twenty-six-hour days. The Prithone equivalent of an hour was close enough to an Earth hour to disregard the negligible difference. These entries utilize the Prithone calendar with the Solar years referenced for convenience. The Vaar utilize the Post-Ascension (PA) metric system to delineate the current calendar from those in the Dawn Era.

# 5A

# THE DAWN ERA

VAAR LANGUAGES WERE FOND of repurposing and modifying words than creating new ones. In most modern Vaar dialects, the word for space and the universe itself was La'kona. Though this word's roots come from a now-dead language, it translated simply as *empty ocean*. The name for the Vaar's home galaxy was La'fona—the Deep Sea—a name given to this lenticular galaxy for its thick galactic disc.

The idea of space as an ocean was an ancient and enduring concept in the Vaar language. Prior to the invention of sophisticated astronomy, early Vaar cosmologists believed that the universe was a great ocean. Prithone's atmosphere was thought to be a bubble in that ocean, and the land a particle trapped in that bubble. The name *Prithone* does not translate as easily but roughly equates to "*the bubble*." As one might expect, the word can be used in many other ways beyond naming the home world.

Similar to the Solar Empire, the Vaar do not have a great deal of understanding regarding their civilization before space travel. In this case, the blame for this lack of knowledge lies solely with the Vaar. Two factors were primarily responsible for the species' lack of history. The first was that the ancient Vaar were extremely poor record-keepers. The second, and more salient reason, was the barbaric method by which the ancient Vaar waged war.

Anagram first placed the Vaar on Prithone sometime before the formation of the Solar Empire. As a civilization, the Vaar began as many do, a tribal species. Prithone's surface in those days was dominated by great jungles save for vast deserts that stretched to the polar regions. The ancient Vaar lived as wandering hunters in these jungles, where they faced a difficult existence.

It was commonly accepted among the Vaar that the far smaller size of the Viss was an evolutionary adaptation. That it allowed females and children to ride on the backs of the males for protection. This conclusion was false. The Viss were deliberately made smaller and with a more simplified anatomy for caloric reasons. With a significantly smaller and simpler body—including fewer digits, as well as a lack of plates—the average Viss requires *far* fewer calories to survive than an adult Vaar. This enabled a Viss to survive, carry, and birth healthy offspring even when food was scarce. That said, the conclusion of the Vaar scientists was not completely without merit. In their tribal days, Viss and children alike spent much of their time riding on the backs of the males, for the jungles of Prithone were full of dangerous predators.

An adult Vaar had little to fear in Prithone's jungles. His body was covered in a carapace of plates that neither fang nor claw could pierce. He was large and powerful with iron bones that did not easily break. An adult Vaar was Prithone's apex predator as soon as the species was introduced to the planet. Viss and children by contrast were constantly vulnerable. For any Viss or child to wander too far from the nearest Vaar was often a fatal mistake.

The worst of Prithone's dangers were the enspa. Enspa were ravenous, multitudinous, and possessed of shockingly little in the way of self-preservation. Enspa reproduced asexually and were born pregnant. They would consume anything that was made of meat, including each other if food was scarce. Even Prithone's largest predators, much larger than any of the carnivorous dinosaurs that ever strode Earth's surface, would often fall prey. Enspa would swarm them, and those that died in the process simply meant more meat for the rest. A common and ancient symbol of masculinity among the Vaar was a pinwheel surrounding a solid circle. It was believed that this symbol stems from the ancient tactics used by the Vaar against the enspa. The pinwheel and its spokes represent Vaar and their spears. The circle represents the Viss and children sheltering within their perimeter.

The Vaar eventually abandoned their tribal ways, with the adoption of agriculture. However as the Vaar were obligate carnivores, this agriculture existed purely to raise livestock. Conflicts over livestock and land suitable to it were more common reasons for war among the pre-stellar Vaar. It takes a great deal of meat to support a predator the size of a Vaar, and a great deal of land to graze sufficient cattle to feed a population.

When ancient Vaar went to war, they did so with a practice known as du'bon. Du'bon was largely responsible for the lack of recorded history in the Dawn Era. The word *du'bon* translated to *erasure*. When one power fell to another, it was not conquered, it was destroyed. Under the practice of du'bon, *all* males of the enemy population were to be killed, irrespective of age or fitness. All females were to be impregnated by the conquerors. Those who could not be, due to age or infirmity, would join the males in death. All cultural artifacts were to be destroyed, including historical records, buildings, artwork, and more. Thus the children of the conquered females would have no culture to embrace but that of the conquerors. If the conqueror did not have the resources to support the conquered females and their war-children, then they, too, were killed. Often they were fed to enspa, whom by this point the Vaar had domesticated to help protect their livestock. In most cases the only cultural artifacts to survive du'bon were those taken as plunder by high-ranking commanders. These were often destroyed when today's conquerors became tomorrow's conquered. Du'bon would remain the rule of war well into the technological age.

The end of the Dawn Era came with the Six Nations War. This conflict was Prithone's closest equivalent to Earth's world wars. The conflict was waged between four nations in the North, known simply as the Northern

Alliance, and two in the southern hemisphere known as the Southern Coalition. This war was a food war, as the conflict began with disputes over fishing and grazing territory. The war was fought on land and sea, with the former being primarily a trench war. This would eventually devolve into twelve years of stalemate, broken only with the entry of Aka'lona.

Aka'lona—roughly, *Prosperity on the Sea*—can be compared in some ways to the United States of America in Earth's world wars. Aka'lona was located in the West, geographically separated from the front lines. It was a wealthy nation, and one of the most heavily industrialized on the planet. Thanks to its isolation and years of neutrality, it had been spared the attrition visited upon the other combatants. Thanks to time and its enormous industry, Aka'lona was able to enter the conflict with the best-equipped army on Prithone. Once Aka'lona joined the Northern Alliance, victory was only a matter of time.

Into modernity the Vaar use the term Aki'doma (*Aklonese bargain*) to describe an alliance made with an untrustworthy partner. No sooner had Aka'lona led its allies to victory than it turned on, and conquered, its depleted allies. The Northern Alliance and the Southern Coalition both were subjected to Aka'lona's du'bon. Aka'lona would however make changes to the rules of du'bon. By this point the Vaar had come to recognize the importance of preserving scientific knowledge. Thus scientists and their works were spared, so long as the conquerors could make use of them.

After the war, Aka'lona found itself in control of nearly half of Prithone's land mass. It was now in possession of unprecedented wealth and scientific knowledge. This began the Aki'tassa, or *Aklonese* Era. Once the Aki'tassa began, any other nation that existed on Prithone existed because Aka'lona allowed it.

Aka'lona would be the first nation to send a Vaar out of the atmosphere to Prithone's rings. Uga'doss remained in surviving records as the first Vaar astronaut, and the first to reach its rings. Much like Earth's space race, this venture was as much about military advantage as scientific progress. Aka'lona had every intention of weaponizing Prithone's rings. Over the following years, Aka'lona would send numerous missions to Prithone's rings, each of them mounting radio receivers and rocket motors to rocks in the ring. When the next war came, Aka'lona would rain death down on their enemies from orbit.

# 5B
# THE RETURN TO ZERO

AKA'LONA WOULD REMAIN THE dominant power on Prithone for over seven hundred years. But like so many other civilizations, Aka'lona would eventually fall into decline. The nation became a naked plutocracy where the rich and poor lived very different lives. The vast legions of the impoverished were in a state of constant agitation, kept from open riot or revolution only by military force and a diligent police state that served the wealthy elite.

The nation's once immensely powerful military and its global reach would decay as the years wore on. The nation's government came to rely almost entirely on its orbital array to handle foreign threats.

The rest of Prithone had not sat idle in the years following the Six Nations War. A coalition of nations on the eastern continent had gradually risen in power and capability. Together they formed the Eastern Coalition, who became not only ideological foes of Aka'lona, but a threat to their world hegemony. The seventeen nations of the Eastern Coalition were united by ideologies built on worker's rights, equality between Vaar and Viss, and centralized control of industry to meet the needs of the citizens.

For its first fifty years of existence, the Eastern Coalition never opposed Aka'lona directly. None of these nations had any counter to Aka'lona's orbital array. Aka'lona had claimed sole dominion over Prithone's orbit and promised to rain fire on any nation that disputed this claim. Thus the Eastern Coalition focused on fighting an ideological war with Aka'lona, spreading its politics to those regions under that nation's control. All the while, they worked on their own super weapon, one that would give them something to rival Aka'lona's orbital array. The atomic bomb.

The Eastern Coalition successfully detonated its first atomic weapon in a rocky valley hidden from observers. Though the weapon worked, the alliance did not immediately announce the development. The entire project had taken place under extreme secrecy. Even the testing site was chosen because it was prone to quakes. If seismic sensors used by Aklonese scientists detected the explosion, it was written off as a minor quake. If Aka'lona knew the weapon was being developed, they would almost certainly attack first before any quantity could be made. The Eastern Coalition created underground factories. The development of rockets that could carry the weapons would surely provoke Aka'lona. So focus was placed on building thousands of nuclear bombs, and bombers to carry them. The doomsday clock was ticking.

The more atomic bombs the Eastern Coalition built, the more confident its leaders became in opposing Aka'lona. Unfortunately, it seemed lost on the Coalition's leadership that a deterrent was not particularly effective when the other side didn't know it existed. Aklonese scientists had conceptualized the atomic bomb, but no effort had been made to develop it as that nation's leadership felt there was no need given the orbital array. Thus while Aka'lona caught on that the Eastern Coalition was vastly expanding its military, it was not seen as a legitimate threat. Aka'lona never realized until too late that the Eastern Coalition had not only developed atomic weapons, but was mass-producing them.

The doomsday clock struck midnight as most Vaar were ringing in the new year. Exactly what provoked Aka'lona and the Eastern Coalition to battle has been lost to history, as has the knowledge of who attacked first. Neither Aka'lona nor the Eastern Coalition survived. While the people were celebrating, rocks were falling from space, and intercontinental bombers were setting up their attack runs. In a single day Prithone was ruined. Of the 250 most populated cities on Prithone, none were spared. Hundreds of millions died either to orbital bombardment or nuclear fire.

The destruction flooded Prithone's upper atmosphere with soot and dust. The relatively low-yield and inefficient nuclear weapons of the Eastern Coalition left enormous quantities of fallout. While the Vaar were one of the most radiation-resistant sapient species in the known universe, the rest of Prithone's fauna were not so fortunate. The particulates thrown into Prithone's atmosphere created a doomsday shroud, blocking sunlight. This lack of light and plunging temperatures that followed led to crop failure, then livestock failure. Far more Vaar would die to famine and the disease that came with it than ever died to bombardment or nuclear detonations. The exchange occurred on the first day of the year, by the last day, more than 90 percent of all Vaar, Viss, and their children were dead.

# 5C
# RISE OF THE SOVARI

THE RETURN TO ZERO should have been the end of the Vaar as a species. By the time the planet's atmosphere had cleared, the planet's once-lush jungles were no more. Most of the plant and animal life had been rendered extinct. Only isolated pockets survived, and their numbers were dwindling. Only a miracle could save the Vaar. But instead of one miracle, the Vaar received fourteen.

Modern Vaar have only an inkling of how dire the species' situation was, or of how they survived. The modern Combine state did not directly censor this information but had no interest in educating the public on this matter. But the survival of the Vaar was due entirely to the intervention of the Sovari. In the handful of surviving accounts, the Sovari bore striking similarities to the prophets found in the religions of many other races.

There were a total of fourteen Sovari. They were the Sovari Anko, El-nan, Felno, Cherek, Gora, Hola, Konda, Kreta, Loma, Putek, Powren, Meek, Vuska, and their leader, the Sovari Soma. Each corresponded to the Vaar's fourteen "unassailable virtues": reason, honesty, loyalty, discipline, conviction, vigilance, patience, temperance, endurance, conservation, acclimation, thrift, resilience, and reverence.

No names were recorded for these first Sovari, nor were the names of their successors recorded. For each Sovari swore an oath, with words known only to them and other Sovari. This oath demanded a level of self-sacrifice and dedication to the whole of their people that each successive Sovari gave up his name. But no matter how much of their accomplishments were written off as myth, it was the Sovari who healed Prithone. The planet's lush jungles, and countless animals rendered extinct, were restored.

The Sovari were said to be miracle workers. Accounts of the time purport that they could speak jungles into existence on fields of barren soil, and could create living animals from drawings and clay sculptures. Most in later eras would go on to simply dismiss this as mythologizing the work of these early Sovari. But they would take on many other, far more mundane tasks that were equally important. Ivex was the language of modern Vaar specifically because that was the language in which the ancient Sovari educated the survivors of the Return to Zero. Many medical terms were inexorably linked with the Sovari because they were the ones who taught medicine in this dark time.

As Prithone and Vaar civilization healed, the Sovari would gradually step back from the task of leading their people, even over that population's protest. When asked why, the Sovari Soma made it clear that they were there to guide, not to rule. The Sovari would establish themselves as an advisory council to governments formed by the population, but never again command their people directly.

Unfortunately so much myth entwined itself around the scant historical records, that the complete truths of the era can never be known. Exactly how the Sovari performed such feats as recreating extinct species remains unknown. Though it would take centuries to restore civilization, even with the Sovari's guidance, the Vaar endured.

# 5D
# THE FIRST STEPS

## Year Zero
## (62,280 AN)

ON THE 600TH ANNIVERSARY of the Return to Zero, two Vaar, Kol'tes and Ru'get, would take flight on the Celestial-7 rocket. Together they were the first Vaar to reach space since the time of Aka'lona. Their mission was to collect data and practice procedures for the raising of the Vaar's first space station. At the urging of the Sovari Council, the Vaar had unified under the Prithone Central Government. Also at their urging, the day of Kol'tes and Ru'get's launch would mark Day 1, Year 0 of the new calendar.

Quality of life on Prithone was still well below what it had been before the Return to Zero. But the Vaar were now unified, they were motivated, and they were ready to claim a new destiny among the stars. Not all was tranquil, as many objected to spending resources on space that could have been used for social programs. But the Sovari Council held great sway in this period, and most followed their urging to focus on space.

No species, humanity included, had pushed into space so far with such limited technology. Fewer than ten years after Kol'tes and Ru'get made their famous trip, the Vaar would raise their first space station. *Destiny* was assembled in orbit beyond the asteroid rings. Within fifteen years, *Destiny* had ten neighbors in its orbit. Within twenty years, that number had grown to fifty-four. Within forty years, the Vaar had built the *New Beginnings*, their first interplanetary colony ship.

The *New Beginnings* was powered by what Solars would consider an Orion drive. The nuclear bombs that had once helped to doom them, were now fuel to carry them to a new world. The nearest planet to Prithone was Heb'ta, where the Vaar would place their first colony. To bioform Heb'ta to be like Prithone was a non-starter with the technology available. But Heb'ta was merely a stepping-stone. Even as artificial habitats were going up and mines were being dug on Heb'ta, the Vaar were looking beyond. The nuclear-pulse engine was capable of more.

The nearest star to Prithone was La'quell—*Sea Diamond*—3.68 light-years away by Solar measurements, and Vaar astronomers were certain a habitable planet lay in its orbit. To reach La'quell, the Vaar constructed the ship *Long Ambition*. On Day 14 of Year 38, the *Long Ambition* set out with ten thousand Vaar, twenty thousand Viss, and eight thousand children to establish the species' first interstellar colony.

The *Long Ambition* would prove to be faster than its designers anticipated, reaching a top speed of 11 percent of *c*. More than thirty years later, *Long Ambition* would arrive at La'quell IV to find that the planet was not simply habitable, but it already supported a fully functioning ecosystem. The Vaar could not have asked for a better planet to establish their colony. The *Long Ambition* took up orbit and deployed its landers to the planet. Not long after, the ship was brought down and scrapped to help fuel the new colony's growth. The colonists would name this planet Sovari in honor of those who had set them on the path to the stars.

When Prithone received word of the success, it encouraged their drive to colonize. The Vaar would soon realize that they were blessed, having arisen on Prithone, surrounded by stars with habitable planets in their orbit. The truth of this matter and the greater hand at work that made it so was a secret the Sovari would never reveal to the population.

The Vaar held the records among all known species for both the longest distance traveled and the highest number of star systems colonized without warp technology. In a span of two hundred years, they would colonize the same number of star systems. The Vaar were further aided in their colonization by the flora and fauna of Prithone. These resilient organisms may have not been able to cope with Prithone's doomsday on their own, but they proved easy to transplant to new worlds and help form stable biospheres where they did not exist. While Sovari was the only naturally habitable planet in its star system, the Vaar would colonize two more planets around that star. Both of which were bioformed with ecosystems grown from life that had been transplanted from the home world.

In 376 the Vaar developed their first warp drive. This device was what humans would refer to as a Weber drive. The Weber drive, or Paka'-lutes'ne, as the Vaar call it (*base-scale drive*) relied on quantum mechanical effects to manipulate space-time than direct manipulation via electromagnetics as with the massless impulse drive. No species used this drive system after developing the MID, as the Weber drive is inferior in almost every way that matters. Some species such as humanity developed the MID first. However, to the Vaar, it was a functional warp drive, and that was enough.

More significant than further colonization was that the Weber drive drastically shortened the transit time between Prithone and its colonies. Up to this point, the colonies had been independent and self-governing. Circumstance forced the Vaar to break up into independent societies. The Weber drive made it possible to reunite them. But once independence was gained, it was not always surrendered easily. This development would lay the groundwork for the Intercolonial War.

# 5E

# THE INTERCOLONIAL WARS

## 1,617 PA–1,647 PA
## (64,198 AN–64,234 AN)

THE INTERCOLONIAL WARS WOULD last thirty years as Prithone and its colonies battled for control. Up until this point, the Vaar had enjoyed centuries of peaceful colonization and expansion. Prior to the development of the Weber drive, interaction with Prithone or other colonies was minimal. The Vaar had not yet developed a working means of faster-than-light communication or travel. Thus individual worlds rarely interacted and had little influence on each other. But with the development of the Weber drive, travel times that had been measured in years were reduced to days.

As travel times shortened, the government of Prithone began providing increasing support for their new colonies. But the government also began asserting control over existing colonies. This would create a divide and alliances with the Old Colonies on one side, and Prithone with the New Colonies on the other. The New Colonies were built with help from Prithone and often with a dependence on it. While the New Colonies did not object to Prithone's actions, the Old Colonies did, loudly.

By this time the Old Colonies had developed functioning societies with little to no help. These colonies even developed their own cultures, in some cases radically different from those of Prithone. The Old Colonies soon resented Prithone's efforts and the taxes the home world tried to enforce on them. But the greatest grievance came from Prithone's attempts to exert its cultural norms on Vaar who had never lived in that society.

Prithone's government was a tightly centralized, bureaucratic monolith where the state saw and controlled all. Private property was barely a concept, the state owned all means of production, and the government made all important decisions. Many of the colonies had established their governments as republics. That said, political franchise in most of these colonies was extremely limited. Viss were legally property. Governments funded themselves primarily through property and trade taxes. Among Vaar, only those who owned taxable real estate or engaged in importing or exporting paid taxes and could thus vote for representatives.

The Vaar had an idiom. *Slay the goza*. This idiom derives from an ancient story of a young Vaar constantly bullied by his older brother. As the two aged, the elder brother's abuse grew worse, and the younger brother took it in stride. This ended when the older brother killed the younger's pet goza by smashing its head with a stone. Enraged, the younger brother murdered his older brother and the parents who had ignored the ongoing abuse for so long. Into modernity, the Vaar used this idiom to refer to the final act in a chain of abuses that provoked a violent reaction.

Ko'ton (*Black Sands*) was one of the Vaar's most successful colonies. It was second only to Prithone in terms of industrialization, and it boasted a wealthy population. This population's wealth only grew when the Weber drive enabled it to export goods to other worlds. Ko'ton became the flash point for the conflict.

As the most successful colony, it was Ko'ton that often drew Prithone's eye. The Black Sands government found itself being levied with one tax after another as Prithone sought to raise capital for further colonization efforts. Black Sands was rich in rare minerals and faced increasing quotas for delivery to Prithone. Eventually, these quotas exceeded what the workers of Ko'ton could produce.

After the third consecutive failure to meet quota, Prithone dispatched a legion of troops to Ko'ton. These troops were instructed to conscript colonists into work brigades to ensure that future quotas were met. The act of conscripting civilians was an ancient practice among the Vaar going well back into the Dawn Era. Much like militia duty or the practice of deputizing in Earth's history, accepting a summons to a work brigade for the good of the community was accepted as being good citizenship. But it did not go over well on Ko'ton.

To the people of Ko'ton, Prithone did not have the authority to conscript its citizens. But the planet's population did not have the military it needed to fight for the people's belief. Nor was this one act enough to push the population in favor of war. It sowed the seeds of resentment that Prithone would water. As Prithone continued raising mineral quotas, it dispatched what were called cultural advisers to Ko'ton. The government of Ko'ton was instructed to place these cultural advisers in teaching positions in all of the planet's major schools. There they would educate the children on how to be "proper Vaar." The parents of Ko'ton did not appreciate this deliberate effort to manipulate their children and change the cultural and political norms of the planet.

The Sovari Council would ultimately warn the Collective Committee it was creating a tinderbox. But for perhaps the first time, the government did not take the Sovari's warnings to heart. Instead they would go on to adopt similar policies on other colonies while turning even more attention to Ko'ton. The next step was the Registration Order. This required all Vaar on colony worlds to register all real estate, weapons, and assets of great monetary value with their governments, who would share the information with Prithone.

These events and more would lead to the leaders of what became the Old Colonies to meet on the planet Shur'tan. There they drafted what became known as the Goza Decree. In this document the colonial leaders spelled out each of Prithone's actions that they considered abuses, and a scathing rebuke of them. The document finished by promising that with its next intolerable act, Prithone was slaying the goza.

One year later the High Minister of Ko'ton broadcast the Goza Decree to Prithone. Realizing that the Old Colonies were on the cusp of rebellion, Prithone would choose the worst option for deescalating the situation. Additional legions were deployed to Ko'ton and to each colony that had signed the Goza Decree. They did not receive a warm welcome.

The Old Colonies had waited a year to deliver their declaration in anticipation of this reaction. That year had been spent readying the colonies to fight for their independence. The first shots of the war were fired on Ko'ton when the dropships deploying new legions were shot out of orbit by surface-to-space missiles. The lines soon formed as the Old Colonies joined in their pledge to fight until Prithone recognized each of them as independent worlds.

After this act of war, things would quiet down. Neither Prithone nor its colonies had ever fought an interplanetary war, and neither was equipped to engage in one. Neither side possessed any true warships. Prithone did not have the means to forcibly seize a planet equipped to defend itself against the landing of troops. Now it needed such ships, and it needed them fast. Most of the colonies did not have shipyards of their own, and those that did lacked facilities equal to those of Prithone. While the few that had shipyards built their own warships, the colonies opted to fight a defensive war. They focused primarily on fortifying their planets to resist invasion or bombardment.

While both sides armed themselves for further hostilities, the Sovari made increasingly desperate pleas for both sides to reach a compromise. But they remained intractable. As far as Prithone was concerned, it was the government for *all* Vaar. As far as the Old Colonies were concerned, independence was the only acceptable outcome.

On Day 166 of the year 1,622, Prithone's newly built and trained fleet launched its attack on Ko'ton. Though outnumbered by more than ten to one, Ko'ton's fleet had the backing of the planetary defense grid. To call the performance of both sides inept was an understatement, and both made numerous costly mistakes in the First Battle of Ko'ton. The home-field advantage was enough to swing the battle in the colony's favor. Prithone's fleet was defeated, suffering more than 50 percent in casualties before retreating.

Prithone's response to this defeat was the same response it had to every defeat it would suffer in the war: raise a larger force and try again. With the shipyards of Prithone being expanded by work brigades and their output rising, it took only a year to replace the losses. On Day 220 of 1,623 PA, the Second Battle of Ko'ton began. The colony proved that it had learned more from the first battle than had the home world. The Second Battle of Ko'ton ended with the colony victorious, so Prithone raised an even larger fleet and tried again on Day 92 of 1,624 PA, going on to lose the Third Battle of Ko'ton.

The fourth time proved no more a charm than the third, and Prithone lost the Fourth Battle of Ko'ton. The answer was to raise an even larger fleet and try a fifth time. Then a sixth. It was only in the Sixth Battle of Ko'ton that Prithone's fleet managed to break through the planet's defenses and land legions on the planet. On the ground, the home world's forces faced intense resistance, the marines that landed found that Ko'ton had raised a powerful army for this situation, and they were unable to secure the planet. The attackers were routed and retreated. The response to this loss was a bigger fleet *and* more marines.

The Old Colonies were doomed by attrition. All of the Old Colonies combined had less than a quarter of Prithone's population. They were never capable of raising as many forces, replacing losses, or building matériel in numbers to match the home world. The colonies made minimal efforts to fight together when it counted most, due primarily to the reasonable fear that Prithone would decide to try its luck on another colony after so many losses at Ko'ton.

After replacing many political and military leaders, Prithone finally found victory at the Seventh Battle of Ko'ton. When Prithone's fleet arrived, it outnumbered the defenders twenty to one. When marines landed on the planet, they outnumbered the defenders five to one. With the most powerful of the colonies subdued, Prithone would turn its attention to the rest. Now with a veteran force, Prithone fared much better in the following battles. But in the few defeats, the solution was the same. More ships, more marines.

The largest battle of the war was the Battle of Kre'shen, Prithone's next target after Ko'ton's fall. With the latter's defeat, the colonies realized they needed to fight together to have a hope of victory. All of the colonies with warships dispatched them to Ko'ton along with ground forces to supplement the defenses of the obvious next target. But by this point, it was too little, too late. These were inexperienced, poorly trained forces against what had by now become a battle-hardened war machine. The Battle of Kre'shen was an overwhelming victory for Prithone.

The only reason Prithone lost a battle after Kre'shen was due to haste to end the war. This led to attempts to seize multiple colonies at once, spreading forces too thinly. Once this mistake was rectified, the Old Colonies fell one by one.

The war officially ended on Day 7 of 1,626 PA with the fall of Sona'me, bringing the last rebelling colony under control. But the will of the colonists to resist had not yet been broken. Though Prithone considered the war over, guerrilla forces on in numerous colonies continued to fight until 1,647 PA. At the urging of the Sovari Council, the leaders of the rebellion were not executed or even tried. In the spirit of reconciliation, each was given a full pardon for any crimes of which they might have been accused. But all were required to move to Prithone, where the state could keep a watchful eye on them. Those who continued to carry out further guerrilla campaigns received no such mercy and were generally executed when they were appre-hended.

In the end Prithone got everything it wanted. The work quotas returned to the colonies, and further colonization resumed. The state confiscated all privately owned weapons. All private real estate became government prop-erty, and all major industries were nationalized. The children of each colony were obliged to state-approved education. The many diverse cultures that had grown in the colonies were eradicated.

As peace returned and colonization efforts resumed, it was becoming clear that the current government was insufficient. Now in a position to dictate any terms it wished, Prithone would reorganize the government into what became known as the Interstellar Collective, a precursor to the Com-bine that exists in modernity.

# 5F
# THE GRAY FLEET CRISES

## 4,026 PA–4,037 PA
## (67,056 AN–67,069 AN)

INTELLIGENT LIFE WAS A relatively rare thing in the universe, particularly when considering species capable of interstellar travel. It was not uncommon for a galaxy to have only one, or even no sapient species residing within it. Meanwhile the fact that a sapient species developed on a world did not guarantee it would never go extinct before, or even after achieving the ability to reach through space. As the Vaar expanded through the Deep Sea, they found no signs of alien intelligence. Though they would find many worlds with native life, none of it was sapient.

The Gray Fleet Crises came at a time of great social transformation among the Vaar. Cultural reforms, most mandated by the state, swept across Vaar worlds. Independent cultures, if not independent governments, had arisen on many colonies, and efforts were being made to reunify the species into a single dominant culture. A strong political movement existed to expand the rights of Viss, who before now had been little more than property. Colonies and the Prithone government tried to reach points of compromise between the amount of authority local governments required to manage their needs, versus the amount of control exercised by the central government. This resulted in a tumultuous political environment.

The influence of the Sovari Council and the respect the public had for them in this era allowed them to keep the peace and stave off more civil wars.

The Collective had a large military. However, this military was not designed to wage war against foreign powers. The Vaar were aware and open to the possibility of other sapient life in the universe, but having failed to encounter any such sapients, doing battle with aliens was not a high priority in military planning.

The Collective military existed to maintain the peace and subdue any world that attempted to rebel against the central government. The overwhelming majority of warships were small and designed for planetary assault. These ships were meant to secure a planet's orbit and then either land or deploy troops from space. They employed mostly short-range and relatively weak weapons systems. The Deep Marines were equipped primarily for urban combat and trained in the subduing of rebelling cities. This was a military in no way ready to fight a hostile outside force.

Some species were lucky. The first encounter with alien intelligence was a wondrous event. Sometimes this first contact led to a friendly relationship between the two species. Other times the lucky species found that their first contact was benign. The Vaar were not so lucky.

On Day 42 of 4,026 PA, the warship *Long Sails* received a transmission from the colony world Abu'sanga. The transmission reported that detected ships were massing on the edge of the colony's sensor range. Shortly thereafter, all contact with the colony was lost. The *Long Sails* raced to investigate and assist the colony.

This was not a short trip. The Vaar were still reliant on the slow Weber drive, and Abu'sanga was a colony on the fringe of Collective territory. The *Long Sails* would need fourteen days to reach the planet, with no other warship able to make the voyage in fewer than thirty. By the time anyone arrived, it was too late.

The *Long Sails* arrived to find Abu'sanga destroyed. The entire surface of the planet had been bombarded into a crater-laden hellscape. The *Long Sails* investigated, and as more ships arrived, they searched for who, or what, had destroyed Abu'sanga. After forty-four days of investigation, no leads were forthcoming.

To avoid creating a panic, the Collective's Collective Committee chose to hide the details of Abu'sanga's destruction. The planet's loss was deemed the result of a massive bioforming failure, implying that those working to make the planet more livable had made a massive blunder that doomed the colonists already present. The military personnel who had arrived at Abu'sanga were forbidden from giving any unapproved statement about what they had seen.

In the following days, more than a hundred more ships went to the area to search for signs of what had transpired. But even after more than a year of searching, no answers were discovered. No matter what the official line was, the Collective Committee knew that an alien intelligence was the only logical explanation.

For the next two years, there were no more attacks, and it seemed that the fate of Abu'sanga might remain a mystery. Certainly many in the Vaar government hoped that was the case. When there were no further attacks and the initial worry subsided, the Collective Committee returned to business as usual. This did not sit well with the military, who urged the Committee to begin expanding the force and developing the weapons needed to face an existential threat. But the Committee was not interested and was still more concerned about possible rebellion within its colonies.

More than 80 percent of the Collective's government was tied up in social programs. Many of these aimed at helping to institute the social reforms the leadership body was pushing. The Collective Committee had no interest in hampering its progress by expanding the military budget and taking resources away from its initiatives.

The loudest voice of protest came from a Vaar named Kopo'tan. Kopo'tan was the chief of staff for the modern Deep Fleet's predecessor, the Collective Fleet. After several increasingly desperate pleas to the Collective Committee to increase the military's resources, he tendered his resignation in open council. The Collective Committee was not amused and classified his actions as an act of political protest by a military official. They charged him with disorderly conduct in a government proceeding. Kopo'tan was arrested, convicted, and sentenced to five years imprisonment.

Kopo'tan had many allies in the Committee but even more enemies. It was only with the protection of his friends that he was not sentenced to a longer term. But his fate revealed another underlying problem. As was often the case in many cultures, the time of wealth and ease had come at a social cost. An air of resentment had grown toward the military, a factor that was always magnified in the absence of a perceived external threat. The military was seen by many citizens as nothing but a place for those too stupid or incompetent to contribute to society to live on the public dole. The expense of the military despite being only a small part of the national budget was seen as a waste that could be put to better use elsewhere.

The military that intervened when the state was displeased with citizens' behavior led to many seeing the military as little more than the cudgel of society's elites. Those same elites often had disdain for the military, and even fear. Though the Collective Committee used the military to maintain order, it feared that the military might turn against it. Leaders were chosen not for command ability, but for political loyalty. Kopo'tan had clashed with the civilian government many times in the past, and this was their opportunity to remove him in favor of a more politically palatable leader.

For many in the military, the Committee's treatment of Kopo'tan was the moment the goza was slain. An alien intelligence had proven its existence and its hostility. The Collective Committee's and the elites' collective abuse had already worn thin the patience of many. But this dereliction of duty was a step too far. The seeds of a coup had been planted, but the military was even less popular than the civilian government. The coup could not begin immediately. Loyal supporters had to be found. Those most loyal to the Collective Committee had to be neutralized. But most important, something had to swing the public's favor toward the military. The burgeoning conspirators had to bide their time.

The unknown menace would return on Day 92 of 4,028 PA when the colony of Stabo'din reported unidentified contacts coming into sensor range. Stabo'din was another outlying colony but far from Abu'sanga, a full quarter the circumference around the Collective's bubble of territory. As was the case with Abu'sanga, the distance to this peripheral colony resulted in a slow response.

Stabo'din was a newly established mining colony. In this era, the Vaar were far from the development of the alchemic printer. Stabo'din was a planet carpeted in active volcanoes. Their eruptions brought many useful minerals to the surface, and the mining of planets and asteroids was critical to Vaar industry. The planet's population numbered twenty thousand living and laboring in orbital habitats.

When the warship *Tall Sentry* arrived on scene, it found no survivors. The orbital habitats had been destroyed, leaving their wreckage in a ring around the planet. As it searched the wreckage, *Tall Sentry* made two unsettling discoveries. The first was that there were no bodies in the wreckage. The second was a piece of metal, a little more than half a meter long. *Tall Sentry* couldn't identify the substance. The ship also noted that the amount of wreckage in orbit was far less than the collective mass of the destroyed habitats.

As had been the case with Abu'sanga, the Collective Committee classified the destruction of Stabo'din as a disaster. The official statement indicated that a large asteroid had struck one of the orbital habitats, and its debris created a domino effect, which destroyed the rest. This explanation did not go over as well for the public. An incredible degree of incompetence would have been required for none of the habitats to see such an asteroid coming, and even more to do nothing to prevent it. The mystery metal was seized by state officials, and all mention of it was forbidden.

The leaders of the Collective Defense Force, now missing Kopo'tan, again urged the Collective Committee to ready the military to fight an alien menace. But again, the Committee refused. The military expected this reaction, and several clandestine recordings were made of the Committee meetings. The footage was kept for when the time was right.

One admiral, Tona'tass, was the Vaar most responsible for formulating the military's response to this second lost colony. As the Vaar expanded in nearly every direction, their nation's footprint in space was roughly spherical. Tona'tass had noted that a nearly 90-degree angle was formed by drawing a line that connected Abu'sanga, Prithone, and Stabo'din. With that information, Tona'tass guessed that whoever was responsible for the attacks was deliberately moving in a roundabout way, scouting to determine the perimeter of Vaar territory. Based on his observations, he deduced that the most likely target for the next attack was Abu'drela. A near 180-degree line could be drawn joining Abu'sanga through Prithone, to Abu'drela.

Tona'tass ensured that five ships were always within thirty hours of Abu'drela. Though he wished to station more ships, doing so risked provoking the Collective Committee to question him since the fringe colony wasn't hinging on rebellion. For the moment, the Committee was in no mood to deal with anyone who tried to pull their heads out of the sand.

Just over two years later, Tona'tass's prediction came true. On Day 109 of 4,030 PA, Abu'drela reported incoming ships. The five ships on duty raced in to protect it. This force was commanded by Yugen'dex, one of several lower admirals picked by Tona'tass to rotate through this post. Abu'drela was a general colony, meant as a place for a large population to eventually live and work. For a fringe colony, it boasted an unusually high population of 927,000.

Unfortunately, Yugen'dex's small force did not arrive in time to save

Abu'drela. But even if it had managed to arrive sooner, it would never have been able to save the planet from its fate. Yugen'dex's force arrived to find thousands of alien ships surrounding Abu'drela—long, conical vessels that dwarfed any ship the Vaar possessed. While some of these ships were actively bombarding the planet, others pointed their mouths toward the colony. With great beams of light, they seemed to suck material into themselves from the planet below. Yugen'dex's forces watched as entire cities were ripped out of the planet and sucked up into the ships' open cones.

To attack such a vastly superior force was suicide, and Yugen'dex appreciated that. He appreciated even more that he had a duty to return with this information. But some of his crew were not so rational. Yugen'dex was forced to put down a mutiny on the *Cresting Wave*. But two of his ships, *Acute Angle* and *Angry Goza*, defied his orders to launch a suicide attack on the unknown fleet. This drew the fleet's attention, forcing Yugen'dex and his remaining ships to beat a hasty retreat. Neither *Acute Angle* nor *Angry Goza* was ever heard from again.

When Yugen'dex returned with irrefutable evidence of hostile aliens, Tona'tass took it immediately to the Collective Committee. The Committee's response was to classify the fall of Abu'drela as a military secret and to raise the military budget by 10 percent. Naturally, the military balked at these crumbs. This time seven admirals and a general were imprisoned for misconduct in open council. The military was told to take the money and justify its existence. This, too, was recorded.

The alien menace was dubbed the *Ecka'fera*, or *Gray Fleet* by the military. The word *gray* in Ivex, though referring specifically to the color, was used as a synonym for the unknown. More specifically, when being unknown took on a negative connotation.

The military needed to be revamped to face this existential threat, and it had been given far too little funding to do that. Anti-ship weapons had to be developed and retrofitted to existing warships. Planetary defenses had to be developed and quickly installed. Tactics relevant to fleet-on-fleet combat had to be developed and quickly taught to existing soldiers and new recruits. The military felt the deep pains of an old human saying: *you fight with the military you have, not the military you want.*

The paltry military budget wasn't enough to build a new fleet of dedicated warships. Meanwhile the hasty studies conducted on retrofitting existing warships showed that the process would take far longer than initially anticipated. These factors and others would lead the Collective Fleet to adopt a doctrine built around carrier ships. Large carriers were expensive but still cheaper than fleets of battleships. Fighters and bombers could be produced for far less than either, and collectively they could patrol large areas. So long as they physically fit in the carrier, new fighters and bombers were easier to design and integrate as their designs evolved.

The construction of the new carriers was a large undertaking and could not be hidden. Rumors began to spread through the population as to the nature of these ships. Did the Collective Committee believe a major rebellion was coming? Or was there some truth to the careful rumors about an alien civilization? Meanwhile friends and family of those lost on the colonies were beginning to openly question the official stories about the loss of their loved ones.

Fear of panic, and its typical totalitarian reaction to being questioned, led the state to swift and harsh responses. The most outspoken of those asking questions were arrested and sent to penal colonies. Those who questioned the purpose of the new carriers often found themselves impressed into work brigades. If they were so curious about the carriers, they could help build them, isolated where they could not cause further public agitation.

Some of those preparing for the coup against the Committee saw this as an opportunity to strike. It was Tona'tass, who had become the unofficial leader of the plot, who convinced them to wait. The Collective Committee's totalitarianism was no secret to the public. For the population to support the coup, they had to see the Committee's incompetence as well. That time would come.

Tona'tass predicted that the Gray Fleet's next attack would take longer to come. If the fleet was indeed probing the edges of Combine territory before picking off colonies, the next attack would be on a colony close to the galactic core. Warp travel was more difficult near the galactic core, especially for the more primitive drive systems of the era. The presence of so many stars, black holes, and other stellar bodies in such proximity created significant warping effects of their own, increasing the difficulty of achieving controlled warp via MID or Weber drive. By analyzing how long their previous efforts had taken, Tona'tass estimated the next attack would come in approximately three years as the Gray Fleet was slowed by efforts to probe the galactic core for colonies.

Tona'tass focused his efforts on ramming the Collective Fleet's new carriers into production as quickly as possible. But Tona'tass had another cat to skin in preparation for the coup. He had become the leader of the movement, and more of its responsibilities were falling on him. A problem that could not be ignored was the Domestic Tranquility Division, the secret police of the era. Not only did he have to prevent the DTD from learning of the coup, but he had to either integrate it into the coup or neutralize it.

Tona'tass focused his efforts on Juma'dee, the new leader of the DTD. Juma'dee was a somewhat controversial figure. Many saw her appointment to leadership of the DTD purely as a political matter and thought she obtained the role primarily because she was female. Tona'tass knew better. Indeed her appointment was political, as she had a long-standing, intimate relationship with a Collective Committee member. But Juma'dee was a cold, calculating Viss who was good at the job she had been given. Juma'dee was also a die-hard loyalist to the Collective Committee. She had to be dealt with.

Tona'tass recruited a Vaar named Tu'seen, a young prodigy in the Collective Fleet. Tu'seen was equally well-known as "Tu'seen the Fabulous" for his striking good looks. Tona'tass gave Tu'seen the order to seduce Juma'dee. He was at best to draw her into the conspiracy, or at least use a relationship with her as the means to gain information about DTD agents in the military.

Tu'seen proved that his military skill paled in comparison to his skills at seduction, and within a week, he had developed a relationship with the much more senior Juma'dee. Tu'seen concluded that trying to draw her into the coup was futile, so he focused his efforts on the second task. In less than a year, he managed to access Juma'dee's personal computer and obtained a full list of DTD agents operating in the military. Tu'seen would not enjoy this work, finding disdain in Juma'dee's interests.

The efforts to bring the new carrier force online were not meeting with equal success. The one high note was that the Collective Fleet had many thousands of drop ship pilots who could be trained to operate the fighters and bombers. But this was all that was going well. It was becoming very apparent that the three-year window Tona'tass predicted would not be enough.

Tona'tass's prediction would prove to be conservative, and it took four years before the Gray Fleet attacked again. This would lead to the Battle of Vok'grela.

## The Battle of Vok'grela

Vok'grela was one of the colonies located closest to the Deep Sea's galactic core. The fight to defend this colony was the Vaar's first experience fighting an alien power in deep space. The battle would also prove a costly disaster for the Vaar.

Tona'tass had managed to convince the Collective Committee to allow him to station a large fleet of ships close to Vok'neka, where he predicted the next attack. With more than twice as much time passing since the last attack, he faced resistance. The Collective Committee was eager to return to normal and believe that the threat moved on. At great risk to his personal freedom, Tona'tass relied on a series of increasingly elaborate excuses to keep the Ninth Fleet stationed near Vok'neka. But his ability to weave passable excuses wore thin. Tona'tass stood before the Committee, scraping the bucket when the news came.

On Day 77 of 4,034 PA, Collective Fleet scouts in the region detected thousands of ships entering Vaar territory. It became apparent that the ships were heading for Vok'grela, not Vok'neka. Admiral So'doka, commanding the Ninth Fleet, scrambled to defend the planet.

The Ninth Fleet never had a prayer of winning this battle. So'doka's fleet of 641 ships arrived at Vok'grela almost simultaneously with the Gray Fleet. But the Gray Fleet had brought 18,726 ships to the fight. Even without this huge disparity, only a handful of So'doka's fleet had been successfully retrofitted with new ship-to-ship weapons, which had been rushed through development and were largely unproven. The majority of the ships were still outfitted for planetary assault, armed with anemic, short-range weapons. Most of the Ninth Fleet was destroyed trying to get close enough to attack.

Why So'doka did not order a retreat as soon as it was clear the battle couldn't be won, was a bit of a mystery. Perhaps he was simply unwilling to leave Vok'neka's colonists to their fate, but So'doka was a member of the coup. Many historians believe that he deliberately sacrificed himself and his fleet, and that the military disaster made it impossible for the Collective Committee to sweep the threat under the rug. Of the 641 ships of the Ninth Fleet, only 131 managed to escape. As they fled, they watched a similar scene to the fate of Abu'drela.

If So'doka's goal had been to force the hand of fate, he was successful. The Collective Committee could bury the loss of one or two ships and their crews. But the fact that hundreds of ships were lost at the same time that another colony went dark was too much. The Collective Committee had no choice but to admit the existence of the Gray Fleet to the public, but to insulate themselves from public backlash, they sought scapegoats. They chose So'doka and Tona'tass.

With So'doka dead, the Committee threw most of the blame at Tona'tass's feet. He was accused of dereliction of duty for not better preparing the defenses of the region. His calm and respectful attempts to defend himself from accusation saw him arrested for misconduct in open counsel. In fewer than twenty minutes, he was sentenced to fifteen years on that offense and awaited a formal trial for dereliction of duty.

Though Tona'tass was still reluctant, this event convinced the coup conspirators that the time had come. With both Tona'tass and Kopo'tan imprisoned, leadership of the plot fell on Tu'seen. Kopo'tan should have already been released from prison by this point. But trumped-up charges for misconduct during his prison stay had been used to keep him there. On Day 107, Tu'seen set the plot in motion.

Tu'seen headed the coup's efforts against the DTD. The first blood was drawn when Tu'seen slew Juma'dee by drowning her in her toilet. With the DTD decapitated, Tu'seen sent the order to the coup agents under his command. By the end of Day 107, more than six thousand DTD agents were killed. On Day 108, marines loyal to the plot raided the prison complex where both Tona'tass and Kopo'tan were imprisoned. On Day 136, the pair led the final stage of the coup to seize control of Prithone.

The culture of abuse the political elite had so long fostered against the military finally came back to bite them. Few loyalist troops materialized, and the conspirators met little resistance in seizing control of the planet. Within twenty days all members of the Collective Committee were arrested. Many of these council members were charged with dereliction of duty by a state official and served life sentences. While the council members were being rounded up, state media broadcasted the many recordings taken of the Council by Tona'tass and others. The Vaar people saw proof that the Council had been aware of the threat all along. Proof that the Council not only knew about the threat but had actively inhibited the military's attempts to meet it. A majority of the frightened population responded in favor of the conspirators.

Though Tona'tass led the coup, he had never done so with the intention of taking power for himself. He nominated Kopo'tan to serve as the head of the new provisional government. Kopo'tan had the better mind for logistics, was forty years Tona'tass's senior, and had many friends outside the military. This, in Tona'tass's mind, made the reluctant Kopo'tan the obvious choice. With the acquiescence of the rest of the military's leadership, Kopo'tan was declared Warlord of the Collective. This made him the dictator of the Collective government.

The Collective Committee and its bungling had been neutralized, but the threat of the Gray Fleet remained. Unknown to the Vaar, the magnitude of this threat was even larger than revealed. But now the military was in control and could openly face the threat.

## The Battle of Pro'kess

After the fall of Vok'grela, Tona'tass estimated another three years before they would encounter the Gray Fleet again. Thus far the Gray Fleet had traveled a fairly two-dimensional path through the galaxy. Tona'tass estimated that the Gray Fleet would continue divning the outline of Vaar territory by moving vertical to the galactic plane. By then Tona'tass hoped that the factories and shipyards being constructed on hundreds of worlds would reach a critical mass and allow the Vaar to release a tide of new weapons to meet the Gray Fleet. Tona'tass was wrong.

Now with the borders through the galactic plane established, the Gray Fleet attacked in force. From the direction of each fallen colony, ships flooded in. Soon their number was established at 267,481. The war was no longer a border matter but a full-fledged and murderous invasion. The Collective Fleet was still not ready to fight this threat. Across the Collective, citizens were impressed into work brigades to build planetary defenses. The Gray Fleet had to be slowed down until the new carrier force was ready for battle. But even with these efforts, Tona'tass would have no choice but to throw masses of his ships to slaughter, all to slow the Gray Fleet down.

The Gray Fleet's warships each measured more than nine kilometers long. The new Vaar carriers, the largest ships the civilization had yet built, measured only two. Neither side was capable of Faster Than Light combat. The most important anti-ship weapon developed to fight the Gray Fleet was the hoshet torpedo, meant to be carried by the bomber force. The word *hoshet* referred to an eel-like predator native to Prithone. Covered in venomous spines, this eel hunted by biting its prey, then constricting around it to slay it.

The hoshet torpedo carried a 5,000-kilogram charge of antimatter fuel. Upon coming into proximity with the target, the fuel was agitated to release anti-protons that annihilated the hull of the torpedo. This weapon was around 42 percent efficient, yielding a detonation of approximately 45,000 megatons.

The Gray Fleet's primary anti-ship weapon was dubbed *travo* by the Vaar. The word *travo* was used to describe a typhoon. Travo batteries consisted of dozens or hundreds of guns firing thrust-assisted 7.2-kilogram slugs at over 5 percent of *c*. This gave each slug just under a megaton's worth of kinetic energy. Each slug was fully guided, thrust-assisted, and capable of maneuvering to hit its target. It seemed as though the new Vaar weapons outclassed the Gray Fleet's, but this was not true. The average travo gun could fire at a rate exceeding 20,000 rounds per minute. Meanwhile the Gray Fleet's ships carried lasers in the gigawatt range for point defense, but at short range, they worked equally well on offense.

The first battle for the Vaar's new carrier force came at the planet Pro'kess. The furious drive to erect planetary defenses, and the sacrifice of thousands of the Collective's older ships, had slowed the Gray Fleet, but it had not stopped it. More than a hundred of the outer colonies had fallen. From three directions the Gray Fleet was closing in on the more densely populated inner colonies. The Vaar were running out of time. The death toll was in the millions and was only going to go up as the Gray Fleet progressed.

The most deeply encroaching force was approaching Pro'kess, an important industrial world with a population of over a billion residents. The Collective could not afford to sacrifice this world without a fight. Tona'tass was forced to send his new ships to Pro'kess in the hopes of defending it.

The Collective had only four operational carriers, each bearing 4,000 fighters and 1,000 bombers. Of the 3,000 additional warships, only 600 had been retrofitted for fleet combat. The force approaching Pro'kess numbered 66,870. Given the criticality of the battle, Tona'tass took personal command of the Second Fleet to try to save Pro'kess.

With its ample industry, Pro'kess had fortified heavily for the attack in a short period of time. Tona'tass planned to keep his fleet close to the planet so that it could provide fire support to his ships. This meant that damage to the planet was a certainty, but no better alternative presented itself. On Day 5 of 4,035 PA, the battle began.

The performance of the Second Fleet's fighter and bomber pilots was described as "a most brilliant effort in a hopeless task." The skill of the fleet's pilots was perhaps the only bright spot in the battle. Faced with what it considered serious opposition for the first time, the Gray Fleet revealed the capabilities it had been holding back. The most important among these was—by the standards of the day—an incredibly powerful jamming system.

Almost immediately after the battle began, Vaar ships found their communications awash in static. This forced the fleet to rely on short-range laser pulses for communications and severely disrupted Tona'tass's ability to coordinate his forces. The hoshet torpedo had been equipped with a fairly sophisticated home-on-jam system that avoided complete nullification of its targeting. But the rushed development and implementation of this weapon came to the forefront.

More than 40 percent of the torpedoes launched by Vaar bombers failed to engage. They lost target-lock upon being fired. Another 25 percent failed to detonate due to a flaw in the systems meant to initiate anti-proton synthesis in their warheads. This left only one out of three as a viable threat to the Gray Fleet. The Vaar watched in dismay as they realized that once the weapons made it past the point defenses and detonated, a single hoshet was not enough to destroy a Gray Fleet ship. They needed at least six hits, with seven to ten being more likely. Even in these cases, the ships destroyed were overcome through the apparent cooking of their electric systems rather than destruction of their hulls. The Gray Fleet's weapons had little trouble smashing the Vaar's primitive defenses.

The Gray Fleet plowed through Tona'tass's resistance. He was forced to order as many ships as he could reach to retreat. For the loss of more than half of his fleet, Tona'tass had managed to destroy two hundred of the Gray Fleet.

Pro'kess fell, and its entire population of 1.34 billion was lost.

## Stillborn Salvation

WITH THE FALL OF Pro'kess, the Vaar's fate appeared to be sealed. The new carrier doctrine had proven it could work, but it was not enough. The Vaar needed hundreds, even thousands, of carriers, millions of fighters and bombers, and to address critical flaws in their weaponry. With the Gray Fleet's progress, there was time for none of this. The Collective was being strangled, and with the fall of Pro'kess, each world to fall next was a major loss. Nearly every Collective citizen who could work was building fortifications, munitions, shipyards, or ships. But there simply wasn't enough time.

The only thing working in the Vaar's favor was the Gray Fleet's thoroughness to find and destroy every single colony. The fleet's ships spread themselves thin into a sort of ring around the Collective before squeezing inward. Whenever a colony was encountered, nearby ships concentrated to destroy it. Afterward they reformed the ring and continued to squeeze.

But after the fall of Pro'kess, something strange happened. The Gray Fleet halted its progress. When scouts were sent to investigate, what they found was not good news. When Tona'tass viewed footage taken by one of his scouts, he watched as a new Gray Fleet ship was seemingly birthed from the mouth of another. The Gray Fleet was using the resources stripped from the worlds they had destroyed to replenish their losses. They had simply stopped long enough to replace their casualties.

But on Day 76 of 4,035 PA, one bomber piloted by a Vaar named Ju'geg made a discovery. Shortly after the Gray Fleet moved on from Pro'kess, one ship had been left behind. As Ju'geg drew closer to this vessel, it did not respond to his presence, even as he came into visual range. Ju'geg had found one of the Gray Fleet's stillborn, a ship that never came online. Efforts were made for a force to slip behind the Gray Fleet's advance and tow this ship.

Vaar marines went first, and scientists were on the ship before the Collective Fleet finished towing it. From this effort, the Vaar learned the nature of their enemy. Once certain that the ship was indeed dead, it was taken to Prithone for study.

The Vaar had inherited someone else's ancient problem. More than half a million years before the Vaar ever left Prithone, three sapient species had arisen in the nearby Disorder Sea. One of these three species called themselves the Po'met Estate. The other two were the Tonn Empire and the Solag Republic. Together the po'met and the solag waged a war against the Tonn Empire and lost. After the solag fell, the po'met began the construction of a doomsday weapon. This weapon would take the form of self-replicating, AI-controlled ships. They were designed to reproduce and destroy all worlds they found populated by any species other than the po'met. Just before the fall of their home world, the po'met launched the first ship of the Gray Fleet to avenge themselves on the genocidal Tonn.

This ship did exactly what it was built to do. In deep space, it strip-mined uninhabited worlds and built copies of itself. Once the numbers were sufficient, the ships attacked the Tonn Empire. Over approximately three hundred years, the Gray Fleet annihilated the Tonn. That was when this crisis was set in motion. There were no solag left, and the last of the po'met died when their home world fell. With no one left to turn them off, the ships of the Gray Fleet continued hunting for sapients to destroy. Eventually this meant leaving the Disorder Sea and crossing the galactic void to the Deep Sea.

The fate of the Vaar and countless other sapients hinged on a programming error. A single AI controlled all ships of the Gray Fleet. Due to an error in the po'met's code, this AI could control a maximum of 267,481 ships. Any built beyond this number never came online, resulting in stillborn like the one found by Ju'geg. Were it not for this error, the Gray Fleet's numbers would have swelled into trillions as it subsumed its home galaxy. Not truly sapient, the control-AI for the Gray Fleet could neither diagnose nor correct this error.

As more scouts were sent behind the Gray Fleet's lines, more and more stillborn ships were found. Soon dozens were being towed back to Prithone. When presented with this information, Tona'tass asked the critical question. Could facilities be installed on these stillborn ships to enable a Vaar crew to gain control and bring them online? As colonies continued to fall, scientists and engineers worked around the clock to answer this question. The answer was yes.

A small compartment near the ship's outer hull, normally used for venting waste, could be jury-rigged into a bridge by installing appropriate control systems and routing the controls through the waste disposal system. Engineers experimenting on the first captured ship brought the ship's propulsion, weapons, and defensive systems online.

A Vaar named Po'klon, considered by many the best pilot in the Collective Fleet, was brought in to test-fly the ship. From his efforts, procedures were written, and Tona'tass began dispatching ships to find as many Gray Fleet stillborn as possible. The ships would bring them online, and the pilots would bring them back to Prithone.

This was a bigger windfall than it may have initially seemed. The Gray Fleet's ships were excellently proofed against their own weapons. Their hulls were well-suited to deflecting the slugs they used for their primary offense. Meanwhile, the more the scouts searched, the more stillborn they found.

Unfortunately, the staff researching the ship found no good means to access the control-AI for the Gray Fleet itself. They had hoped that some means to attack the AI through its own network would enable the Vaar to disrupt its control. Indeed this *was* possible, but the Vaar of the time did not have the expertise needed to do it.

A handful of other positive developments were occurring. Analysis of the hoshet torpedo revealed its primary flaw. Its tendency to lose its target-lock after launch was a simple fix. The culprit was electrical feedback, which occurred when the torpedo's engine came online. The solution was as simple as installing stronger resistors in key portions of the missile's guidance system—a flaw that would have certainly been found sooner had the weapon not been rushed into service at such a breakneck pace.

The danger had not yet passed, but now the winds of fate seemed to be shifting.

## The First Battle of the Triangle

THINGS WERE GETTING BETTER for the Vaar but were still very bleak. Even with the enormous windfalls they had received, the war was progressing poorly. By the start of 4,036 PA, there were no fringe colonies left. Only the densely populated core colonies remained. Vaar, Viss, and children alike worked side by side to manufacture weapons and install planetary defenses. With the primary flaw of the hoshet resolved, much greater casualties were being inflicted on the Gray Fleet.

But even so, it was not enough. Even the most optimistic projections showed that the Gray Fleet would reach Prithone before the Collective Fleet was strong enough to stop them. The Vaar needed to throw a roadblock in the fleet's path, and it needed to be a big one. To that end, Tona'tass began massing his forces at what was known as the Triangle.

The Triangle was considered either a natural wonder of the universe or evidence of ancient aliens operating on immense scales. Three planets, Balta, Dehon, and Cas'na, all shared the same orbital diameter around their local star. The relative position of these planets formed a triangle orbiting the star. The three colonies were some of the most prosperous and important in the Collective. The planets' positioning made them well-suited to defending each other and to working with nearby fleets.

Tona'tass concentrated his forces on the Triangle in the hopes that he could draw enough of the Gray Fleet to battle to slow its progress around the Collective. Once again he took personal command of the battle, hoping to give his people their first victory against this menace. For now, he chose to leave the salvaged Gray Fleet ships, now dubbed *black ships* out of the battle. Their numbers were still too few to be a deciding factor.

Tona'tass had twelve carrier ships with complete wings available to him, including his flagship, *Collective Vengeance*. On Day 28 the Battle of the Triangle began as 22,000 Gray Fleet ships approached the Triangle. Now with more reliable weapons and experience purchased in blood, the Vaar fleet of 1,200 warships, 48,000 fighters, and 12,000 bombers met the Gray Fleet.

Tona'tass stationed his carriers in close orbit around the local star and divided his remaining ships among the planets. The Gray Fleet approached the star system from above, relative to the star's and planet's poles, coming down to attack all three planets at once. As the Gray Fleet began to divide, Tona'tass launched his bombers.

The resulting battle lasted for three days. Tona'tass said, "All glory for the frenzy at the Triangle must go to our bomber and fighter pilots. Without their skill, their courage, and their sacrifice, no victory would have come."

Indeed it was the daring of the bomber and fighter wings that made the difference. To overcome the Gray Fleet's jamming, the fighters flew in formations meant to spread from the planets to the bomber formations. This allowed each fighter to serve as a relay for laser-point communication and, in turn, enabled positive command and control over the bombers.

Bomber crews showed great courage by pressing their attack runs dangerously close to the Gray Fleet ships before launching their weapons. This put the bombers in great danger and resulted in many being destroyed by the fleet's point defenses. But by withholding their weapons until close range, the bombers gave those point defenses less time to track and intercept incoming torpedoes. These daring and well-coordinated attacks were responsible for the bulk of the enemy ships destroyed.

The Gray Fleet made nine separate advances on the system, each time retreating when the number of damaged or lost ships began to compromise their combined point defense. The attrition was working both ways, and by the time the Gray Fleet retreated, the Vaar had lost more than half their bombers, a third of their fighters, and a quarter of their warships. Celebration erupted across the planets of the Triangle and throughout Tona'tass's fleet when the enemy finally retreated.

Tona'tass did not celebrate. He already knew what was next, and his deep space scouts confirmed his suspicions. The Gray Fleet moved two hundred light-years away from the Triangle and began to thin their perimeter around the Collective, concentrating their forces for a much larger assault. All the while they were producing replacements for the ships they had lost. The Vaar had destroyed 3,600 Gray Fleet ships. Each time casualties had reached the point that more than 50 percent of torpedoes made it through their point defenses, the Gray Fleet retreated.

The Battle of the Triangle was the turning point of the conflict. The Vaar had stood toe to toe with the Gray Fleet and forced it to retreat. The fleet's greatest weapon up to this point had been fear, and they were losing their power. News of the victory spread rapidly across the Collective. The Gray Fleet was not unstoppable.

Tona'tass had observed the fleet's actions in battle. He speculated that perhaps the fleet's behavior was a symptom of the problem that cost the po'met their war and led to the fleet's creation in the first place. Whoever had programmed the Gray Fleet's AI was a poor tactician. Overwhelming force was the fleet's *only* tactic. His analysis of the battle would reveal that the fleet was extremely conservative, did not take even favorable risks, and quickly prioritized retreat if it lost the status of extreme advantage. Perhaps it had been an intentional design feature for the fleet to run from any superior foe and come back later with a larger fleet. The Vaar were no strangers to the use of overwhelming force, however, it was not their only tactic.

## The Second Battle of the Triangle, and the Long Burn

AFTER THE FIRST BATTLE of the Triangle, the Gray Fleet identified the region as the center of Vaar resistance. The Gray Fleet began to draw in its ships from across the Collective for an overwhelming assault. This took a great deal of time as the fleet's ships went around other points of potential resistance. Tona'tass sent many of his ships out to harass the Gray Fleet in the hopes of pushing them into even more roundabout paths to their rendezvous.

Tona'tass had fourteen carriers, most of them with full wings. But this was as many as he was going to get. The Collective had used up its reserves of necessary materials, and it was a year or more before construction of another carrier could begin. The older carriers in his force were suffering constant technical breakdowns. Like the bombers' torpedoes, they had been rushed through production and into service. Design flaws were rearing their heads, but many of these did not have simple solutions. Though Tona'tass had fourteen carriers, no more than nine were generally available at any given time.

The Gray Fleet was massing the bulk of its force in preparation for the second attack. To Tona'tass and others, it appeared that a decisive battle was about to occur. Tona'tass ordered all the black ships, now numbering 350, to join the defense at the Triangle. With no more carriers to bear them, additional fighters and bombers coming off the assembly lines were sent to the planets of the Triangle. Entire cities were leveled to produce ramshackle space ports to host these incoming wings. Civilians slept on the floors where they labored, and even on the sidewalks outside the factories as more and more fortifications were built.

The Second Battle of the Triangle began on Day 6 of 4,037 AN. Two hundred thousand ships of the Gray Fleet moved up to initiate the battle. From the view of some historians, the long road of the Vaar to becoming a great power began in the Second Battle of the Triangle.

Tona'tass's plan relied heavily on the black ships. Analyses had shown they were well-proofed to their own weapons and were difficult for other Gray Fleet ships to destroy. Tona'tass positioned the black ships into a protective sphere around his other warships and launched them at the Gray Fleet in a counterattack. Between his carriers and the planets of the Triangle, he commanded a force of 244,000 bombers and ten times their number in fighters.

They hoped that the Gray Fleet might not recognize its own ships as a threat until too late. This did not work, and the fleet fired on the black ships without hesitation. But between their point defenses and their incredibly durable hulls, they proved quite capable of absorbing punishment from their parents. Their point defenses helped shield the warships sheltering in their perimeter.

While Tona'tass's warships met the Gray Fleet head-on, the massive bomber forces attacked them from the flanks. What ensued was effectively a deep-space wrestling match. While Tona'tass force-fed the Gray Fleet their stillborn offspring, he struck at their flanks with his bombers. Each time the Gray Fleet tried to move back or reposition itself, Tona'tass had to move with it so that the grapple was not broken. Just before 05:00 on Day 7, Tona'tass's fleet broke through the perimeter of the Gray Fleet and pushed through its center.

The Gray Fleet ships were protected against their own weapons but not invincible to them. Outnumbered by thousands and taking fire from all directions, the black ships incurred serious damage with several becoming disabled. Tona'tass revealed the second surprise he had waiting for his enemy. Up until now, he had only attacked with the bombers from his carriers.

The order was given, and massive waves of bombers and fighters stationed on the Triangle's planets were launched. With thousands of bombers approaching, the Gray Fleet had no choice but to reorganize its formation to prepare for the incoming attack. Once penetrating the perimeter, his ships enjoyed protection from the black ships. The short range allowed them to strike the Gray Fleet with their torpedoes.

The wrestling match ended in the dawn hours of Day 7 when the Gray Fleet's formation finally broke, and its ships retreated. The Second Battle of the Triangle had been won, but it came at a great cost.

Of the black ships sent to battle, only five remained operational. Of the 244,000 bombers, 111,000 had been destroyed with ten times that number of losses among the fighters. Of the Vaar's actual warships, more than 50 percent were either destroyed or damaged beyond repair. But of the two hundred thousand Gray Fleet ships, only seven escaped.

Across the Deep Sea, the remaining ships of the Gray Fleet rapidly withdrew from Collective territory. The Second Battle of the Triangle was the last major battle the Vaar would fight against the Gray Fleet. The battle had bought the Vaar the time they needed. The factories were opened, the workers were trained, and production was in full swing. Fighters and bombers rolled off the assembly lines by the thousands per day. The only bottleneck was in crew training, as the Collective had exhausted the supply of drop ship pilots it could retrain even before the First Battle of the Triangle. But the Collective found no shortage of volunteers eager to sign up.

Many more battles were fought as the Collective Fleet scoured the Deep Sea for remnants of the Gray Fleet—to forever eliminate it. This task would not be accomplished in full for another four hundred years. But the Gray Fleet would never again feel confident enough to launch an attack on the Collective's worlds. The long and arduous process of hunting them down came to be known as the Long Burn.

The Vaar had to face certain realities. Lack of preparation to fight an existential threat had nearly cost them their existence. While indeed the Collective had rallied to face the threat, it had survived only through strokes of incredible luck. The flaws in the Gray Fleet's control system, the discovery of its stillborn, and the tactical ineptitude of the fleet's programmers—without any one of these, the Vaar would have almost certainly been exterminated. If ever faced with such a dire situation again, there was no reason to assume such incredible fortune would favor them twice.

The Vaar later learned that their fortune was more vast than they thought. The Gray Fleet was slow to rebuild its numbers. Many of the ships that had survived the battles in the Triangle were among the most ancient in the force. Due to millennia of wear, a significant number were no longer capable of manufacturing replacements. This critical factor would buy the Vaar the time they needed to hunt down the remainder without being on the defensive again.

Attitudes toward the military and its importance changed throughout the Collective. More importantly, the Vaar resolved to make themselves a strong people. They hoped to never again be at the mercy of an alien power, but this event also poisoned the already dim view the Vaar held of AI.

After the Second Battle of the Triangle, Tona'tass returned to Prithone to give his report, and there he met his end. Tona'tass was assassinated on Day 44 of 4,037 PA by a Collective Committee loyalist as he dined in a restaurant just outside of the Council's former meeting place. The assassin was quickly apprehended and beaten to death by the restaurant's other patrons. Tona'tass's body was interred on Prithone in a monument that stood into modernity.

# 5G

# THE DEEP REPUBLIC AND THE AGE OF DECADENCE

## 3,038 PA–12,105 PA
## (65,884 AN–76,641 AN)

WITH THE END OF the Gray Fleet Crises ending, the Vaar had to decide what to do about their long-term government. Kopo'tan had been appointed warlord, and many wished for his tenure to become permanent. But Kopo'tan was not one of them. He proposed that the Interstellar Collective be abolished entirely and that a new government be erected in its place. He would be one of the founding fathers of what became the Deep Republic.

At Kopo'tan's invitation, representatives of every colony were called to Prithone, where they established a constitution for the new government. The idea of representative government was always a difficult one for the Vaar. The idea of universal suffrage was anathema as some citizens contributed a great deal more to society than others. Even with this idea firmly in mind, the Vaar often disagreed over how much franchise the most contributing members should have, versus how little should be accorded to the least contributing. The fact that the representatives summoned to Prithone were able to hammer out an agreement in only two years was astonishing even to them.

The Tax Council replaced the Collective Committee. This council was made up of elected representatives headed by a prime minister. Voting rights for the citizenry were tied directly to their taxation. Every Vaar would have a vote—the more taxes a Vaar paid, the more weight his vote would carry on his home world. The more taxes the central government drew from a planet, the more representatives it was entitled to on the Tax Council. Viss were not granted a birthright vote as they were exempted from the laws of conscription drawn up by the representatives. But like their male counterparts, if they earned a wage and paid taxes out of that wage, they would receive voting power proportional to the amount of their tax. Civil liberties, which were virtually unheard of in the Collective, were also written into the Republic's constitution. These included rights of life, property, speech, and trial if accused of criminal wrongdoing. This new government became known as the *Jeem'fona*, the Deep Republic.

Perhaps the greatest controversy the representatives faced was what to do with the Sovari. Not all were keen to give them the place of esteem they had held in the Collective. These representatives saw the Sovari as enablers of the Collective that had helped to establish it in the first place. This was not at all true. The Sovari never involved themselves in the creation of government, and their code required them to offer their counsel to whatever government existed for the Vaar. Many forgot or ignored the fact that the Sovari had been warning about the need for a better military long before the Gray Fleet ever arrived.

The Sovari still held great, borderline religious sway among a significant portion of the population. But a bit of their charm had been lost in the Gray Fleet Crises. The Sovari always had answers before the crises. If there was a problem to be solved, their solutions were not always taken, but they always had solutions to offer. When the Gray Fleet came, the Sovari knew neither what they were, nor any weaknesses to exploit. The higher a pedestal on which one was placed, the easier it often was to knock them down. The Sovari image as the all-knowing advisers had been tainted.

Modern Vaar scholars generally wrote off the entirety of the Republic's duration as a time of hedonism, debauchery, decadence, and immorality. This was not at all accurate and was mostly the modern and totalitarian Combine justifying its existence. While the Republic became an incredibly decadent realm, it did not reach this point immediately.

The Deep Republic presided over the longest period of uninterrupted peace the Vaar had ever known. The last Gray Fleet ships capable of self-replication were destroyed by 3,047 PA. The last Gray Fleet ships in the Deep Sea were destroyed by 3,120 PA. In the following years, the Vaar reached hitherto unknown standards of living without the Collective to depress them.

The Vaar had a concept known as *Pritho'tel*, literally *Fire of Prithone*. This concept revolved around the Vaar being the apex predator of an incredibly hostile planet. This concept stressed the need for a Vaar to face adversity, trials, and suffering to be whole. For his home was an environment that ruthlessly culled the weak, the stupid, and the foolish. Few in modernity remembered it, but this concept was taught by the Sovari. Throughout the passing years, the Vaar would learn that there was some truth to it.

This was the only era among the Vaar where automation truly flourished. The technology was there, and the Collective was no longer around to inhibit it. Within two hundred years, the Republic faced its first major social crisis: mass unemployment. Efforts were made in education to create new employment opportunities in science, engineering, and similar fields. A society could only support so many workers in each of these, and not every citizen was capable of such work.

It was easy to believe that laziness and lack of work ethic were the same. They were not. The Vaar were enormous creatures; their bodies required a lot of energy and calories to function, such a creature is naturally prone to conserving that energy when possible.

A saying shared by both Solars and Vaar goes "Necessity is the mother of invention." Among the Vaar, in the field of medical science, necessity was a neglectful mother. A Vaar's immune system was a phenomenal thing. Precious few bacteria or viruses had any prayer of surviving in their bodies unless the host was starving. Their regenerative capabilities could heal wounds that would slay most other sapient beings. Only degeneration of brain tissue with age, along with the reduced ability to regenerate, prevented the Vaar from being biologically immortal.

As automation replaced jobs and made existing jobs easier, the Vaar grew lazy. When overeating led to mass obesity and chemical imbalances in the body, medical science was not in a position to meet the problem head-on. The Vaar grew up in comfort and forgot how to handle adversity. For that matter, they forgot what adversity was.

The Deep Republic Council on Education kept careful records of standardized cognition tests given to all students. These tests were similar to IQ tests used by humanity long ago. These tests operated on a base score of 1,000 for the average citizen. The council would note that by the Republic's third generation, scores were changing.

The declining intelligence of young Vaar and Viss eventually became a serious concern. Thousands of studies were conducted on the subject, and political movements grew around them. A Vaar proverb would emerge in this era. *Politics is finding greater profit in problems than solutions.*

Over the Republic's lifetime, the structure of society changed. The idea that the rich got richer while the poor became poorer had never been more true than in the Deep Republic. This was unintentionally written into the constitution when a citizen's tax contribution directly affected the magnitude of his vote. Only a handful of wealthy Vaar could outvote hundreds of thousands of middle-class and millions of poor. By its thousandth year, the Republic was a naked plutocracy.

The poorly-scoring were not simply winning the reproduction race in this era; they were dominating. While the elites of society generally maintained scores well above 1,000, the scores for the average citizen continued to plummet. By the year 4,800, the average Vaar had a score of 750. This score was considered severe mental impairment when testing began. The Vaar were once a pair-bonding species. That practice was heavily discouraged by the Collective. Pair-bonding made a brief return in the Republic's early years and remained a hallmark of the elite, but it died a painful death among the common people as promiscuity and uncontrolled childbirth ballooned into their social crisis.

The state boarding school system that existed in the modern Combine found its roots in this era. It was an outgrowth of the sheer number of abandoned children the state was forced to care for. Added to this were the children who had to be taken from parents who couldn't properly raise their offspring.

There was a finite number of strains, burdens, and crises that any society could endure before it became too much. The fact that the Deep Republic managed to last as long as it did should speak to how resilient it was. But that resilience could not change the decline the Vaar eventually found themselves in.

With dropping intelligence came declines across the whole of civilization, but perhaps the most significant was technological decline. Automation could be a wonderful thing when there were people to maintain the machines. When it became difficult to find workers who could do basic math, automation started to become a liability. Food shortages emerged as the automated farming systems broke down, and each generation brought forth fewer people who could repair them or design replacements. Shortages of consumer goods manifested for similar reasons. Even basic infrastructure such as electric grids and sanitation systems began to degrade. Due to the Vaar's disdain for AI, the possibility of building advanced machines to perform this work was not seriously considered until it was too late.

One branch of society had largely managed to avoid declining while the rest degraded like rotting corpses. That was the military. The military's immunity was due in large part to the influence of the Sovari. Their influence had grown since the Republic declined. People who could not think for themselves were often eager to accept whatever an expert or a leader told them. The biggest problem for the Sovari was that they were trying to guide a population that was more willing than ever to listen but was, at the same time, becoming too brain-dead to follow the advice they were given.

Thanks largely to the Sovari, however, the Republic's military managed to avoid a fate that had often plagued some of humanity's armed forces. Namely to be hijacked as a welfare program to provide jobs to unemployed and unemployable citizens. The Republic military was careful to accept only high-quality candidates. Rumors came from this era that the Sovari employed some method to raise the intelligence of certain recruits.

# 5H
# RISE OF THE INTERSTELLAR COMBINE

## 12,105 PA–13,805 PA
## (76,641 AN–78,658)

SOME NATIONS DIED IN fire and calamity. Others like the Deep Republic passed like a wasting patient until nothing remained. The bottom fell out for the Deep Republic in the 6,800s. By this point, the military had been forced to take increasing responsibility for society. The military operated nearly all power plants, sanitation, and even food production.

Those who learned that the Combine was overseen by the military often assumed that there was some dramatic moment where the military seized control. But the reality was that the military gained control over time, picking up more and more of society's burdens as the general public became unable to handle them. By 6,845 PA, the military's responsibilities included control over the election system.

The Republic had originally established its supreme military rank as Warlord of the Republic. This rank was meant to be granted only in times of war, to provide a supreme commander. By this point, the military had taken on so many responsibilities that it was necessary to have an individual in the role, even in peacetime. In 12,105 the role was held by a Vaar named Kal'ron, who had been handpicked and guided by the Sovari. A career member of the Republic Marines, Kal'ron had spent his entire life in service to the Republic. He had also seen its accelerating decline.

At the start of 12,105, Kal'ron began transitioning to the official abolition of the Republic government. This process would take time but, in many ways, was easier than one might have expected. The only real resistance came from the social elite, the wealthiest and most affluent of the Vaar citizenry. Many of them could see exactly what the military was writing on the wall. Some supported change, but many turned their focus to protecting their wealth and preparing to fight the incoming reforms.

Rather than engage in an armed coup, Kal'ron chose to use the election system, which the military already controlled. Carefully selected candidates ran in all major elections, and the military—thanks to their control of the elections—ensured their victory. Many of the wealthy class attempted to rally the population against these efforts. These attempts generally met with little success. Too few in the population had any real motivation. Many of the Vaar's less affluent citizens had adopted the mindset that if the wealthy did not like it, it must be a good thing.

By year 12,200, the military had near total control over the Republic government. This had entailed a massive amount of voter fraud given that the voting system favored the wealthy based on their taxes. With the top 10 percent owning more than 70 percent of the wealth, and with it, the vote, the military could not have accomplished its electoral control legitimately.

On Day 13 of the year 12,240, the Republic Council officially voted to abolish itself and hand all government control to the military. The reaction from most of the citizenry was ambivalence. The average citizen foresaw little change. In their eyes the military already controlled everything that mattered. But not every world went along with the transition peacefully.

On Day 15 Warlord Kal'ron formally declared the abolition of the Deep Republic and the institution of the new Interstellar Combine.

The social elite had been ready for this move. A total of fifty-two planets declared their independence from the Combine on Day 16 of the year 12,240. These worlds were some of the most commercially wealthy, and home to many of the same elites who had been preparing for this move. Under the name Heirs of the Republic, this group of wealthy citizens promised to defend their territory from encroachment by the Combine.

The Heirs of the Republic did not make an idle boast. They had been raising a technologically sophisticated military to protect themselves. However, legions of imbeciles did not make for an effective fighting force. The Heirs of the Republic had chosen to build an automated, AI-controlled military. The Heirs revealed this fighting force on Day 67 when they attacked the starports on the planet Rusnaga.

The Combine military had been massing forces of the Deep Marines on Rusnaga in preparation to subdue the rebelling worlds. Though the military was aware that the elites had been arming, they had not realized just how far it had gone. A total of 168 warships were destroyed, mostly at their moorings as they were hit by AI bombers and interstellar missiles. This was at a time before the Vaar had mastered astranet-like technology. Thus the masses of marines gathered on Rusnaga were temporarily trapped on the planet.

The newly christened Deep Fleet responded to the Heirs' actions on Day 148 when a fleet of over six hundred ships, including sixty-four fleet carriers, arrived at Rusnaga.

There were very few major battles of the War of the Fifty-Two, as it would later be known. The construction of interstellar warships was not a task the Heirs were able to carry out in secret. As a result, the rebelling planets had few ships with which to contest the Deep Fleet. The only real challenge to the Deep Fleet for orbital superiority was in the missile batteries that had been erected on the planets, their moons, and in asteroid fields. While it proved time-consuming, the Deep Fleet used its masses of fighters and bombers to gradually break down these defenses and move in on the rebelling planets.

The true nightmare of this conflict was found in the ground campaign. When Deep Marines landed to seize control of the planet, they found themselves awash in combat drones. These ranged from AI-controlled infantry units to tanks and artillery. The greatest threat came from suicide drones barely the size of a Viss's fist. They flew at high speeds while skimming the surface. Their low altitude and small size made them difficult to track and detect for units in space or orbit. They would attack in swarms, diving on their targets. Each had enough explosives within to defeat any personnel defense that existed in the day. In groups they could present a serious threat to armor and drop ships.

The sensor technology available to the Vaar in this area was not especially good. This left orbital units largely unable to find the points where the machines would concentrate or the factories where they were built. Most of these factories had been converted from other tasks and continued manufacturing their original product in token quantities to keep up appearances. Other factories had been constructed deep underground. This often left the Deep Marines with no choice but to go city by city, factory by factory, to find the points of manufacture so they could be destroyed, an effort they had to accomplish while under constant attack by the drones.

The Heirs had always planned to fight a war of attrition. The long eras of peace and the lack of good recruits had winnowed the military's numbers significantly. The Deep Fleet and the Deep Marines had only 2.21 billion personnel between them. By Day 1 of 12,245 PA, the Combine had subdued twenty of the fifty-two remaining worlds. The rapid design and deployment of new laser point defense systems helped defend against the drones. By this point, the Combine War Forces, as they were now known, had suffered over 240 million casualties. Many of these casualties had come when the Heirs ceased attacks to give the appearance that their forces had been neutralized before resuming attacks when more forces showed to occupy the planet.

This rate of attrition was unsustainable and led Warlord Kal'ron to issue what was recounted in history as the Bombardment Order. No further attempts were made to land the Deep Marines on hostile worlds. Instead, once local space defenses had been neutralized, these worlds were bombarded. Targets included all major sources of power generation, sanitation, transportation infrastructure, and off-world communication. The planets were then subjected to blockade.

Over the following year, the military dropped simple communication devices, along with pamphlets promising food to any citizen who used the coms units to report on the locations where drones were being constructed and where they massed when not in action. Though the military received many false leads, as the blockades continued and hunger mounted, more useful tips came in. The Deep Fleet soon destroyed an increasing number of the Heirs forces from space.

The rebellion ended on Day 12 of 12,246 PA, when the last planet, Gruzo, was occupied by the Deep Marines. Many of the rebellion's leaders were successfully captured, handed over by starving civilians in the hopes of food. On Day 111 of 12,246 PA, the surviving leaders of the rebellion were publicly flayed for their treason against the Combine.

Winning the war to keep the Vaar united under one government was the easy part. The military knew all along that winning the peace was going to be a monumental task. The war, however, resolved questions that had split the burgeoning Council of Warlords, including whether to revive the police state that had existed under the Interstellar Collective. The fact that wealthy private citizens could assemble such vast forces in secret was the factor that resolved the issue. The warlords ordered the creation of the State Security Service as the new agency to monitor for disloyalty in the Combine.

The Combine still possessed a population made up primarily of citizens who couldn't hold gainful employment or contribute to an advanced society productively. No agency in the Combine had kept a closer eye on, or conducted more studies relating to, the serious decline in intelligence among the population. This led the early warlords to face some very tough decisions.

The military's studies attributed the declining intelligence to two primary factors. The first and most salient was that those with lower intelligence were out-reproducing the others. The problem was exacerbated by the ease and comfort in which young Vaar and Viss lived, effectively stunting their mental development in their childhood and adolescent years.

The newly formed Council of Warlords felt that it had no choice but to write off the current generation. In the hopes of reversing the decline, the Combine instituted a strict licensing requirement for all citizens to reproduce. A step further was the creation of a military-run boarding school system that all children were required to attend. The military did its best with both to accomplish the task with minimal backlash.

The majority of the population was sterilized simply by placing a birth control supplement in the drinking water of each planet. This was supplemented in consumer drinks to ensure the formula reached the entire population. It had no significant effect on the Vaar, but even in small doses, it was effective for the Viss. Meanwhile females approved for a breeding license were required to take "supplements" they were told would help the child mature without defect. In reality these supplements simply counteracted the effects of the birth control.

The effort to convince the public to give up their children for attendance to boarding school proved much simpler than some had anticipated. The majority of the population became so decadent and selfish that plenty were willing to ease the burden on themselves by surrendering their children. The few who showed an unwillingness to do so were given the choice to remain near their children in exchange for helping to operate the growing state school system.

The majority of the teachers in this school system were drawn from the military. These officials ran a rigorous program to educate the children in their care. Immediate results were seen by ensuring the young Vaar and Viss had proper challenges to stimulate their young minds.

These schools were practically prison camps. The children were not permitted to leave until graduation, barring school-sponsored activities. Free time was tightly regulated. The modern Combine boarding school system would find its genesis in these early schools. While results came quickly, they were still small. Generations would pass before the intelligence rate would return to pre-Republic norms.

The Combine War Forces had no interest in managing every affair of the civilian population. While there were enough intelligent civilians left to administer a government, there were not enough to run the bureaucracy beneath what was responsible for carrying out the leadership's decisions.

The War Forces maintained the totality of their control for eleven generations. By this point, the intelligence of the general population still had not returned to pre-Republic norms, but the numbers had risen high enough that the military began offloading some of its responsibilities. Early failures in handing infrastructure back to the civilian population led the military to commit to long-term control. Even in modernity, civilian workers in the power, water purification, and similar sectors labored under the supervision of military engineers.

By 13,805, the Interstellar Combine was ready to expand.

# 51
# PRELUDE TO EXPANSION

## 13,805 PA–14,277 PA
## (78,658 AN–79,218 AN)

MORE THAN A THOUSAND years had passed after the fall of the Deep Republic. Eventually the flame of Prithone burned once more. The Council of Warlords was determined never to let the days of decadence and indolence return. The warlords determined that to prevent such an era from returning, the Vaar required an unending mission. The Council determined that mission was the exploration, conquest, and colonization of the universe.

The Deep Sea had a total of four irregular satellite galaxies. The Vaar focused their first extragalactic colonization efforts here. But unlike the Deep Sea, these galaxies had a dearth of habitable, or easily adaptable, planets. The Vaar made great strides in developing their bioforming technology to seed colonies throughout the Deep Sea's satellites.

Most of the colonization efforts in these galaxies went without serious difficulty. There were a paltry few planets with native life, and none of them supported sapient life. The Combine War Forces continued to grow, and the military trained extensively. The Gray Fleet had proven that there was other intelligent life out there. The Vaar intended to be ready to conquer it once they found it.

The Vaar began sending probes toward the Proximity Sea to map the region. The Council of Warlords had every intention of expanding its control. The Vaar even began the construction of massive sleeper ships to carry a vanguard force into the Proximity Sea.

The Vaar would soon join the short list of sapient species that colonized a second prime galaxy, not an orbiting dwarf, without the aid of the transpatial drive. This would also bring the era of bloodless expansion to an end.

# 5J
# THE LONG VOYAGE

## 14,277 AN–14,504 AN
## (79,218 AN–79,487 AN)

THE COUNCIL OF WARLORDS intended to colonize the Proximity Sea, one way or another. The preparations to do so created a massive works project for the civilian population. This culminated in what came to be known as the Reach Fleet, a collection of twelve of the largest ships the Vaar had built and the largest they would build until the Rethan War. These ships would leave from the Deep Sea satellite galaxy of Nen'daj (*Broad Lake*). These ships would then make the journey toward the Proximity Sea.

The Vaar had only recently begun to phase out the Weber drive in favor of massless impulse drives. The MID was new technology for the Vaar, immature, and had a great deal of room left for improvement. The MIDs available were considerably slower than the Weber drives the Vaar possessed, but far more fuel efficient. The twelve ships for the long voyage were thus built with MIDs, while the smaller ships they carried were equipped with Weber drives.

The Proximity Sea faced the Deep Sea at a perpendicular angle, allowing the ships to advance on it from above or below, depending on perspective. Each ship laid a series of navigation buoys and pre-fabricated "advancement depots." These depots were stocked with supplies by faster ships launched from the Deep Sea or its satellites. With the ability to refuel at these depots, the Weber-equipped ships could make the transit in less time once the path was complete.

The trip required a total of 224 years before the first ship, *Strident Voyager*, arrived on the rim of the Proximity Sea. Three of the twelve ships never made it to their destination. The *Bold Voyager* suffered a critical malfunction in its warp drive that forced the ship to turn back. The *Sleeping Voyager* exploded halfway to the destination as it deployed a buoy. Exactly what caused the explosion was never determined.

The final ship to fail on its trip was the *Ardent Voyager*. The ship made the trip, but none of the crew survived to see it. The ships utilized an interesting crew rotation. The Vaar were not willing to completely trust AI to handle the journey. Thus the Vaar crew worked in shifts. Most of the crew were kept in stasis, while two team members were awake to monitor operations.

Each two-person team handled a six-month rotation before going into stasis as the next team was automatically awakened.

A malfunction in the life-support system doomed the entire crew. The alert system designed to notify the crew of such an issue failed. The next shift realized too late that the problem existed and asphyxiated as a result of a critical buildup of carbon dioxide. Each subsequent team awakened and realized the issue but with too little time to perform the necessary repairs. Thus each team awoke, only to asphyxiate a few minutes later. *Ardent Voyager*'s autopilot brought the ship to its destination in the Proximity Sea, but by that point, no crew remained to begin operations.

The remaining ships made their trips in a relatively uneventful fashion. From each vessel, 144 cartographer probes were launched to begin mapping the galaxy and searching for sapient natives. The massive ships began the process of converting themselves into space stations. Each was the reception point for the waves of Vaar that prepared to stream between galaxies.

Scans given by the probes were relayed along the buoy network, and they soon showed that the Proximity Sea was home to an advanced sapient species. This species controlled approximately a third of the galaxy. The information obtained by the probes suggested the presence of a species more technologically advanced than the Combine. The native's ships operated with massless impulse drives that were considerably faster than any warp drive the Vaar possessed. The probes made several attempts to pick up the communications of the galaxy's natives but could not find anything intelligent in the data they received.

All of this information was transmitted down the line of buoys to the Deep Sea and the Council of Warlords. This kicked off a new debate in the military leadership about whether to conquer the native species or exterminate it.

Most of the Council of Warlords was in favor of extermination, having no desire for the Combine to be responsible for a large alien population. But there were enough on the Council who opposed this option. Grand Warlord Joln'kar petitioned the Sovari for their advice on the matter. The warlords were surprised to learn that the Sovari knew a great deal about this previously unknown alien species. The Sovari knew their home world, the species' age, and a significant amount about what their technology was capable of. But when pressed on the issue, the Sovari refused to disclose how they knew this information.

The Sovari rebuked the warlords for contemplating the annihilation of a sapient species. It was unknown which Sovari said it, but a quote survived into modernity among the Vaar:

*If they have not sought to bring annihilation to your home, what becomes of you who brings it to theirs?*

The Sovari's judgment was enough to inform the Council's decision. They would conquer the natives of the Proximity Sea.

# 5K
# THE PROXIMITY WAR

## 14,545 PA–14,620 PA
## (79,536 AN–79,625 AN)

EVEN AFTER THE DECISION was made to conquer the Proximity Sea, it was some time before the Vaar were in a position to do the deed. Even with the buoy network that existed between galaxies, even the fastest ships could only make the journey in fifty-two years. The warlords were not optimistic about the implications. Ships would have to go on journeys of many decades just to reach the battlefield. To hold such a distant conquest would prove difficult.

Never ones to back down from a challenge, the Vaar went forward with their plans to conquer the Proximity Sea. The native population controlled only a third of the galaxy, and by simple coincidence, none of the original ships had finished in their territory. The natives had noticed many of the probes entering their territory. These probes had been designed to self-destruct to prevent their capture, but they had alerted the natives that another sapient species was watching them.

The Proximity Sea's natives came from a world near the galaxy's rim and had gradually expanded outward. The Combine focused on its voyager star bases farthest from their territory. These stations became the depots as supplies for an invasion were sent down the buoy lines.

The Vaar spent years building the great armament used to subjugate the Proximity Sea. This would culminate in the most massive armada the Vaar had yet assembled. Four hundred six fleet carriers carried seven thousand bombers and forty-nine thousand fighters each. Six thousand escort ships were designed to protect the carriers and provide fire support for the carrier's forces. Forty thousand transport ships carried munitions, additional craft for the carriers, and matériel to build additional outposts. Twenty thousand assault transports carried one billion marines to secure objectives.

Warlord Oron'gor was chosen as the leader of this vanguard. He made the initial trip with his forces across the intergalactic void. The Combine war machine continued building forces for him and sending them down the buoy lines every two hundred days. Oron'gor would receive his first reinforcements two hundred days after his invasion began, with more every two hundred days thereafter. Oron'gor and his personnel went into stasis to begin their trip toward the Proximity Sea. The buoy network made all the difference, and only a pair of transport ships were lost on the journey. The fleet arrived on Day 73 of 14,545 PA.

Vaar military planners had divided up the galaxy into four lateral quadrants referred to by the cardinal directions north, south, east, and west. The natives resided in the galaxy's north wing. Oron'gor concentrated his forces on the east and west quadrants. Roughly a third of his forces were concentrated in the west, with the remainder in the east.

Oron'gor's selection to lead the invasion had been a difficult choice among the Council of Warlords. The Combine had been at peace for so long, they lacked battle-tested troops and commanders to guide them. Wargames held during his time had shown that Oron'gor was competent as an admiral but was neither the best tactician nor strategist in the Combine. He was chosen primarily for the iron discipline in which he had always held his forces, which was essential for a journey so far from home. However, Oron'gor's flaws as a commander would take their toll.

Oron'gor planned to launch a probing assault from the western quadrant of the galaxy. This assault could gauge the enemy's strength. Equally important, it would draw defenders to the western quadrant and out of position to defend against an attack from the east. The downside of this plan was that it divided Oron'gor's forces, reducing the maximum strength he could concentrate at any one point. Fortunately for the Vaar, they faced an enemy completely unprepared to defend itself from an extragalactic invasion.

The natives of the Proximity Sea were a semi-vertebrate species that looked to some almost like plant life. These tentacled creatures lacked any semblance of vocal cords and communicated through a combination of pheromones and selective color control of their flesh. The Vaar would eventually dub these creatures quorim, a word meaning *weird* in the ancient tongue.

The quorim had very sophisticated technology. Their tech was well beyond that of the Vaar and, in the hands of a competent military, could have been a deciding factor in the conflict. However, the quorim had little experience in warfare before reaching the stars, and even less afterward. Much as the Elrua were to the Solar Empire, they were a vast enemy without the knowledge or expertise to win. But unlike the Elrua, the quorim had the will to make a fight of it.

Some historians look back on the conquest of the Proximity Sea as a military gift to the Vaar. The quorim put up enough of a fight to make the invaders work for it, but not so much that the invasion was ever in real danger of failing. This allowed the Vaar to gain an excellent grasp of what tactics worked and what did not.

With more than 4,800 worlds under quorim control, it took many years for Oron'gor's fleet to dominate the region. Despite the sheer size of this conquest, major battles were relatively few in number. The quorim lacked the logistical expertise to quickly organize, deploy, and concentrate their forces, but they fought without reservation or even a sense of self-preser-vation. This would earn a measure of respect from the Vaar as the saying came: *quorim don't surrender.*

Oron'gor did not survive to see the end of the invasion. While the quorim were having a hard time organizing mass fleets and armies, they proved much more capable in terms of small operations. The quorim had proven to be excellent code breakers, and intercepts of Vaar communica-tions were responsible for their only significant victories.

Oron'gor was killed on Day 300 of 14,619 PA. The invasion was pro-ceeding well with the eastern and western forces closing in on the quorim home world from two directions. Oron'gor took a bomber from the eastern force to inspect the western quadrant in preparation for the push on the quorim's home planet. The quorim's code breakers learned about Oron'gor's upcoming inspection and tracked his bomber through its flight. This al-lowed an ambush force of quorim ships to break through the escort and destroy Oron'gor's bomber, but the mission was a sacrificial one.

Oron'gor's death was a setback, but it came too late to have a mean-ingful effect on the outcome of the war. The invasion of the quorim home world was delayed by forty days as the force waited for word from Prithone to determine who would replace Oron'gor.

The conquest of the quorim was declared officially complete on Day 6 of 14,620 PA when the species' home world was declared secured. After the conquest was complete, the Council of Warlords and others began to see value in the Sovari's stance on conquest or extermination. The quorim were ahead of the Vaar in many areas ranging from propulsion, to communica-tion, and they even had the foundations of an FTL weapon system under development. Had the conquest come a few decades later, the Vaar may have faced an insurmountable problem.

The integration of the quorim into Combine society was a long and difficult process. Not only were the quorim less than thrilled about aiding their conquerors, but many in the Combine were not thrilled about working alongside aliens. Were it not for the Sovari, the issue might have exploded into a social crisis. The Council of Warlords was eager to begin incorpo-rating as much of the quorim's technology as possible into the military. At the urging of the Sovari, they instead used quorim and their technology to improve Vaar infrastructure, communications, and consumer goods to ben-efit the civilian population. The Council of Warlords did not like this idea, but the Sovari still held great sway. None among the warlords were ready to openly act against their counsel.

The Vaar who had manned the invasion force became the first colonists in the Proximity Sea. The Vaar had taken the galaxy in the near term. But as far as the warlords were concerned, to hold it in the long-term, they had to dominate it. That meant growing a huge population in the new galaxy.

For the quorim who lived in the conquered galaxy, the war was just the beginning. The quorim had carefully cultivated their technology to conform to the natural environment of their planet. Most quorim lived in homes built into the giant fungi that dominated their home world and which they transplanted to their colonies. Giant forests of these fungi, and the homes they contained, were leveled to make way for Vaar settlement. Efforts by the quorim to form resistance cells or otherwise rebel were dealt with harshly. Even passive resistance, such as refusing commands, was often met with extreme force.

The quorim were held to strict reproductive limits. The Council of Warlords had been very careful to balance the genders of the invaders. Almost as soon as the war was over, the birth quotas were handed out. These restrictions would not be lifted until the Rethan War. Though the quorim would eventually gain a measure of standing and respect in Combine society, that would not come for many more years.

Oron'gor was remembered by Vaar historians as the warlord who gave the Vaar their first successful conquest of a new galaxy. The Vaar renamed the quorim home world Oron'gor'segwa, or *Oron'gor's Island*, in his honor.

# 5L
# SAILING THE EMPTY OCEAN

## 14,856 PA–16,925 PA
## (79,905 AN–82,359 AN)

AFTER THE CONQUEST OF the Proximity Sea, the Vaar found themselves in possession of two major galaxies and many smaller satellite galaxies. But no sooner had the conquest of the Proximity Sea been completed than debate spawned over what the next step should be. When they initially made it into space, they had expanded with a frenzy across their home galaxy. Now they had a second galaxy to colonize.

Some among the Council of Warlords wished to begin sending their people to a third galaxy. Others argued that this was folly and that seeding many colonies separated by decades was certain to result in their new empire disintegrating as distant and isolated colonies pushed for independence. The Council was already dealing with domestic issues, including a nascent rebellion hoping to restore the Deep Republic.

These years were a busy time for State Security as these movements were stomped out only to reappear elsewhere. This problem was exacerbated by the need to send many agents to the Proximity Sea. There they had to not only ensure that the distant colonists did not entertain thoughts of rebellion, but to ensure that any efforts by the quorim to rebel were stamped out before they could mature. The Sovari urged the Vaar to consolidate their holdings before looking to expand. That was enough to settle the debate—until a new development arose.

On Day 43 of 14,856 PA, Vaar and quorim scientists tested the Interstellar Combine's first transpatial drive aboard the ship *Joyous Expedition*. The ship successfully made a transpatial jump from the Deep Sea to the Proximity Sea, which meant the . The Vaar had a fast lane to reach new galaxies. This development reignited the debate in the Council of Warlords as to whether or not the Combine should focus on expanding to a third galaxy. This time when the Sovari were questioned, they advised exploration. But they advised strongly against starting any war that could not be handled with ease.

The Vortex Sea was the next closest after the Proximity Sea, but the Vortex Sea's core hosted two supermassive black holes in close orbit to each other. This was a problem for the Combine's new transpatial drive. The drive could not adequately separate the gravitational warp of the two to form a safe jump point. The Combine thus set its sights on the Disorder Sea.

The Disorder Sea was formed when two large galaxies warped and distorted each other in the long process of merging. While this galaxy had multiple supermassive black holes, several were far enough apart that they could serve as suitable navigation points for a transpatial jump. The first transpatial explorer ships entered the Disorder Galaxy in 14,871.

Galactic collisions could be spectacular sights but were not as violent as one might expect. The vast distance between stars meant that even in such a collision, it was unlikely that two stars or planets would meet. The Vaar knew this and were not surprised that they found life. What startled them was how *much* life they found in this galaxy. Of all the galaxies known to the Empire or the Vaar, none held more indigenous sapient species than the Disorder Sea.

The Vaar's experience was very similar to that of the Empire as it expanded beyond Andromeda and Triangulum. Many of the species in this galaxy were sapient, but only a handful were capable of leaving their atmosphere. If the Vaar claimed dominion over the Disorder Sea, none of these species were in any position to challenge them. The Vaar examined these species to varying degrees, often taking samples off their world for study. In at least one notable instance, the local species detected a Vaar ship in orbit and launched a trio of nuclear weapons at it. With shielding plenty strong enough to survive the hit, the ship ignored the attack and went about its business.

The Vaar concluded that many of these species, while sapient, lacked the intelligence necessary to achieve space travel in any foreseeable future. The Vaar went on to annex those already capable of leaving their atmosphere. As for the rest, monitoring stations were left to watch for any sign that the observed species left their world. They were otherwise ignored while the Vaar worked to stake their claim on the galaxy.

The most difficult task for the Vaar was in keeping their population in line. A bit of a division began in this era between the Council of Warlords and the Council of Sovari. The Sovari still held enough influence with the population that the warlords were not willing to openly defy their counsel, but the warlords increasingly began to view them as doddering old men and began working to undermine their influence. They taught the children in the state schools to trust the judgment of the warlords over that of the Sovari. These efforts did not bear the fruit the warlords hoped. The Sovari continued to accept petitioners from the general population, often giving them excellent life advice. The Vaar and Viss so aided went on to spread their praise through the Combine.

The quorim exerted a serious influence on society as this period drew on. Though they had no political power, their contributions to the advancement of Combine science continued. Sometimes the quorim were an uncomfortably logical people. They understood all too well how bad things could be for them if the Vaar failed to see them as an asset. Thus they actively worked to contribute to Combine society, gradually adapting to their new role.

The contributions of the quorim helped the Combine's technology grow steadily through this era. It was a mistake to think the quorim were smarter than the Vaar, but the quorim had a natural affinity for technology that made them excellent technicians and engineers. They also excelled at contemplating possibilities that didn't occur to Vaar researchers, making them particularly helpful in research and the development of new technologies.

The Vaar visited more than four dozen galaxies in the Deka'Seda (*Proximity Chain*), known as the Virgo Cluster to humanity. Many of these visitations were just a quick jaunt through the galaxy to release probes before venturing on to the next. But in others, the Vaar established outposts to await the day when the Combine would turn its colonial gaze that way.

The Vaar finally entered the realm of FTL combat in this era, developing sensor and missile technology appropriate to the task. They would need it, as the Vaar were rapidly approaching what many in the Combine considered the nation's darkest hour.

# 5M
# THE RETHAN WAR

## 16,926 PA–16,933 PA
## (82,361 AN–82,369 AN)

DESPITE ITS RELATIVE CLOSENESS to the Deep Sea, the Vaar could not visit the La'sora, or Vortex Sea. The invention of the transpatial drive had nullified interest in reaching new galaxies via buoy lines and supply depots. This resulted in the Vortex Sea being neglected until a major development in transpatial technology in 16,926 PA. There existed a single black hole, smaller than supermassive but quite large for a stellar mass in the arms of the Vortex Sea that the new drive technology made reachable. The Vaar wasted little time making good on this new capability.

It was important to understand the reasons one might have to invade a planet. There may be valuable resources or scientific expertise to capture. There may be other items and artifacts of value that risked destruction in heavy bombardment. But in the end, the main reason to invade a planet was the same reason one might invade a city—to take control of it and ensure that the local population could not do anything to aid the enemy's war effort.

There was a common conceit that ground armies were obsolete in a time of interstellar travel and space-borne warships. This idea posited that warships needed only relatively light marine forces to be deployed by star ships for the occasional ground mission. This idea further posited that if warships controlled the space around a planet, then they automatically controlled the planet. If a planet did not surrender or otherwise capitulate, it could simply be bombarded. The same applied if an already subdued planet caused trouble. While it was easy to see the logic that led to this belief, it was a flawed and very naive belief.

It was built on a mountain of bad assumptions and ignored the many non-military factors that often influenced how military forces needed to conduct themselves. The first bad assumption was that star ships could lock down planets on their own. It assumed the military and political leadership were willing to accept the consequences of bombardment. The second bad assumption was that the warships could always and completely neutralize opposing planetary defenses without having to land ground forces to do it. The third bad assumption was that the aggressor would always have a surplus of warships available. Every ship spent babysitting a planet was a ship that is not somewhere else, performing other missions. One of the benefits of a ground army was that it freed up warships to do warship things.

The Rethan War at the beginning, at least, was one of the few conflicts where all of these assumptions were valid. The character of the Rethan War was different from many of the conflicts fought by the Empire. But in terms of hostility, bloodshed, and malice, it compared unfortunately well with the Therican War and the Conquest of Triangulum.

The Vaar entered the Vortex Galaxy on Day 202 of 16,926 PA with a force of three explorer ships. The vessels made contact with the Rethan Republic, which held most of the galaxy in its sway. The Vaar had learned lessons in the conquest of the Proximity Sea about not gathering sufficient intelligence on potential enemies. So the explorer ships took pains to gather as much information as possible on the Rethan and their ships.

When this data was analyzed by the Bureau of Military Intelligence, it concluded that the Rethan had a significant tech advantage over the Combine. These reports were enough to convince the Council of Warlords that an immediate conquest was not the best option. The Combine had domestic issues on its plate that it did not need to complicate by starting what would certainly be a major war.

In the prior years, the Council of Warlords had relaxed the reproduction restrictions for the general population. This was done in the hope of boosting birth rates and helping the Vaar to populate the worlds they had obtained. The measure worked too well. The population exploded, and the Combine couldn't keep up with the growing demands in infrastructure. The most acute issue was a worsening energy crisis.

Contact with the Rethan had gone peacefully, and the species had even shown an interest in opening a trade relationship with the Vaar. To that end, the Vaar were allowed to establish an outpost around the black hole they had used to enter the galaxy. The Vaar dubbed this black hole Vera'donna, or *Gate of the Vortex*. The Vaar erected a transpatial gateway in the region as trade between the two powers commenced.

An area where the Rethan were well ahead of the Vaar was in the production of antimatter-decaying fuels. These were effectively primitive forms of modern xenomatter meant to serve as a storage-safe, containment-safe source of antimatter. With their need for as much energy as possible, the Vaar began trading with the Rethan for their fuel. Neither side had mastered the alchemic printer, and thus the trade focused on goods. The Vaar traded primarily in gold, silver, copper, and other rare metals.

There was a big difference between the rarity of a material like gold to an interstellar civilization and a species confined to a single planet. The former could strip-mine entire planets and asteroids for these materials. The Vortex Gate saw a massive influx of traffic as Vaar cargo ships bearing precious metals came in, and Rethan ships bearing antimatter fuel went out. Meanwhile many enterprising merchants from both sides set up shop in the region to facilitate the trade of other goods. The small region of the galaxy controlled by the Vaar rapidly became known as *Kaguna*, or *the Bazaar*.

Unfortunately the trade between these two powers was mired by bad faith. Rethan society was not one to value traits like honesty and fairness over maximizing personal gain. The Rethan created accounting measures to supply fewer tons of fuel than promised, but the Vaar quickly learned to exploit the Rethans' lack of morals and ethics. This allowed the Combine's intelligence services to collect data on this potential foe. The sometimes flagrant cheating of the Rethan, however, riled feathers from the traders to the warlords. But the Rethan did not worry. The Vaar needed Rethan antimatter more than the Rethan needed Vaar metals.

The goodwill that had been established with a peaceful first contact eroded as the Rethan looked for more ways to cheat on their end of the trade. The matter was not helped by the growing disdain between the two populations. The Rethan were a quasi-avian species that relied on both vocal language and pheromones for communication. The Vaar found the Rethan mercurial, rude, and possessed of an atrocious stench. The Rethan, meanwhile, considered the Vaar dull, plodding, and rude.

The Vaar's need for imported fuel only grew. As years passed, the quantities requested outstripped the surplus production the Rethan were using to meet the demand. The spark found the tinderbox when, instead of increasing their production, the Rethan chose to cheat harder than they already were.

The Rethan began cutting their antimatter fuel with inert additives to provide less fuel for the tonnage of product delivered. When the Vaar discovered this, they were less than pleased. The Council of Warlords put a halt on the next shipment of rare metals, demanding that the Rethan make up the difference in fuel lost due to their additives. The Rethan countered that the additives were

a safety feature. The Rethan halted the next fuel shipment, resulting in over a hundred tanker ships stopping in the Bazaar.

The Council of Warlords had tolerated all it cared to. The body decided that a clear message needed to be sent to the Rethan. The Vaar had a small number of warships in the area, primarily to discourage any form of pirate activity. Over the advice of both the intelligence services and the Sovari, the warlords ordered their forces in the Bazaar to seize the tankers and their crews.

On Day 287 of 16,926 PA, the Deep Fleet warships in the Bazaar carried out their orders. This would mark what most historians considered the beginning of the Rethan War. The Rethan were initially shocked by this action but still felt that the advantage was with them, and they had no intention of backing down. While the Rethan outwardly negotiated, a special team was assigned to go into the Bazaar and rescue the captured tanker crews.

The Rethan could not have botched their rescue operation any harder had they tried. The prisoners were being held in a converted supply depot orbiting an otherwise unremarkable star in the Hrus'ta system. To clear the way for boarding craft, the Rethan tried to bring down the shields. Instead, they accidentally destroyed the depot. All personnel, including the captured tanker crew, were killed.

Rather than admit their mistake, the Rethan leaders in charge of the operation reported to their superiors that the Vaar had destroyed the station to prevent the rescue. When news of this hit the Rethan public, the demand for war was loud and clear. The Yonora Council of the Rethan Republic formally declared war against the Interstellar Combine on Day 392 of the year 16,926.

## The First Battle of the Bazaar

THE RETHAN HAD PREPARED better for a possible conflict with their trade partners. This led the Rethan to spend the intervening years carefully staging forces for a rapid response against any sign of Combine aggression. The Sovari had advised caution in dealing with the Rethan. The Combine's intelligence services had warned them away from direct confrontation. But the Council of Warlords did not listen. Centuries of easy conquest and exploration had led them to arrogance. Too many believed the Vaar were unstoppable in their destiny to claim dominion over the universe. Others had swallowed their own propaganda that had painted the Rethan as weak and cowardly.

Both sides employed fleet doctrines based primarily around carrier ships with bomber craft serving as the main strike component. Though the Rethan had an edge, both sides were broadly comparable to what the Solar Empire had been in the years immediately following the Kaurken War. Failure by both sides to develop better sensory capabilities had left them highly dependent on fighters and bombers to strike distant targets and secure large volumes of space. Most non-carrier ships were either escorts designed to protect the carriers, or assault ships designed to deal with targets too tough for the carrier's craft to handle.

Though both sides relied on a carrier doctrine, the similarities diminished from there. The Vaar favored lightly armed and defended carriers to maximize the number of craft they could carry. Rethan carriers were well armed and hardened, meant to follow their craft into battle and provide them with fire support. But as a consequence, these carriers often carried half or fewer fighters and bombers as their Combine opponents.

The Battle of the Bazaar began on Day 4 of 16,927 PA. The Vaar had a single fleet carrier and twelve escort ships in the region. This was supplemented by an additional two hundred bombers and 1,400 fighters. The Rethan entered the Bazaar with twelve fleet carriers and forty-eight escort ships. With little hope of winning the battle, the Deep Fleet did its best to delay the Rethan to buy time to evacuate Combine citizens in the region. Unfortunately the sacrifice of this force was in vain, as slow mobilization resulted in too few transports arriving in time to process the evacuation.

Despite having taken the region, the Rethan fleet did not destroy the local transpatial gateway. Nor did they make any effort to hinder the communications of the Combine civilians in the region, as if daring the Combine to launch an assault to retake the region. The Vaar took the bait.

## The Second Battle of the Bazaar

WHEN THE COUNCIL OF Warlords realized the truth of the defeat in the Bazaar, they ordered the Third Wing of the Deep Fleet to move in and secure the region. This was not a realistic objective, with more and more of the Rethan fleet mobilizing and ready to defend their territory. Placed in command of the Third Wing was Warlord Hur'sem. He had been given command of this force due to being one of the few fleet commanders with actual combat experience, though it had been against inferior opponents.

Hur'sem was wise enough to send scout probes through the local gateway before jumping in with his fleet. These probes were promptly jammed and destroyed before acquiring any relevant information, which left a clue about what kind of opposition awaited them. But with orders to proceed, Hur'sem had little choice. He sent a few bombers through in the hopes of leading the Rethan to believe he would follow while jumping his fleet to Vera'donna.

Hur'sem's deception worked, not that it did him much good. His force of twenty-four carriers and 154 escorts arrived in the Bazaar to find a force of sixty-two Rethan carriers with 460 warships waiting. Hur'sem's diversion had granted him the first strike, and he rapidly turned his fleet away hoping to slip out of the Rethan's sensor range while they dealt with his attack. It was a good plan, given the options available to him, but his efforts were in vain.

The Rethan utilized a primarily automated military. Their fighters and bombers were all AI-operated, Vaar equivalents were manned platforms operating with AI assistance. The Vaar were suffering a bad case of what they called *peace sickness*. Their inexperienced pilots and flawed tactics resulted in a massacre. Of the thousands of bombers Hur'sem launched at the Rethan fleet, none scored successful hits on a warship. The handful that made it through the protection of the Rethan fighters watched point defenses strike down their attacks.

The Rethan were quick to counterattack, hurtling their own bombers at Hur'sem's fleet and giving chase to keep it in sight. The folly of the assault became apparent when Hur'sem was cut off by a second Rethan fleet more than twice the size of what he had already been facing. The Second Battle of the Bazaar began and ended on Day 34 16,927 PA. None of the Third Wing's ships or bombers survived.

# The Invasion of the Deep Sea

IN THE AFTERMATH OF the Second Battle of the Bazaar, the Rethan were less than impressed with what they had seen of the Vaar's fighting ability. The Vaar had been trounced so heavily in both battles that the Rethan contemplated an invasion of Vaar space. The Rethan had only one approach to fighting a war with an alien power—to kill everyone until they surrendered or none were left.

Combine intelligence had not been alone in studying the opposition. The Rethan's intelligence network had ascertained a great deal about the Interstellar Combine. The Rethan were aware of the Combine's size and the sheer industrial power it could muster against them. To the Rethan, it seemed clear that their only option was to invade and put a knife through the Combine's heart. Otherwise it would only be a matter of time until the Vaar overwhelmed them.

Unfortunately neither the Deep Fleet, nor the Council of Warlords had learned their lesson. The Rethan victories in the Bazaar were written off as the inevitable result of overwhelming numbers. Thus the Combine focused on massing its forces to launch an invasion of Rethan space, but the Rethan were prepared to go on the offensive first.

On Day 222 of 16,927 PA, the bulk of the Rethan fleet made the transpatial jump into the Deep Sea. The Combine had assumed that any attack by the Rethan would come after a transpatial jump to the galactic core, but the Rethan surprised the Vaar with a show of just how much more sophisticated their transpatial systems were. Rather than jumping to the galactic core, the Rethan jumped to a stellar-mass black hole in the galactic disc. The Rethan arrived with 468 fleet carriers, twenty-four thousand warships, and millions of fighters and bombers with which to press the assault. The strategic situation was made all the worse by the jump into the galactic disc, effectively nullifying the heavy defenses the Vaar had arranged in the Deep Sea's galactic core.

The Vaar used a six-point system to map their galaxies. Cartographers divided the galaxy into quadrants. Elevation above or below the galaxy was determined as positive or negative after determining each side. The Rethan had arrived in the northern quadrant, less than five thousand light-years from Prithone.

The Rethan's choice in jump point had been about more than bypassing the defenses in the Deep Sea's galactic core. Their jump point had brought them within two hundred light-years of the Dre'zoma shipyards. These were not only the largest shipyards in the Combine at the time but were the primary mooring site for the Sixth Wing. The Sixth Wing was the Deep Fleet's force dedicated to defending the home galaxy. Intent on not wasting the element of surprise, the Rethan emptied their carriers on Dre'zoma.

The massive shipyards orbiting the planet were blasted out of the sky, and more than half of the Sixth Wing was destroyed at their moorings before the ships could get underway. The rest were destroyed as they attempted to rally for a counterattack. With a single well-executed strike, the Rethan had neutralized the force most responsible for protecting the Deep Sea. Dre'zoma was bombarded shortly thereafter, with casualties exceeding 400 million as the planet's cities were razed. The Rethan fleet began around-the-clock strikes, targeting every Vaar planet in their proximity.

Heads rolled after the initial attack. Gurga'tot, the admiral in command of the Sixth Wing, was charged with dereliction of duty and gross incompetence for allowing so much of his fleet to be in port during time of war. Many more in the Combine's intelligence community faced charges for failing to ascertain the capabilities of the Rethan's transpatial drives.

As had occurred in the Gray Fleet Crises, the call went out across the Deep Sea. Billions of citizens were conscripted into work brigades to build planetary defenses. The Deep Fleet scrambled to grow their forces in the defense of the Deep Sea.

## The Battle of Trae'ton

Upon entering the Deep Sea, the Rethan advanced on Prithone. The path to the capital went through star sectors housing a great deal of the galaxy's infrastructure. When compared to more modern warfare like the fighting in the Hourglass War, the dynamics of fleet combat made it difficult for an aggressor to bring an opponent to battle who was not willing to commit. One needed to advance in a front narrow enough to keep forces concentrated, yet wide enough to force a flanking enemy to go on wide, time-consuming paths to do so. This bought plenty of time for the enemy to be spotted and for the front to meet the counterattack. All of these difficulties expanded with operations in three spatial dimensions.

The Rethan moved through the Deep Sea on an especially wide front, allowing them to strike more Vaar worlds without diverting from their line of advance. This broad front was vulnerable to counterattack as it approached the Trae'ton Cluster. This was a star-dense region of space. Only the galaxy's core exceeded it in the number of stars per cubic light-year. This region was also a colonial dead zone, with relatively few colonized worlds.

The Rethan launched bomber strikes deep into Vaar territory to strike at transports, supply depots, and other logistically vital facilities. This affected the Vaar's ability to concentrate their forces for an effective defense. Raids launched by the Vaar met with much less success. On average the Vaar lost fighters at a ratio of 2.6 to 1 against the Rethan, and none of the Rethan's vital carriers had been successfully neutralized.

A warlord named Von'tu was placed in command of the defense of the Deep Sea. Von'tu, relatively young for a warlord, was considered by many to be the Combine's foremost expert in carrier-based fleet combat. Von'tu planned to engage the Rethan with a full counterattack in the Trae'ton Cluster, hoping to keep the Rethan engaged in this relatively low-population region.

This was the first time the Deep Fleet would face the Rethan without being on the wrong end of the element of surprise, and with comparable numbers to the enemy force. Placed in command of the First Combined Wing, Von'tu had a force of 320 fleet carriers and 5,600 warships. Though he was significantly outnumbered in terms of warships, Von'tu had a slight edge as the primary striking force for both fleets in his bombers. Von'tu's force had just under 4.5 million bombers to throw at his enemy, with over 31 million fighters to support them. This was in addition to another 1.5 million bombers with matching support deploying from hastily assembled star bases in the region. The Rethan had just under 3 million bombers and 20 million fighters.

One star in the Trae'ton Cluster had recently undergone a stellar event where two black holes of substantial mass collided. Von'tu hoped to use the distortion the event caused to the relatively primitive warp sensors of the era to mask much of his fleet's presence from long-range sensors. The Rethan were ruthlessly scouting every cubic light-year ahead of them and spotted Von'tu's force well before either side could strike the other.

The Battle of Trae'ton began on Day 290 of 16,927 PA, with the Rethan using their faster, longer-ranging attack craft to launch the first strike on Von'tu's fleet. The Rethan's bombers were the pride of their fleet, and the best on either side at this point in the conflict. They were stealthy by the standards of the time but were also relatively fast. If given the time to accelerate, these bombers were capable of outrunning the Vaar's bombers or fighters. These bombers also carried a potent armament. Neither side of the conflict had developed working inflation charges yet, leaving both to fight with vortex-charged warheads. The torpedoes carried by the Rethan bombers were more than twice as fast, had 70 percent more range, and held more than double the Combine bomber's destructive power.

The Rethan fighters were lighter and more compact than those of the Vaar. They were also faster, more agile at warp, and though more fragile, they equipped longer-ranging anti-fighter/bomber missiles. In the Vaar force, as much as 40 percent of all fighter and bomber pilots serving in the battle were made up of undertrained reservists.

At 0340 hours, the first strike of the Rethan fleet approached the First Combined Wing. Von'tu was forced to commit most of his fighters to the defense effort in the hope of staving off the attacks on his carriers. Unfortunately Von'tu had fallen for a diversion. While the Rethan had concentrated most of their fighters on this first wave, only 20 percent of the bombers were present. The rest, with a lighter escort force, had launched more than two days before and were circling around to bypass the wall of fighters Von'tu had thrown up to defend his fleet.

Plant-based bombers serving as scouts spotted the main attack as it formed up on Von'tu's fleet. Most of Von'tu's fighters were already engaged with the diversionary force. This forced Von'tu to recall many of those fighters to intercept the main attack. This effort was only partially successful, and enough Rethan bombers made it past the defense to land heavy blows against the First Combined Wing. The attack cost the Vaar sixteen fleet carriers, and thirty were sufficiently damaged enough that they were forced to retire from the battle. In addition to the loss of carries, thirty-six escort ships were destroyed, with forty five more sufficiently damaged as to retire from the battle.

The Rethan had over-committed their fighters to the main assault, and Von'tu attempted to punish them for this mistake. He launched his bombers in a counterstrike along with any fighters that still possessed the fuel reserves to make the trip and escort them. What could have been a golden opportunity to make the Rethan pay dearly for a tactical error was ultimately stymied by poor pilot experience, flawed tactics, technical limitations, and the Rethan's skill in defending their ships.

The Vaar bombers were significantly inferior because they were slower, easier to detect, and armed with only a single inferior torpedo. The only real advantages of the Vaar bombers were marginally superior shielding and an extremely heavy sensor package. The Vaar fighters were even more heavily outclassed. The kind of breakneck maneuvers and fast-paced engagement one may think of when contemplating fighters did not apply to those doing battle at FTL. Rapid maneuvering and dogfighting simply were not possible, particularly with the limitations of the era. A fighter's primary task was either to intercept bombers before they could come within range of their targets or to protect their bombers from interception. When fighters fought fighters, speed, positioning, weapons range, and sensor range generally determined the outcome.

Rethan fighters were marginally faster but had superior sensor capabilities. While they carried fewer weapons in total, their weapons possessed superior range and speed. When combined with poor decision-making by inexperienced pilots, Vaar fighters fared poorly against their opponents.

Von'tu had sent a relatively lighter fighter escort with his bombers. His own fighter force had suffered significant casualties defending from the initial attack, and of the survivors, many were forced to return to his surviving carriers to rearm and refuel. He had hoped that the Rethan's over-commitment of their fighters to the attack would leave few to defend their fleet so the bombers could make it through. Unfortunately for the Vaar, things did not work out that way.

Despite being outnumbered by Von'tu's fighters, the Rethan defenders decimated the approaching bombers. This was due to bad tactics and lack of information, as the Vaar did not realize the Rethan weapons had such an extended reach. As a result, Vaar fighters were too close to the bombers to properly intercept for them, while the Rethan happily fired through the defense screen they were supposed to provide. This resulted in heavy attrition for the bombers before they reached the Rethan fleet. Once the bombers came close enough, the situation did not improve.

The Vaar pilots were largely unprepared for the volume of defensive fire. This resulted in many bomber crews losing their nerve and firing their weapons at the far edge of their range. This not only resulted in many torpedoes running out of fuel before they could chase down their targets but left ample time for intercept systems to do their job. To compound problems, insufficient counter-jamming capability and lack of crew training to operate in such an environment made it difficult for the bombers to accurately pick their targets. Many torpedoes were launched at the far less valuable escort ships.

Von'tu's counterattack failed, and he lost 35 percent of his bomber force. No Rethan carriers were destroyed, with only two suffering significant damage. A few dozen escort ships were destroyed, but it didn't hamper the Rethan's capabilities. The only bright spot was that the Vaar fighters were able to intercept and destroy a force of approximately six hundred Rethan bombers. These bombers had been part of the first attack, separated from the rest of the force on their way back to their carriers. This left them ripe for attack.

The most prudent move in Von'tu's situation would have been to withdraw his fleet and avoid combat until he could replace his losses. However Von'tu was more concerned with keeping the Rethan pinned down in the Trae'ton Cluster. Every day he could keep the bulk of their forces tied up was more time the planets behind him had to fortify.

Both fleets recovered their attack craft and rearmed for a second strike. Von'tu switched gears to put himself in a defensive stance. Rather than rearm his bombers for ship attack, he ordered them armed for fleet defense. Whereas a bomber could only carry one effective anti-ship torpedo, it could make an effective missile truck bearing dozens of light warheads for destroying fighters or other bombers.

The second wave came at 2500 hours as 290 drew to a close. Much more confident after the first encounter, the Rethan grouped all their attack craft into a single strike and launched them against the First Combined Fleet. This time the Rethan warships advanced just behind. Their obvious battle plan was to shatter the First Combined Fleet with the bomber attack before engaging in ship-to-ship melee.

Many in that era and later in history questioned or condemned Von'tu's actions to follow, believing that he should have withdrawn his fleet. Von'tu was not the best tactician or even the best the Vaar had. But he was perhaps the best strategist in the Combine and was keenly aware of the strategic situation. In his mind, it was worth sacrificing the entire First Combined Fleet if it meant delaying the Rethan's progress.

The defensive measures of the Combined Fleet blunted the attack by the Rethan's strike craft, but the result was still brutal. More than a hundred of the Combine Fleet's carriers were destroyed or critically damaged. So many were lost that the remaining carriers could not adequately service the now orphaned attack craft from those ships. Many fighter and bomber pilots found another carrier in which to dock, only to see their craft jettisoned shortly after as the space and technical crew to service them was unavailable.

The ship melee began at 06:00 on Day 291 as the two fleets closed within weapons range of each other. The Vaar acquitted themselves marginally better in this encounter. While Vaar carriers were not designed for ship-to-ship combat, their escort ships were much more capable. Escort ships in this period often had to choose between armaments suitable for defending against strike craft or focusing on ship-to-ship combat. Whereas the Rethan heavily favored the former, the Vaar had designed their escorts with a roughly equal split in capabilities.

Despite their advantages in ship-to-ship combat, the First Combined Fleet was too heavily outnumbered, and the Rethan retained the advantage in strike craft, which continued to run sorties during the melee. Von'tu sounded the retreat at 09:30 on Day 291. He had planned to make a fighting retreat all the way to the region known as the Black Ring. But to the surprise of Von'tu and many others, the Rethan did not pursue.

The Vaar had managed to destroy six Rethan carriers and several hundred escort ships during the fleet battle. One of the six carriers destroyed had been the Rethan's flagship, which was too far toward the front line due to a poor decision by the fleet's admiral. The Rethan military was mostly automated, but it still retained an organic command staff to oversee the machines. The destruction of the Rethan flagship, *Pride of the Republic*, had wiped out the leader of the invasion and most of the command staff. The admiral who took over the fleet worried that Von'tu's retreat was an attempt to lure the Rethan into an ambush at the Black Ring, and he chose not to pursue. Von'tu did not realize it at the time, nor did anyone else, but his decision to engage the Rethan in ship-to-ship combat had bought the Combine critical time that it needed.

Shortly after the battle, Von'tu found himself in a fight for his military and political life. Many in the military and the Council of Warlords criticized his actions at Trae'ton. The battle had cost him millions of bombers, fighters, and thousands of warships. Many of the surviving ships were effectively useless. The destruction of the Dre'zoma shipyards had left a critical lack of space in the Deep Sea for the surviving ships to be repaired. Many were too damaged to seek refuge in the Proximity Sea until receiving some modicum of repair. More than half of the warships and carriers Von'tu had taken to the battle were stripped of their propulsion systems and converted to space stations to add to the growing defenses in the Black Ring.

Von'tu held his position due largely to the support of Grand Warlord Tu'slen, one of the few who agreed that Von'tu had made the correct decision. The uncomfortable fact was that the Rethan now had fleet superiority in the Deep Sea. The initiative was in their hands for the immediate future, and the Vaar was no longer in a position to contest the pace of the war.

# The Black Ring

THERE WERE A TOTAL of nine defensive perimeters maintained around Prithone. Technically globes rather than rings, these zones encompassed not only the Vaar home world but the oldest and most well-developed colonies the Vaar had. The White Ring formed the outermost defensive perimeter, while the Black Ring formed the innermost perimeter, with the Infrared, Red, Orange, Yellow, Green, Blue, and Violet rings between them. The name *Black Ring* was commonly used to refer to all of the perimeters.

Still in charge of the Deep Sea's defense, and now with a critical lack of ships, Warlord Von'tu focused his next plan of action on the Black Ring. Things were going to get worse for the Vaar before they got better.

Many of the star systems in this region were already defended with surface-to-space missile batteries, complex sensor grids, and the logistics chain necessary to handle a prolonged battle. The moment the Rethan entered the Deep Sea, work began in earnest to enhance these defenses. Billions of citizens had been impressed into work brigades, working alongside the Deep Marines to further harden the rings. The coming battle would be a turning point in the war.

Von'tu's actions at Dre'zoma had bought the defenders time by forcing the Rethan into a blunder. The death of the invasion's commander at Dre'zoma had created a political divide that stalled efforts to name a replacement. The Rethan wasted seventy precious days picking a new leader for their invasion, who was then dispatched to the Deep Sea.

On other fronts, communications specialists finally penetrated the Rethan's communications protocol and decoded their transmissions. This portion of the intelligence division worked so rapidly and efficiently that Von'tu and his field commanders sometimes had the orders for Rethan units in their hands before those orders had filtered down to the units they were meant for.

Additional shipyards were being erected within the Black Ring. The destruction of the Dre'zoma shipyards had seriously crippled the Vaar's efforts to build more ships and maintain their fleet. The Combine had learned a painful lesson about over-concentrating and under-defending their strategic assets.

The bulk of the Rethan's efforts was concentrated in the Deep Sea. With Grand Warlord Tu'slen's support, Von'tu convinced the Council of Warlords that the bulk of the new shipbuilding facilities should be concentrated in the Proximity Sea, where they would not only be safe from attack, but their activities would also be difficult to spy on.

Some praise must be given to the work brigades laboring in the Black Ring. In addition to the defenses they were building, they raised so many new shipyards that the Rethan would conclude that the Vaar were concentrating their new shipbuilding capacity within the Black Ring.

Von'tu had a simple but controversial plan to defend the Black Ring.

Grand Warlord Tu'slen faced an attempt to remove him from office for supporting the effort. While it was unsuccessful, it showed just how many the objecting warlords were and how seriously they took the matter. Tu'slen's tenure as grand warlord came down to a single vote, with a recent addition to the elevated warlords breaking the tie. Ku'yen, a bomber pilot decorated for valor in the fight for Dre'zoma, ultimately cast his vote in favor of Tu'slen, settling what was effectively a proxy vote on Von'tu's leadership.

Von'tu's plan to keep the Rethan bound to the Black Ring moved forward. He fed enough forces into the region to keep the Rethan occupied. Meanwhile, in the Proximity Sea, he focused on building an overwhelming fleet to counterattack and smash the Rethan at the correct moment.

Von'tu's strategy was put to the test in the Battle of the Black Ring.

## The Battle of the Black Ring

THE BATTLE OF THE Black Ring began on Day 21 of 16,928 PA. By this point the Rethan had managed to concentrate more than three-quarters of their fleet in the Deep Sea for the drive to Prithone. On Day 21 more than a thousand carriers led the fleet to the White Ring, which formed the outermost layer of defense. Through the efforts of Combine intelligence, Warlord Von'tu knew exactly when and where the attacks would come. In one of the most controversial decisions of his career, Von'tu didn't send reinforcements to repulse this attack on the first line of defense. He'd decided to let the White Ring fall so as not to tip-off the Rethan that their communications had been compromised.

By sacrificing the White Ring, Von'tu had effectively signed the death warrants for billions of Combine citizens on the colonies in that perimeter. As their defenses were overcome, these planets were thoroughly bombarded by the Rethan. The Rethan focused its attacks on power generation, food storage and distribution, industrial sites, and transportation systems—as opposed to the populations. While millions would die in the bombardment, billions would die in the resulting lawlessness and famine that broke out on the afflicted worlds.

The relatively easy fall of the White Ring lured the Rethan into a false sense of confidence about the grim task ahead of them. To breach the remaining rings meant breaking through millions of surface-to-space missile batteries, thousands of deep space weapons platforms, hundreds of space stations, and missile-launching minefields. The Vaar had concentrated so much sensor capability into this region that the previously significant stealth advantages of Rethan bombers were diminished.

So many new defenses were erected in such a short time that Von'tu was quoted as saying "The ancestors who filled the brigades to fortify the Deep Sea against the Gray Fleet would weep with pride at what their descendants accomplished in the Black Ring."

But there was a stark and much darker reality to the activities of the work brigades. The Vaar suffered heavy civilian casualties in more than one major conflict. The responsibility for many of these lay with the leadership. Even when the capacity to evacuate was there, civilians were rarely allowed to leave conflict zones. They were instead herded into work brigades to build defenses and assist the military. It kept the civilians concentrated in points of conflict where casualties were inevitable. The citizen work brigades labored throughout the battle in the Black Ring, and billions of them gave their lives in the process.

The few operational warships Von'tu kept in the region were concentrated on the true Black Ring. There the carriers sent out strike craft to assist in rebuffing Rethan assault but were forbidden from exposing themselves to danger. Von'tu was an energetic commander, but he could not be in every place at once. He focused the bulk of his efforts on building his new armada in the Proximity Sea and improving the training of the Deep Fleet. To directly oversee the defense of the Black Ring, he appointed an admiral named Jos'no. Jos'no followed Von'tu's orders to the letter.

One of the facets of the battle that gained the most attention from historians came from the "skeleton ships." The bulk of these skeleton ships were *Yoppen*-class (roughly *shield* or *aegis*) destroyers. These ships went through a crash course to provide the fleet with the maximum defense against strike craft. While not as effective as an equivalent mass of fighters, they could remain on their stations longer, carry armaments with longer ranges, and better survive the attention of enemy fighters.

The *Yoppens* became known as skeleton ships because the need for them on the front line was vastly outstripping the capacity to produce them. To get as many into the field as quickly as possible—and ease production at the shipyards in the Black Ring—the designers removed everything considered unessential from these ships. The word *everything* in this context was not chosen lightly.

The *Yoppen*-class destroyers built in the Black Ring were often called pano ships by their crews. The word *pano* was roughly analogous to the way humans often used the term *hell* to describe extreme discomfort. These ships were often sweltering hot, as no more heat-sinking capacity was installed than absolutely necessary. Their crews often slept on floors to save the time of fitting out proper berthing facilities. Most crews ate the same prepackaged rations as the Deep Marines. Bodily waste and garbage were generally deposited in the same receptacle to save the time of installing proper toilets.

The crews of these vessels often began their toil before boarding the ship. Officers were often promoted from enlisted personnel on other Deep Fleet ships, but the actual crews were generally conscripted from the population. They worked double shifts, training to operate the ships, then reporting to the shipyards to help build them. Once their hasty training was complete, they would deploy on the first available ship. Many Vaar would fight and later die on skeleton ships they had helped to build.

These efforts and the suffering of their crews were not in vain. Some of the shipyards in the Black Ring hit rates of production that enabled them to turn out a functional skeleton ship every fifteen days. These ships were concentrated on the vital areas of defense to repel attacks.

Despite these efforts, the Rethan began to systematically dismantle the rings as their approach to Prithone continued. On Day 109 of 16,928 PA, the Infrared Ring was breached, and the Rethan launched assaults on the thirty-four colonies in the ring's expanse. Many of these worlds had especially high populations of quorim. The fall of the Infrared Ring brought with it the deaths of over 240 billion citizens.

Morale in the Black Ring wavered. The Rethan were painstakingly careful to protect their carriers and use only their expendable and unmanned strike craft because factories in the Vortex Sea churned out constant replacements. With space superiority in the region, the Rethan had little difficulty moving these replacements from the Proximity Sea to the Deep Sea, and up to the Black Ring. To the overburdened defenders, it seemed that the supply of Rethan strike craft was never-ending.

Jos'no made a handful of attempts to disrupt the Rethan supply lines, sending bomber groups on long-range missions beyond the ring to intercept the transports jumping in as they made for the front lines. These efforts met with little success as Vaar fighters lacked the range to escort them. The Rethan expertly patrolled the space through which the transports traveled, rebuffing the majority of these assaults.

Despite how it seemed to those in the Black Ring, the attrition affected the Rethan. The Republic built these strike craft faster than they could mine the material, resulting it growing depletion of their strategic reserves. The effect was negligible at first but compounded as the battle wore on.

In the Proximity Sea, the work to build the great armada ran around the clock. The Vaar had designed new carriers, new bombers, new fighters, and new escorts to face the Rethan. Much of the esteem the quorim held in the modern Combine descended from this effort. Many quorim volunteered before ever being called into brigades. Technicians and dockworkers accepted long hours, with many working themselves to death. But the moment that solidified the quorim's position in the modern Combine came thanks to the Rethan.

The Rethan intelligence network had made considerable efforts to contact community leaders and other influential people in quorim society. They promised to split the Combine's territory between Rethan and quorim if the latter's leaders rebelled against the Vaar. It was not love for the Vaar, nor fear of State Security that led to this refusal. Any hope of an alliance between the Rethan and the quorim died with billions of the latter killed in bombardments.

Back in the Deep Sea, the battle for the rings was going poorly. On Day 270 of 16,928 PA, the Red Ring was breached. Sixteen more colonies were bombarded, and another 41 billion civilians were killed. The scourging of the Vaar planets was meant to break morale, but it had the more salient effect of destroying war industry with each world that fell. The interdependent rings weakened as factories and planetary populations to draw from were being lost.

Just after the fall of the Red Ring, Jos'no transmitted the following message to Von'tu:

"Our situation is dire. Rethan supply proceeds unimpeded. The rope of morale frays. Crew casualties immense. Whispers of mutiny have reached my ears. Viss and children starve on heaps of ash that were their worlds. The soldiers believe themselves dead already. Even the warriors doubt our prospects for victory. I cannot hold the Orange Ring without immediate assistance."

Von'tu answered:

"Under no circumstance must the Orange Ring fall. Acts of valor are to be publicly praised, by you. Any who refuse to work or fight are to be executed publicly. Talk of mutiny is to be punished in equal measure. The Council has lowered the age of conscription to thirteen. New personnel to be available to you soon. Will send reinforcements that can be spared. Hold the Orange Ring."

The Combine had gathered ships from across its territory and amassed a significant fleet. Von'tu, however, had chosen to keep this fleet in the Proximity Sea. While the Rethan showed minimal interest in that galaxy, he did not wish to leave his new shipyards and burgeoning armada unguarded. Jos'no's appeal prompted Von'tu to send many of these ships back to aid in defense. None of his new assets were to be sent. One flight of bombers was even recalled as it had mistakenly been deployed with the Deep Fleet's new anti-ship torpedo. Von'tu wanted nothing to alert the Rethan of what was going on in the Proximity Sea. Under Von'tu's orders, sixty-four carriers and 896 warships were dispatched to the Black Ring. All of these forces were crewed overwhelmingly by new and inexperienced personnel. Von'tu kept the most experienced in the Proximity Sea to help train his new force.

The Orange Ring fell on Day 369 of 16,928 PA. Despite the additional forces dispatched by Von'tu, the Rethan were pushing through. The Orange Ring was the most sparsely populated, and four billion citizens were lost when their worlds were scourged. With each ring that fell, the volume of the battlefield shrank. The areas the Vaar had to defend became smaller, but it allowed the Rethan to focus more of their forces on fewer points.

With little fleet presence to challenge their movement, the Rethan had sent many task forces out to bombard planets beyond the rings. The primary focus for these groups had been to interdict supplies attempting to reach the rings, but as the Vaar defense became more concentrated, more and more of these task forces returned to the front line to help press the assault.

The Vaar gained a small amount of time to breathe in the early days of 16,929. The Rethan had been producing a constant stream of strike craft to keep up their ceaseless assault, which required skilled labor to produce. Early in the year, many of these workers went on strike, protesting their grueling hours and insufficient wages. The strike lasted only nine days, but the Rethan fleet ceased their attacks, not knowing how long it would go on. This bought Jos'no a critical window of time to plug holes the Rethan had punched into the Yellow Ring. The Yellow Ring was a critical layer of defense, as it was here that the majority of the shipyards producing the skeleton ships were found. If the Yellow Ring fell, then the fall of the remaining rings would certainly be only a matter of time.

The Yellow Ring fell on Day 72 of 16,929 PA. This led to the most historic tragedy of the battle, the destruction of the Triangle Worlds. Balta, Dehon, and Cas'na were some of the most culturally significant worlds in the Combine. Their existence was considered a natural wonder. They were old colonies and some of the most prosperous of any in the Combine. The planets were home to many high-status personages throughout the Combine's history, Von'tu among them.

In the space around these planets, the war against the Gray Fleet had been decided.

The Rethan bombardments had caused numerous deaths. But up to this point, it was possible to argue that they had been military in nature. The bombardments had focused on factories and critical infrastructure, all things that contributed to the military's resources. But from the beginning, the bombardment of the Triangle Worlds was intended to kill every Vaar, Viss, and child residing on these planets, and they had succeeded.

The destruction of the Triangle Worlds was meant to break the Vaar's will to resist. It had the opposite effect. The collective population whiplashed from the brink of despair to open rage at the destruction of these treasured worlds and the malicious extermination of their populations.

Jos'no denied requests by bomber and fighter wings to launch themselves into rage-fueled attacks on the Rethan. Though he denied their requests, he soon found that his forces were growing more motivated than they had been even before the battle began.

The Rethan were ultimately disappointed by the reaction to the destruction of the Triangle Worlds, but the event also served to encourage them. The Rethan knew the Vaar had more warships and assumed more were being built in the other galaxies. But they believed that if anything would motivate those forces to intervene, it would be to protect the Triangle Worlds. This combined with misinformation disseminated to them by Combine intelligence convinced them that the Combine was beginning to break up—that other galaxies were looking to defend themselves and leave the Deep Sea to its fate.

The thing about making a mistake was that sometimes it took years for it to compound and explode in one's face. The Rethan had been *too* focused on destroying Prithone and the Combine's leadership. Bombers intercepted scouts deployed to the Proximity Sea. If they weren't destroyed, they were repelled.

The Rethan had relied on other methods of gathering intelligence— their methods often led to them being made the fools by Combine counterintelligence. The lengths to which the Combine went to misinform the Rethan were immense. Von'tu had multiple body doubles, many altered to better resemble him. These doubles made frequent inspections and communications in the Black Ring to lead the Rethan to believe he was actively guiding the defense. With the help of the Council of Warlords, the intelligence services created the fictional office of the Governor of Proximity and placed an aged warlord in that position. This warlord, Uhn'dee, opened secret talks with the Rethan for the Proximity Sea to form a separate peace with the Republic. Once those talks began, intelligence moved in and "arrested" Uhn'dee, all to build and later enhance the Rethan delusion of unrest.

By the time the Yellow Ring fell, Von'tu had enough of a force in the Proximity Sea that he *might* have been able to eject the Rethan from the region. Indeed he faced great rebuke from many in the Council of Warlords and even an assassination attempt by one of his troops for not intervening. But Von'tu remained focused on his goal to amass enough forces to fly into the Deep Sea and bag the entire Rethan fleet before they could retreat. He also faced the reality that neither the Proximity Sea nor any of the others were as well-defended as the Deep Sea. If the Rethan turned their attention to the Proximity Sea before he was ready, Von'tu could not have defended it.

It took two more years for the Rethan to grind their way through the Black Ring and face the final line of defense before Prithone. By that time, Von'tu commanded a larger armada than the Deep Fleet and Republic Fleet combined at the war's onset, but such a massive force took time to mobilize, especially with the limited communications and logistics capacity of the era.

The true Black Ring was the most heavily fortified, and Von'tu assumed that it would take the longest to fall. He had originally set the date for his armada's intervention on Day 60 of 16,931 PA. Rethan intelligence caught wind that the Vaar had something prepared for that day, and Combine intelligence learned that they knew. This forced Von'tu to delay the operation until Day 91 in the hopes of catching the Rethan off guard. This decision nearly doomed Prithone.

The collapse of the Violet Ring occurred earlier than Jos'no had anticipated, and the Black Ring came under assault while he was still trying to withdraw as many troops and supplies as possible. The result was an inadvertent breakdown in communications that threw the relocation and defensive efforts into disarray.

Once they managed to breach the defensive perimeter, the Rethan intended to head directly for Prithone. This occurred on Day 65 of 16,931 PA. More than forty Rethan carriers and four hundred escort ships slipped through the Black Ring and advanced on Prithone. After Von'tu learned of it, he gave the order for his armada to jump to the Deep Sea.

Transpatial travel was fast, but it was not instant. It took at least two days for his force to arrive at Prithone. By then it was too late. The salvation of Prithone came at the hands of those known in modernity as the Golden Fourteen.

The Vaar operated on a base-14 system of mathematics. Perhaps it was a coincidence that this was the same number of fingers a Vaar had, or perhaps it was not, but fourteen was also considered a lucky number. The Golden Fourteen referred to the Fourteenth Bomber Wing, a force of 1,400 bombers and their crews. Nearly every pilot in the unit was a warrior, not a soldier. Their status as the most successful bomber group in the Deep Fleet had made them popular with Combine war propaganda. The unit had seen constant action in the Battle of the Black Ring. The only reason they were not in the Proximity Sea training on new bombers or training new recruits was that their presence was deemed vital to the defense of Prithone.

The Fourteenth Bomber Wing was pulled back to Prithone to be granted a brief period of rest after more than a year of uninterrupted front-line duty. When they received word that the Rethan had broken through the Black Ring, they did not wait for orders. Under their own initiative, the bomber wing armed and took flight. The bombers flew for nineteen straight hours, slowing only to rendezvous with refueling tankers.

These were some of the most skilled and experienced pilots in the Combine. With no real escort to speak of, they launched themselves into an attack run on the advancing Rethan. The crews of the bomber wing proved in their final battle that the stories the Combine media told about them were not exaggerations. Despite having no fighter support, they attacked the advancing Rethan force. Though they suffered significant casualties, the Fourteenth successfully penetrated the advancing force's defenses. Pilots braved fighters and missiles to press their attacks dangerously close to lower the odds of point defenses intercepting their torpedoes. More than half of the Fourteenth was lost in the attack, but they succeeded in landing hits on all forty-three of the advancing Rethan carriers. Unfortunately, none of these hits inflicted critical damage.

As the Fourteenth pulled back to assess the results of their attacks, the wing commander Ral'du made a final broadcast. "I won't order any of you to do this. For our children, I ask you to follow."

The Golden Fourteen turned back toward the Rethan fleet and launched into kamikaze attacks. Every bomber in the unit was destroyed, but they inflicted significant damage on thirty-six of the forty-three carriers. For twenty of these ships, the damage was severe enough that they were forced to drop out of warp. Not knowing what kind of defenses waited for them at Prithone, the Rethan made the fateful decision to stop and make repairs, just out of striking distance.

The Golden Fourteen's sacrifice bought Von'tu the time he needed. His armada poured out of the nearby Gro'gan gateway ready for battle. Against such overwhelming force, the Rethan never had a chance. But Von'tu brought more than numbers to the battle. Research and development had been busy, and nowhere was this more clear than in the development of the deep-range torpedo.

For most of the war, Rethan bombers had enjoyed a significant advantage with their larger and more powerful torpedoes. The Vaar's new multistage deep-range torpedo was more than twice as powerful, boasted three times the range, and was equipped with the most advanced interceptor-avoidance protocols used by either side of the conflict. In an unusual methodology for the Vaar, the torpedo was designed before the bomber that carried it. With this powerful new weapon and several others, the Vaar quickly overwhelmed the battle-weary Rethan.

Of the more than half a million warships the Rethan had in the Deep Sea, fewer than two hundred would escape. Some of the organic commanders attempted to surrender, but as far as mercy, the Vaar showed none.

## The Invasion of the Vortex

WITH HIS DESTRUCTION OF the Rethan fleet, Warlord Von'tu transformed from the controversial and sometimes despised military figure to a national hero almost overnight. Jos'no was recognized as the Hero of the Black Ring and was soon elevated to the status of warlord, but Von'tu's choice to sacrifice so many lives and so many planets remained deeply controversial for many years. Most eventually recognized that he saved more lives than he sacrificed. By keeping the bulk of the Rethan's forces glued to the Black Ring, he had kept them away from more vulnerable regions of similar population density. Moreover he had taken what was likely the only realistic path to eventual victory. With the casualties suffered early in the conflict, the Vaar simply had no other choice but to fight on the defense.

The Battle of the Black Ring was over, but the war was not. For many in the Combine, from the warlords to the common laborers, victory was no longer enough. Von'tu already had his invasion plans drawn up for the Vortex Sea. He had the fleet necessary to do it, and the Deep Marines were itching for a fight.

Even with his newfound status, Von'tu found several detractors for his invasion plan. He intended to enter the Vortex through the Bazaar, his only path, then advance on a broad front. The Rethan's fleet had been gutted, and they would not be able to concentrate enough forces to hold him back. Von'tu's contemporaries favored advancing in a narrow front, intent on carefully dismantling whatever defenses waited in the alien galaxy. But Von'tu had led the Vaar to victory thus far, so his plan was executed.

No single battle could serve as an example of Von'tu's brilliance. His success was not rooted in his tactical or strategic acumen. Von'tu was neither a creative nor innovative player in the game of war. He was a player who had mastered the fundamentals and used them to maximum effect. When he had the choice, he favored steady incremental gains over huge, but risky, tactics and strategy. He had that luxury. The Rethan's space forces were in ruins, and he had the massive industry of the Combine at his back.

Von'tu waited for half a year, fitting out more of his ships and preparing the Deep Marines for the task, before launching his invasion. He had wished to wait longer but was pressed by Grand Warlord Tu'slen not to give the

Rethan more time to prepare.

After the destruction of their fleet, the Rethan attempted to open peace talks with the Vaar. The Vaar flayed their diplomats and sent their skin back. None were in the mood for peace. Von'tu's invasion began on Day 1 of 16,932 PA.

# The Battle of Rethes

THE RETHAN HAD LONG worried that the Vaar might launch an attack on their galaxy in the hopes of drawing their fleet home from the Deep Sea. Thus they had taken measures to fortify many critical sectors. Most of this effort focused on the Rethes Cluster, which housed their home world. The level of hardening in the rest of the galaxy was nowhere near sufficient to stop the forces Von'tu brought to bear. Von'tu's new 1st Combined Fleet swept over the Rethan so quickly that outrunning their supplies was the primary factor that forced them to occasionally stop and slow down.

By the end of 16,932 PA, the First Combined Fleet was knocking on the door of the Rethes Cluster, which housed the species' home world. The Deep Marines had invaded over a thousand planets, facing relatively weak resistance in the process. The Rethan had gambled nearly everything on control of space and had precious little to defend their planets on the ground.

As 16,933 PA approached, Von'tu did not believe that the Rethan possessed the ability to go on the offensive. While they had kept roughly one-quarter of their total fleet home—and were building new ships—the replacement rate simply was not fast enough. Every ship the Rethan had, they needed to defend their worlds. The general pace of the invasion had slowed. Time was on the Combine's side, and they were content to use it. They focused on bolstering the invasion forces in preparation for the assault on the well-defended Rethes star cluster.

The Rethan had done everything they could to prepare for the final invasion. In a sharp reversal of fate, the Rethan built what amounted to skeleton ships in the hopes of defending their core worlds. Meanwhile they had devoted every resource to erecting as many defenses as possible. Most of the Rethan's efforts had been on the Rethes Cluster. It had always been assumed that if the Vaar did attack the galaxy, then the brunt of the attack would come here. The Vaar would jump into the Bazaar, then as quickly as possible, jump to Rethes. With the fortification the sector already had, combined with the feverish work ongoing, the star cluster had been well fortified.

There was a creature native to Prithone that the Vaar called *ugo'sat*. It was a small creature with many barbed, retractable spines and an unusual hunting method. Many animals on Prithone ingested rocks to aid in their digestion. The ugo'sat retracted its spines and lay among the rocks until an animal ingested it. Once that occurred, the ugo'sat spread its spines and anchored itself in the prey's digestive system. There the female of the species laid its eggs, and both genders proceeded to eat the victim's innards. Prior to the invasion into the Rethes Cluster, Von'tu would send the following message to the Council of Warlords:

"Maximum force is at hand, and I am prepared to use it. But let me impress upon the Council the bitter reality. The Rethan are not defeated yet. This battle will not be the glorious final stroke that many are hoping for. The moment I enter Rethes, we take an ugo'sat into our collective throats. We shall pass it and feel the pain of the effort for some time thereafter."

There was little brilliant or artful about Von'tu's assault. The Rethan proved that they were no less capable of fortifying their territory than the Vaar. There was no quick or easy path for Von'tu to take to seize control of the sector. Instead it was a slow grind through the defenses, systematically dismantling them on the way forward. But unlike the Vaar when they had been in this position, the Rethan did not have an entire second galaxy raising forces to save the day.

For 217 days, the Vaar ground the Rethan, cluster by cluster and planet by planet. But on Day 303 of 16,933 PA, the Vaar finally cleared the way to Uk'hu, the Rethan home world. The situation for the Rethan had gone beyond hopeless. Their defenses were shattered. Stories of Vaar cruelty on the occupied worlds were creating mass unrest from the panicked population. As Von'tu prepared for the final strike on Uk'hu, he received a message from the Rethan government, asking for the terms of surrender. Von'tu answered:

"I offer you no terms. I will accept no surrender. Beseech your peace from the ghosts of Balta, Dehon, and Cas'na. Prepare your defenses. I come to kill you, whether you defend yourselves or not."

As Von'tu's forces advanced on Uk'hu, panicked civilians sent open broadcasts begging the Vaar for mercy. Others resorted to holding signs asking the same toward the sky, hoping Vaar scouts might see them. Von'tu's mass of fighters and bombers swarmed Uk'hu on Day 305 of 16,933 PA. But with these strike craft was the modified destroyer *Ghost of the Triangle*. The fighters and bombers cleared away the defenses, and the *Ghost of the Triangle* delivered its payload.

The Rethan on the planet were killed instantly as they were incinerated by intense heat and electromagnetic radiation. Vaar ships watched as over several hours Uk'hu collapsed into a new black hole. The Vaar had developed the compression bomb, and the Rethan Republic had fallen.


# Aftermath


WITH THE DESTRUCTION OF Uk'hu, the nightmare was just beginning for many of the Rethan. When the Deep Marines landed on other worlds, many Rethan had come out of their homes with offerings of food, gold, electronics, and other trinkets. Anything and everything that might mollify the invader's wrath. But the Vaar were in no mood to be appeased.

Well before the war's end, the Sovari Council had impressed upon the warlords to show temperance in their handling of the Rethan. But the political reality was that the population wanted blood, lots of it, and they wanted it now. Most of the warlords were already keen to punish the Rethan, but anti-Rethan sentiment in the general population had grown so strong that they feared a rebellion if they did not brutalize the Rethan. Many openly called for the wholesale extermination of the entire species. The warlords were not prepared to go that far, but the public had to be mollified.

Ever since the victory at the Black Ring, the warlords had planned to use the Rethan to help rebuild the Deep Sea. With this in mind, Warlord Von'tu had been forbidden from destroying or engaging in massive bombardment on any Rethan planet but Uk'hu, and the Council had given strict guidelines to the Deep Marines on how to conduct themselves. In reality, fear of public backlash for enforcing these guidelines saw many violations go unpunished.

If a Vaar sergeant decided that live Rethan made good target practice, his officer was unlikely to make a fuss about it. If soldiers decided to alleviate their boredom by seeing who could kill Rethan in the most creative ways, that left fewer mouths to feed in the occupation zones. But even in terms of the atrocities committed, the warriors comported themselves much better than the soldiers. While they held the same hate, they had their discipline. No matter how much they hated the Rethan, their fate was now the warlords' to decide.

The intelligence services went to work raiding existing government records for the names of any surviving Rethan soldiers. Their numbers were few as most of their military was automated, but they were out there. The destruction of Uk'hu had taken many records with it, but there were sources in other locations. No surviving Rethan soldier was safe. Those the intelligence services found were never seen again.

Within a year, the first prison ships arrived in the Vortex Galaxy. Many Rethan saw the demolition of their home cities before boarding ships, soon referred to as *death ships,* as most were so overpacked that many of the passengers died in transit. Massive prison camps had been constructed in the Deep Sea for the Rethan, where they spent the rest of their lives repairing the worlds that had been destroyed in the invasion.

Most of the Rethan transported to Deep Sea were females and children, as occupation forces were quietly killing as many of the military-age males as they could. The Vaar had no intention of fighting a resistance. Those in the work camps faced a brutal existence with equally brutal work quotas. Failure to meet a quota meant one did not eat. Repeated failure was construed as sabotage and resulted in execution. Many of the laborers were worked to death as time went on. The right hand often coordinated poorly with the left, exacerbating the misery of the camps as they were routinely packed with more Rethan than they were designed to hold. Guards usually solved this problem by liquidating the least productive workers when a new batch came in.

Billions of Rethan delivered to the work camps made trinkets, tools, or any manner of thing that might improve the lives of the countless Combine citizens touched by the war. Rethan who grew too old or infirm to work were liquidated.

Even this was not enough to satisfy the hate in the population. The Council of Warlords ordered a census of the Rethan population, with forced numbering of each citizen. After this task, a lottery was held. The winners received nothing. The losers were sterilized. The few fertile Rethan remaining were subjected to the most brutal reproduction limits in the Combine. A series of fifty marginally habitable worlds were designed as reservations. The few Rethan who could still reproduce were relocated to these worlds. The rest of the Rethan's planets were earmarked for Vaar colonization. Priority was given to veterans and the few survivors of Rethan bombardment.

In modernity the Rethan were only found on these reservation worlds. No Rethan was permitted to travel off-world without a state-issued permit. As a rule, centuries at a time passed with no permits being issued. These Rethan reservations were overpopulated, under-serviced, and impoverished slums. No Rethan in modernity had the skills or education to build something like a star ship. For many, even basic literacy in their native language was elusive. In all respects, they were a broken people.

For his command of the Black Ring, Jos'no was elevated to the rank of warlord. He later became warlord of the Deep and served as the chief of staff for the Deep Fleet. He held this position until dying comfortably of old age seventy-six years later.

The Wall of Victors was raised as one of the greatest monuments on Prithone. Names of warriors and soldiers were etched on this wall—those who had delivered the Combine great victories over hated enemies. Tona'tass of the Gray Fleet Crises was the first name etched on this wall. Von'tu and Jos'no would stand together, etching their names as the second and third entries. The fourth was made collective for the Golden Fourteen, who would also receive their own monument nearby.

Warlord Von'tu was eventually hailed as the hero of the war. Much of the Combine came to see him as the warrior willing to make the hardest decisions for the greater good. Not long after the war ended, his public favor elevated him to the position of grand warlord. He proved much less capable as a statesman and served most of his term as a figurehead. His most important policy contribution was to order the creation of the Planetary Defense Force to protect Vaar worlds going forward. Beyond that he was effectively put out to pasture, strongly encouraged to make the most of his warlord privileges. Many modern Vaar considered him their species' greatest commander.

Reproduction became Von'tu's full-time job. By the time old age and massive circulatory failure claimed him, he had fathered over six hundred thousand children at an average conception of eleven per day. Von'tu was likely the most reproductively successful sapient male in the known universe who was not a roliam. A duty he carried out while a senior citizen.

The Rethan War in modernity was a controversial subject among both students and historians. Modern Vaar tend to view the war with a mixture of pride and shame. Great pride was taken for their people's resilience in the face of adversity and their resolve to see the war through to its end. Even the Gray Fleet never reached a position to threaten Prithone in the way the Rethan had. But this was not why so many Vaar considered this war their darkest hour. Instead it was viewed as such because of what the war made of them, and the terrible fate visited upon the Rethan. Others saw the war as nothing but a great triumph and maintained that the Rethan were shown more mercy than they deserved.

# 5N
# THE HARD PEACE

## 16,934 PA–17,597 PA
## (82,370 AN–83,157 AN)

THE END OF THE Rethan War marked the end of one struggle and the beginning of another. The Combine's economy had been left in ruins. The Vaar had committed to total war with the Rethan, subordinating all other concerns of society to the war effort. But the war had gone on for too long. The central government had created so much money to pay for the war that hyperinflation was in swing before the conflict ended. Many of the Vaar colonies destroyed in the Battle of the Black Ring were old, prosperous colonies, and their destruction hurt the Combine's overall economy. The Combine at the time was by no means a free market economy—far from it—but it was closer to one before the Rethan War.

The destroyed worlds had to be salvaged, many required bioforming to repair their livability, and then the worlds would need to be recolonized. Some such as the Triangle Worlds were too far gone for the capabilities of the era and would ultimately become nothing more than mass graves. The Vaar also had a new galaxy to begin colonizing. This meant children, and many of them. This also meant birth subsidies, new state schools, and countless more expenses pertaining to the colonization effort.

The Council of Warlords also had to contend with a growing dissident movement. Grand Warlord Von'tu was hailed by many as a national hero. But the Council of Warlords was not in the general public's favor. In much of the population's eyes, the warlords were responsible for causing the war and for the poor results in the early years that had allowed the conflict to become so devastating. The flailing economy only hurt the image of their leadership further.

A wedge was driven deep between the warlords and the Sovari when the former asked the latter to intercede on their behalf. The Sovari refused to endorse the warlords to the rest of the Combine's population. The Sovari's code forbade them from establishing a government for the Vaar. Endorsing any government trod too close to violating their code. Moreover the Sovari were not in complete disagreement with the population. They had warned the warlords about needlessly escalating the war. They had warned the warlords about taking the Rethan more seriously as a threat. They had given several warnings, and the warlords had ignored them.

The greatest point of contention was the use of the compression bomb to destroy the Rethan home world. Though Vaar scientists had conceptualized the weapon without aid, they had run into several problems that halted their progress. The Sovari provided the knowledge that helped the scientists to overcome these problems, but they had done so under the agreement that the warlords would only use it if Uk'hu proved too costly to invade. This simply was not the case. The Deep Marines could have taken Uk'hu and done it with acceptable losses, but the warlords chose to destroy the planet to avenge the deaths of the Combine civilians killed in the Rethan bombardment. This act would have consequences going forward, with the Sovari less willing to aid in scientific developments.

A sort of cold civil war began between the warlords and the Sovari. This was not the first time they had come into conflict. The warlords had many years ago decided that the Sovari were a potential threat to the legitimacy of the Combine government. The warlords' past efforts to indoctrinate young Vaar and Viss away from the influence of the Sovari failed to produce the desired results. The warlords doubled down on their efforts to restrict Sovari influence. This included ordering the Domestic Tranquility Service to keep them under close observation, and for the intelligence services to restrict their access to secret information. The warlords, unaware that the Sovari were telepaths, did not know that their plans were revealed the first time one of them thought about them in a Sovari's presence.

The Hard Peace would ultimately be defined by the economic collapse that came after the Rethan War. Beyond the myriad of problems already mentioned, others were growing in severity. So much emphasis had been placed on building up the War Forces that critical infrastructure had been neglected. Countless Vaar had missed out on completing their education as they were pulled out of school to fill work brigades or military programs. Billions of Vaar and Viss had fought in the conflict, and with the war over, their jobs were no longer necessary.

The warlords were happy with their new, fearsome military, and were reluctant to dismantle it or cut back its size despite the desperate need for resources.

A degree of infighting broke out between the Council of Warlords and the Collective Committee. Both sides could see the massive economic problems and disagreed vehemently over how to address them. In truth, neither side had the correct answers, and their dispute ultimately amounted to two parties conflicting over whose bad policies to adopt. Because the civilian government answered to the military, the Council of Warlords' bad policies would ultimately go into effect.

The Hard Peace resulted in one of the worst economic collapses ever suffered by an interstellar species. The attempted solutions only exacerbated the problem. Unemployment was a severe problem for the Combine. Every citizen had a duty to work, and the state was obliged to provide each citizen with work to perform.

The warlords' decision to use what amounted to Rethan slave labor to rebuild the Deep Sea was not a sound decision. This ultimately resulted in millions of jobs being done that would have otherwise been given to unproductive citizens. Whether the warlords liked it or not, they would have to drastically shrink their new military. Billions of citizens were left unemployed in the short-term, and other economic problems threatened to make it long-term.

The warlords chose to battle the rampant inflation with increasingly strict price controls on all goods and services. The problem with this idea was that it invariably created artificial scarcity in some economic sectors, while resulting in artificial surplus in others. When this was multiplied out over thousands of worlds, this became a large problem. The Combine economic system of modernity was a result of the increasingly totalitarian control the state would ultimately exert.

The solutions in place weren't working, but the stubbornness of leadership only prolonged their problems. It was a rude and inconvenient truth about species with extremely long lifespans. Those who were married to bad ideas took longer to do things like retire and die. As a result, their bad ideas often took longer to die out as well.

An economic crisis that should have taken only a couple of generations to solve would instead require many. The economic contraction of the Combine lasted for over six hundred years. All as the economic system was effectively reset and forced to rebuild into the new normal. This would significantly stymie the efforts to further explore and expand.

More than any other event, the Hard Peace would change the Vaar attitude toward expansion. The Vaar already occupied more territory than they controlled. Large empires that were built quickly often had a finite lifespan. This left systematic weaknesses across the empire. It was not uncommon for such empires to contract as quickly, or even more so than they expanded in the first place.

Whereas the Vaar had previously raced to expand as quickly as possible, their focus shifted to a slow and gradual expansion of their people and civilization. They began carefully cultivating the territory they controlled before moving on to seize more. The belief in a destiny to dominate the universe was not gone. Instead it was simply a realization that pursuing this goal quickly and carelessly was unsustainable.

How successful they were was debatable as the Combine often lost its presence in a galaxy and had to establish it anew. It often resulted from isolated colonial populations choosing to return to their home territories, though occasionally it resulted from a deliberate effort by another species.

# 50

# EXPLORING THE EMPTY OCEAN AND THE ALCHEMIC TRAGEDY

## 17,598–22,238 PA
## (83,158 AN–88,663 AN)

THE COMBINE EMERGED FROM the Hard Peace as a nation easily recognizable economically and culturally. The Vaar were more concerned with holding what they had rather than acquiring more, but their spirit of exploration remained alive and well. There were thousands of galaxies in the Virgo Cluster, and the Vaar were intent on exploring many of them.

Of the known universe, the Virgo Cluster had by far the highest concentration of sapient life. Granted, much of this was a result of intentionally creating or seeding it, but the Vaar had no concept of this and simply explored the space around them. This often came in the form of galaxy hopping. Ships capable of transpatial travel would jump to one galaxy, begin exploration, and then use that galaxy as a stepping-stone to the next.

As they explored the Virgo Cluster, the Vaar came to several realizations. They were the most powerful species they knew to exist, but they were not the only significant power in their corner of the universe. The Zal Empire, the Sora Collective, the Unean Union, and more existed in the Virgo Cluster. Nearly all of the significant powers were limited to single galaxies, even in instances such as the enigmatic Zal who could go beyond if they wished.

This was a relatively calm period for the Vaar as they explored their local universe. Cartography probes went first, and crewed missions came after. The Vaar did not give up on expansion during this era. They set seed colonies in many of the galaxies they encountered for gradual growth. Without the directed efforts the state had made before, many of these galactic holdings would take centuries or even millennia to mature, but they still had plenty of exploited territory to focus on.

The Combine fought in small-scale conflicts against regional powers during this era. As the Vaar planted seed colonies, they often did so close to the territory of any interstellar civilization they found. This was effectively a form of area denial meant to stymie these civilizations' growth, easing the ability of the Vaar to eventually overtake them in their native regions. Most of the conflicts fought in this era came around when these civilizations tried to bypass Vaar territory to continue expanding, or to force the Vaar out. But very few of these powers were able to mount effective challenges. To the average Combine citizen, these wars were distant matters of the state that did little to nothing to affect their daily lives.

Not all was quiet and peaceful over this long era. As the years passed, the warlords continued to indoctrinate the population to be loyal to them and the Combine. This came at the expense of the people's faith in the Sovari and their guidance. The Sovari were not helping themselves by becoming increasingly withdrawn from public affairs. Their mission had been to put the Vaar on the path to expanding through the universe, and that goal had been achieved. The Sovari always had a somewhat parental view toward the rest of the Vaar, and in their eyes, the children were growing up. They had to chart their own path.

One of the great social crises of this era came from the development of the Vaar's first alchemic printer. To say that the military and civilian governments were displeased about this development was an understatement. The number of jobs that would be destroyed by the proliferation of the technology was seen as the greatest internal threat the Combine had ever faced. The technology was still in its infancy and could not create any element with an atomic number higher than iron's twenty-six. The scientists who had developed the technology were confident that further development would lead to the ability to synthesize all known elements.

The Council of Warlords classified the technology as a military secret. The lead developers of the project were soon taken into military custody, all of their research records and prototypes were seized, and their laboratory was destroyed. The Council turned to the Bureau of Domestic Tranquility to find dirt on the lead developer, a Vaar named Chu'kon, but Chu'kon was cleaner than most BDT agents. He couldn't be charged with anything, so the Council did what many a totalitarian has done when they had issues with a private citizen. The BDT was again ordered to find dirt on Chu'kon or suffer severe consequences for failure.

To ensure the warlords kept a degree of deniability, the BDT handled the task of manufacturing charges against Chu'kon without blatantly disclosing that they were doing so. The BDT fabricated charges, accusing Chu'kon of everything from academic fraud in his scholastic years to a myriad of heinous, violent crimes in adulthood. The BDT's claims ended in Chu'kon's imprisonment. Chu'kon later escaped and vanished, eluding all BDT efforts to recapture him.

The Council of Warlords blamed the Sovari. They believed the Sovari aided Chu'kon in the development of the technology to destroy the Combine and force a change in government, and that they helped Chu'kon escape. The warlords had no evidence, but they were correct on two counts. The Sovari had aided Chu'kon in one of their increasingly rare interventions in science. The Sovari also helped Chu'kon escape from prison and obtain a new identity. But the warlords were wrong in their speculation of the Sovari's motives. Their aid to Chu'kon had been meant as a sort of final gift to the Vaar as a people. A technology that could vastly improve their quality of life in the days ahead. How this technology would affect what government the Vaar employed did not even enter their concerns.

Chu'kon was not the only victim of this heavy-handed suppression. A Viss named Tuma'zee had been integral in the design work as a lab researcher. She also had a close relationship with Chu'kon. The two had a genuine friendship and, when faced with the high reproductive quotas placed on scientists, chose to create most of their children together. She knew, as well as the rest of Chu'kon's employees, that the charges against him were lies. But unlike the rest, Tuma'zee spoke out. This would see her charged as an accessory to many of the crimes for which Chu'kon was accused, and she, too, was imprisoned. She escaped shortly after Chu'kon and vanished into obscurity.

The warlords were not pleased with how events played out, and the BDT continued to hunt for both Chu'kon and Tuma'zee until well after both must have died from old age. The warlords consoled themselves by believing that they had dealt with the problem. Without state resources, the two would never be able to bring their invention to any form of proliferation.

The problem with the warlords' self-assurance was that science was always there. The laws of physics did not change because they were inconvenient, and they did not care how anyone felt about them. The more scientific understanding gained, the more inventions slid toward inevitability. Chu'kon had come forward in the year 18,000 PA. By the year 18,200 PA, seven different scientific teams had come forward with their own claims to the invention of the alchemic printer.

Each time this occurred, the scientists involved received what became known as the Chu'kon Order in the BDT. One of these was even a warrior-turned-scientist named Hax'nen. He was given something close to a warrior's death. A Bureau of Military Intelligence agent picked a fight with Hax'nen and killed him. This was seen as the closest to a warrior's death that could be offered, and a greater mercy to the warlords than a life spent in hiding. The event continued to occur as those imprisoned by the BDT found ways to escape and disappear.

The warlords went to increasing lengths to slay what they considered a mortal threat to the Combine. This included mandating changes to the science taught in the state schools in the hopes of making the alchemic printer seem like a scientific impossibility. It did not work. Those who were educated, intelligent, and understanding routinely saw through the errors of what they were taught. This forced the BDT into even more overtime to suppress the scientific literature these personages attempted to publish on the matter.

The personnel of the BDT were becoming fearful that they would pay the price if this monster was not put away for good. This led to heavy scrutiny of many scientists with the potential to build an alchemic printer. The BDT became proactive in this regard, even disappearing some scientists who trod too closely to this forbidden knowledge. The quorim paid an especially heavy price here, as the BDT found it easier to stomach assassinating non-Vaar. But even so, many Vaar who did not heed the warnings found themselves in an early grave.

Despite all the BDT's efforts, the warlords were eventually forced to admit that the issue of the alchemic printer was not going away. Some in the Council wished to exploit it in a limited capacity. This manifested in the hopes of keeping the technology exclusively for the military to produce matériel, particularly in the event of a major war. A majority of the Council was opposed to this, fearing that the leaking of the technology to the general public became an inevitability.

A sad reality was that the warlords were making this a much greater problem than it was. Through the state-run education system, they had successfully convinced the majority of their people of the dangers of returning to luxury and indolence. Most Vaar would have spurned the technology as something to be used outside of emergencies, seeing it as an invitation to social ruin. This was the only reason the Sovari were willing to guide Chu'kon in the first place. But all the warlords could see was a return to the decay that had existed in the time of the Deep Republic.

By the year 19,000, the faction of the Council favoring limited use of the alchemic printer had reached a majority. The technology was incorporated only in specialized and highly secretive military facilities. These were hidden away from civilization. In a multi-galactic nation, space came in excess. These facilities would officially be classified as mines. They would produce only raw materials, and Vaar workers would still be required to turn those materials into goods. Further they were used only in times of war. To prevent leakage of the technology to the public, the warlords fought another cultural taboo. The facilities were to be completely automated with no living workers, and the Bureau of Military Intelligence was responsible for guarding them. So, too, would all transport of materials from these mines be supervised by the BMI or BDT.

The Council proved unable to resist using the technology as time went on. Were the miners not meeting their work quotas, resulting in shortages affecting the military? The alchemic printer could make up the shortfall, just this once. An unexpected shortage of a rare mineral was creating an economic disturbance? The printers could provide, and the minerals could be labeled as coming from the strategic reserve.

Rather than reserving the technology for when it was truly needed, the Council turned to it as a tool when it was convenient. This led to leaks in the existence of the technology. For many years the Combine government did everything it could to discredit the idea, but the warlords could not help themselves.

In 19,200 PA, the Vaar fought a war to claim possession of the Ink Sea from the native Unsaan species. The Vaar were never in real danger of losing the war. The conflict had become a tedious grind through the defenses of a stubborn enemy determined to see the war through to its bitter conclusion.

It caused shortages in materials. Gold was used in copious amounts in this era for communications and weapons systems. Production quotas for that metal had fallen short of expectations for the year, causing issues that threatened to explode in magnitude if the shortage was not alleviated soon. The warlords chose to print a large quantity of gold and release it into circulation, claiming it was from the strategic reserve.

The warlords had underestimated their civilian government's bureaucracy. Gold was part of a collection of precious metals that were scrutinized to help prevent shortages. When a large quantity was suddenly released, the Bureau of Minerals defecated an ugo'sat trying to figure out where it had come from. The BM could not reconcile the sudden influx with their records. This kicked off a massive audit to determine how so much gold had been misplaced, or who was embezzling terrific quantities of the substance from the strategic reserve. Like flame consuming oil, that audit expanded to dozens of agencies in the Combine before the warlords or anyone else could stop it.

By the time the warlords realized they had thrown a lit match into oil, it was too late to put a stop to the audit without causing a great deal of suspicion. Rumors of alchemic printing technology had already leaked into the population, and a significant portion believed it existed. To quash the audit would be seen by many as exactly what it was, a desperate attempt to cover up a secret.

It was fortunate for many that a Vaar named Wal'voon had recently been named grand warlord. State Security was already manufacturing evidence of a grand embezzlement conspiracy and picking their fall guys. Wal'voon was the one who finally said *enough*.

On Day 406 of 19,206 PA, Wal'voon did what the warlords should have done in the first place. He went on Combine media and admitted that the technology existed. He further admitted that the technology was being kept under strict control by the military and out of the hands of the general public. He claimed that it would protect the jobs of Combine citizens and ultimately stave off another, and perhaps fatal, return to the ages of indolence and decadence.

Wal'voon did not do this unopposed. His most ardent opponents on the Council attempted to assassinate him before he could make his announcement. The only thing that saved Wal'voon was the panic causing several warlords to act quickly and independently. So many assassins converged on Wal'voon at once that they detected each other's presence in this parody of intrigue. Several of the assassins interpreted the others as BDT or BMI agents acting against them. This was enough to draw the attention of actual BMI agents assigned to Wal'voon's protection and enable them to intervene.

The reaction these warlords expected never came. Some protested the denial of this incredible technology, but the majority of the Vaar was fully indoctrinated against consumer culture, into the need for work to give meaning to life. But most of all, into the importance of preserving their way of life and never returning to decadence. The collective reaction of most of the citizenry was a metaphorical nod before everyone went back to work.

It was debatable whether or not the warlords learned their lesson. Chu'kon, Tuma'zee, and many others who had independently developed their own alchemic printers never received a posthumous expunging of their false criminal records. Nor were they ever given the credit for their work. Into modernity, a military scientist named Raz'nelo was officially credited with the invention of the alchemic printer. The true history of the technology was known only among the warlords and the remaining Sovari.

# 5P

# THE RE-EXPANSION ERA

## 28,000 PA–30,000 PA
## (95,499 AN–97,872 AN)

BY THE LATER YEARS of Millennium 27, the Council of Warlords sought once again to expand the Combine in force. The galaxies the Combine held were institutionally sound, and the lot of easily colonized planets had been collected. Once more it was becoming more appealing to move on to new galaxies than work to bioform increasingly unsuitable worlds. The warlords were much more concerned with how long it had been since a major conflict or expansionary period. Though the Vaar found plenty of fights to pick in this period, only one stood out.

Improving transpatial drive technology allowed ships to make longer jumps while transitioning through fewer galaxies. The conquest of the Ink Sea was opening the door in a direction that precious little colonization or exploration had gone. The Vaar had already seeded distant colonies in many galaxies, but the Council wanted to go further.

The Vaar set their sights on the Ideal Sea. This galaxy was given its name by Vaar astronomers for its well-defined spiral shape. This galaxy was also home to the Zal Empire. *Zal* was an Ivex word that loosely translated to *stranger*. The Vaar knew precious little about the Zal or their galaxy. The Zal intercepted every explorer ship and probe that entered the galaxy.

Distance and many technical factors had forced any ship traveling to the Ideal Sea to do so after a series of lengthy galaxy hops. But with possession of the Ink Sea in hand, the Vaar had the means to jump a sizable force into the galaxy. The warlords decided to send multiple explorer ships with an escort of warships to perform proper reconnaissance. This effort was achieved on Day 36 of 28,000 PA. It ended poorly.

The Deep Fleet dispatched a total of 140 warships plus another seven dedicated explorer ships to the galactic core of the Ideal Galaxy. Almost immediately these ships came under attack. The Zal had erected a myriad of defenses in the core, including thousands of battle stations orbiting the local stars. Hundreds of thousands of missiles came in on expeditionary force from all directions, resulting in a predictable outcome.

Only one ship, the *Traveling Eye*, was spared from destruction. When the missiles stopped, that ship received a single transmission: "Our isolation is our treasure. Your presence is unwelcome. Return and warn. All you send, we will kill."

The message was sent only in text format, and most disturbingly, it was already in Ivex. The Vaar knew next to nothing about the Zal, but the Zal knew enough about the Vaar to know their language. The *Traveling Eye* fled the Ideal Galaxy and delivered the news of what transpired.

The intelligence services tore into the Traveling *Eye*'s sensor records, identifying no less than 22,000 battle stations and many times their number in what were almost certainly smaller automated weapons platforms. The analysis of the trajectory of missiles fired at the fleet revealed something far more disturbing—many could not have originated from any of the stationary platforms. They could have only come from warships. At first it was thought that these ships were attacking from beyond the range of the Deep Fleet's sensors. Analysis of the missiles' speed, however, showed that this was not possible. The ships firing those missiles had been much closer, and they had been numerous. Yet they had gone completely undetected.

Many in the Council of Warlords panicked when they received the news. Many a warlord was kept awake at night by thoughts of Zal ships or even entire fleets flying carelessly and undetected as they happily spied on the Vaar. At first this inflamed passions to invade the Ideal Sea and dismantle whatever threat the Zal posed, but therein lay the problem. The Combine had no idea how big of a fight they might be picking.

The Zal had gone to great lengths to harden themselves against the dangers of extragalactic invasion. The Deep Fleet had proof that the Zal utilized some incredible stealth technology that had denied any ability to analyze their ships. Combine scientists had deemed stealth technology that advanced to be impossible.

The Vaar had long been capable of FTL combat. The natural growth of their society and industry allowed them to maintain a fleet of millions of sophisticated warships. A fleet that, until now, had enabled the Vaar to declare themselves the masters of any galaxy in which they found themselves.

The Council of Warlords' goal to expand was not always about pursuing some destiny of the Vaar people to dominate the universe. Survival had always been a significant factor. The Virgo Cluster was dense in sapient species, far more so than the Solar or Near Galaxy clusters. The Vaar had a common mentality with the Praetheen in at least one respect: just because a species did not pose a threat yet, did not mean it would not in the future. So often the best defense was a good offense, and dominating the species around them was a means to ensure they didn't grow into something that could threaten the Vaar people.

With the destruction of the Combine's expeditionary force, the Zal had proven they were a threat *now*. But the Vaar were leery of picking a fight with this unknown, capable species.

Four black holes were identified outside the Ideal Sea's galactic core, which made for useful, albeit risky, navigation points for a transpatial jump. The Deep Fleet made seven more attempts to slip explorer ships into the

Ideal Sea, but none returned. Two were lost due to the hazards of unacceptably precise transpatial jumps. The rest were destroyed by the Zal.

The Council's fear of the Zal only grew and would precipitate the vast fortification of all the Combine's galaxies. The Deep Fleet expanded, and the galactic cores of both the Deep Sea and the Proximity Sea brimmed with battle stations and weapons platforms. All of which were packed with as many weapons and sensor devices as would fit. But the fear of the Zal only grew after what came next.

On Day 64 of 20,005 PA, a lone Vaar walked into BMI headquarters on Prithone and announced himself as Kal'to. This caused a little bit of an uproar, considering that Kal'to was the captain of the explorer ship *Studious Eye*, reported lost in the Ideal Sea the previous year. The intelligence agents were a little more disturbed when an examination of Kal'to showed that he was medically dead. His arteries were not contracting to pump blood through his body, his lungs were not circulating air, and his brain showed no signs of activity. The personnel at the station took a blood sample and referenced it against personnel records for the Deep Fleet. The result was a perfect match for Kal'to. The BMI office called special agents to take Kal'to to a research center where he could be interrogated and studied. When officials arrived to take him, Kal'to delivered a message:

"Our isolation is our treasure. Your presence is unwelcome. All you send, we will kill. The next invasion means war."

After delivering his statement, Kal'to became unresponsive. His body, which had previously shown no signs of decay, started to rot as he was transported to the research center. An attempt to perform an autopsy on his body accelerated the destruction. This was not an accelerated form of natural rot; Kal'to's plates and iron bones remained intact. But the entirety of his body's soft tissue spontaneously dissolved down to their base chemicals.

A recording of Kal'to's brief interrogation found its way up the chain of command to the warlords before the day had ended. The Council's viewing of the recording ultimately decided the issue of the Ideal Galaxy. Whoever and whatever the Zal were, the Vaar were not ready to pick a fight with them. The colonization of the galaxy was put on an indefinite hold. Massive new funding went into research to improve the Deep Fleet while the Zal became a sort of boogeyman for the War Forces. The ever-present threat ensured that no military expenditure was too great, and no standing army too great in the face of such an enigmatic threat.

There was one source of information that the warlords had hoped might provide answers. Grand Warlord Hep'hu approached the Sovari and asked what, if anything, they knew about the Zal. But the Sovari knew little, only speculating that the Ideal Sea was not their original home. This answer was not taken well by the warlords, who had grown up in a state school that portrayed the Sovari as an obsolete relic. The Sovari retained their seats on both the Council of Warlords and the Collective Committee, but their advisory presence in both had dwindled to little more than a ceremonial capacity.

With colonization of the Ideal Sea off the table, the Council turned their attention to other galaxies. A considerable secondary task faced the warlords: enhancing the military to deal with the potential threat of the Zal.

# 5Q
# THE TIME-LOST SEA AND ORIGIN'S REJECTION
## 30,209 PA–30,336 PA
## (98,120 AN–98,270 AN)

ON DAY 62 OF 30,209 PA, a Combine exploration vessel made the Vaar's first entry into the Time-Lost Galaxy. This was considered a major technological achievement. The Time-Lost Sea should have been made easily accessible via the Ink Sea that the Vaar held, but reaching this galaxy had proven an extremely difficult task. Vaar astronomers had noticed weird readings and observations about this strange galaxy, but for thousands of years, their ambition to visit it had remained unfulfilled. No attempt to establish a transpatial lock on any of this galaxy's black holes or neutron stars had met with success. The ships that attempted it were lost. In the end, the galaxy, known as the Anomaly Sea, was reached neither through transpatial jumps nor through buoy-telescoping.

The Combine reached the galaxy by constructing a mammoth ship known as *Rur'peth* (*Seeker of Mystery*). This massive ship composed primarily of fuel tanks crossed the intergalactic void from its closest major neighbor, the Vortex Sea. The journey took more than fifty years before the *Rur'peth* managed to reach the galactic periphery.

The crew of the *Rur'peth* realized quickly that this galaxy was far stranger than any had thought. As the ship charted the galactic arm it had reached, it left a series of navigation buoys. Something caused the clocks in these buoys to lose synchronicity with each other, and with the *Rur'peth* itself. After accounting for all relevant factors leading to known causes of time dilation, the crew was left with an inescapable conclusion. Something in this galaxy regularly altered the flow of time.

The clocks on *Rur'peth* ran slower the closer they came to the galactic core. It seemed obvious that this unknown cause was radiating from the center of the galaxy. Its influence strengthened the closer they approached. At the core, the *Rur'peth* saw the nucleus of the galaxy, which generally appeared as a bright globe lit by many old stars packed close together. As the *Rur'peth* plunged through this globe of stars, they found an inexplicable void. A zone of nothingness fifty light-years across. This zone didn't emit radiation, yet it possessed a very discernible gravitational center.

The *Rur'peth*'s crew was at a loss to explain what they had encountered.

The ship's captain, Kro'det, declared it *the hole of reality*. The ship fired numerous probes into this hole, none of which returned. All contact with the probes was lost the moment they crossed the threshold. Unable to probe the anomaly, the *Rur'peth* took what measurements it could, departed the galactic core, and prepared to return to the Vortex Sea.

As the *Rur'peth* departed the galaxy, the crew realized that they had badly misjudged the increase in time dilation as they approached the center. According to the clocks on the ship, the crew had spent just over a year in this galaxy. But when the crew managed to establish contact with the Wide Range Network, their clocks suddenly sped forward. The crew of the Rur'peth had lost twenty-two years relative to Prithone. This led the crew to name the galaxy the Time-Lost Galaxy, and the name stuck.

The *Rur'peth* returned to the Vortex Galaxy, shocking the rest of the Combine. More than twenty years overdue, the vessel and the crew had been declared lost. The vessel's unexpected arrival was met with celebration, and the data she had gathered was delivered to some of the brightest minds in the Combine.

Information about this galaxy spread to the public, and the Time-Lost Galaxy even became a staple in Combine fiction for a time. The Council of Warlords took a much more militant interest. Something in that galaxy was altering the flow of time, something that did not correspond to the known laws of physics. The Council ordered new expeditions to establish a functioning transpatial gateway in the galaxy, no matter what it took. If a warrior could control time, he might just be invincible. The warlords were determined to see if the Time-Lost Sea could teach them how to do that.

Their order resulted in the creation of the *Rur'okam* (*Conqueror of Mysteries*), which was the largest ship the Combine had ever built until the construction of the *Caustic Reverie*. It took nine years for the new expedition to be ready. Vaar engineers spent a lot of this time designing a transpatial gateway that they believed would not be nullified by the unusual phenomena. Slightly faster than the *Rur'peth,* the *Rur'okam* made the journey in forty-four years, arriving on Day 101 of the year 30,336. The ship began construction of its gateway in what became known as the Turga Arm of the galaxy. This gateway was the most powerful the Vaar had ever built, meant to bludgeon the local interference and enable linkage to gateways in other galaxies.

The moment the gate opened, a tsunami of exploration, scientific, and military vessels poured through. The Council of Warlords wanted to know the secrets of this galaxy, it wanted to know now, and it wanted to ensure no native life would interfere. The Council was disappointed. No effort to penetrate the hole was successful. Countless hypotheses were offered by Vaar researchers to explain this galaxy's strange effects on time, but not one survived when put to empirical testing. The Vaar, it seemed, had found a puzzle they could not solve.

While the bulk of the early forays into the galaxy focused on studying the anomaly, the exploration division of the Deep Fleet carried out its regular duties. This new galaxy had to be mapped to determine the potential for colonization. Any natives needed to be noted and their threat analyzed.

The explorers found an appreciable number of planets ripe for colonization. The time-altering effects of the galaxy rapidly diminished farther from the galactic core. If colonies were kept primarily in the galactic arms and the outer edges of the galactic disc, they would suffer what was deemed an acceptable level of deviation from the Wide Range Standard.

The Deep Fleet worked tirelessly to find sapient natives. It found three. These species were confined to a single arm on the galaxy's opposite side relative to the Vaar's point of entry. These species were deemed too primitive to be of immediate concern.

As exploration of the galaxy continued, the Vaar eventually found the planet that later became the focal point for conflicts. This planet was located close to the point where the galactic arm, now known as Auchard by the natives, merged with the galactic disc. Long-range probes spotted structures on the surface of this planet but no other signs of sapient life. Intrigued by this discovery, the Deep Fleet dispatched a survey team to investigate.

Almost simultaneous to this event, on Prithone, the Sovari Council bid a meeting with Grand Warlord Bonn'ko. The Sovari advised Bonn'ko to declare this planet forbidden. In a clear sign of how far the influence of the Sovari had diminished, Bonn'ko ignored their advice.

The survey team landed on this new planet, and attempts to date the material used in constructing the ancient structures often gave nonsensical results. Sometimes the equipment rendered negative dates, and other times they spat out dates older than the age of the universe. This event and others only stoked the thirst for discovery, and additional scientific teams were dispatched to the planet.

As the explorers made inroads into the vast labyrinths beneath the planet's surface, more discoveries followed. The scientific teams soon learned of the planet's nature as a nursery for sapient life and that it had been producing such beings and depositing them on other worlds for countless years. These scientists wondered if the Vaar were one of these species. This information was quickly classified and passed up the chain, eventually reaching Bonn'ko.

The grand warlord called all the senior warlords and the Sovari to summit. There he asked the Sovari what they knew of this world. Speaking on behalf of his fellow Sovari, the Sovari Soma refused to answer in open council. He would share with Bonn'ko, and only Bonn'ko.

This sowed seeds of mistrust, which were later exploited by an outside force. Bonn'ko opted to meet with the Sovari privately and learn what they knew. The Sovari revealed the Vaar's nature as a created species, the purpose of the planet that they dubbed Origin, and the importance that it be left alone. Bonn'ko did not agree with their position. To Bonn'ko, this planet was part of the great story of the Vaar. More than a simple part, this was the beginning of the story. Though Bonn'ko did not share what he knew with the rest of the warlords, he ordered additional teams to the planet to confirm the Sovari's story.

But by this point, the planet had begun to respond to the trespass on its surface. The Vaar immune system was a powerful thing. Serious infection from bacteria or viruses was generally a risk only to heavily malnourished Vaar. But the Vaar and Viss on the planet found themselves awash in infectious diseases that mysteriously vanished as soon as the infected left the planet. The explorers resorted to environmentally sealed suits and continued probing the planet's underground. The next stage of the defense was environmental, as massive hurricanes and tornadoes became daily occurrences. This was upstaged by massive quakes and volcanic eruptions.

Back on Prithone, the Council of Warlords grew increasingly irate that the Sovari, and now Bonn'ko, were keeping secrets from them. The Council threatened a vote of no confidence in Bonn'ko to compel him to share what he knew. That vote began when word reached the Council of the cataclysms unfolding on Origin. The Council concluded that an alien intelligence must be involved, and they threatened to bring charges against the Sovari for withholding information that potentially endangered the Combine. The urgency for knowledge was compounded by the stories about the planet, which leaked to the general public.

One could easily conclude that Bonn'ko had little respect for the Sovari. This was not true. While he often differed with them, he was one of the few Vaar left in a position of leadership who felt their continued council was important to the Combine. Bonn'ko chose to maintain the secrecy the Sovari desired, and his last act as grand warlord was to issue a writ of immunity on their behalf, barring the Council of Warlords from bringing charges against them. Bonn'ko then prepared to end his own life to avoid the shame of being forcibly removed from his position. Before he did, the Sovari Soma ultimately decided to reveal the information to the senior warlords.

The warlords' reactions were mixed. Some rejected the statement, unable to believe that they had been created by an alien intelligence only to be abandoned on Prithone. Others were keen to know what purpose their creators had meant for them. Others were irate that the Sovari had concealed this information for so long. This latter group ultimately formed a faction that would adopt the belief that the Sovari existed to limit the Vaar, rather than enable them to shape their own destiny.

With a degree of self-awareness, the Council of Warlords saw how the issue divided them. They agreed that telling the public would prove even more, divisive but the Council could not simply conceal the issue. Largely through the civilian scientists sent to the planet, far more information had reached the public than the Council wished.

Ultimately the Council chose to honor the Sovari's request to abandon the planet. The information they gave the public was more fiction than fact. The Council invented the story of an ancient species known as the Vo'tanen (Ancient Ones) who once called the planet home. This forbiddingly ancient species was said to have progressed beyond its reason and destroyed itself through runaway technology. The great works that remained on the planet were said to be too great, even for the Vaar. They were not ready; such capabilities were beyond what the Vaar or any species could safely handle.

Thus the Council created what was known as the Origin Quarantine Zone, a 150-light-year radius centered on the planet. The Deep Fleet would not allow anyone to enter this region—not the Vaar, nor any other species.

The scientists who had examined the planet were told in no uncertain terms that they would support the story. State Security watched to ensure their compliance. Any who deviated from the official line were severely punished.

To the relief of the Council of Warlords, the public accepted this story. Much of the fiction created in the intervening years had coincidentally conditioned the public for such a discovery. Many even lauded the Council for having the wisdom to know when to back away from potential danger. The Deep Fleet set up warning beacons to mark the new quarantine zone and stationed ships to enforce it.

Politically, all was not nearly so easy. Deep resentment remained in the Council of Warlords, both against the Sovari for concealing the origin of their species for so long, and toward Bonn'ko for refusing to share their secret when called. Though Bonn'ko would not face a vote of no confidence, his influence in the Council was broken. He resigned from his post and retired the following year. Meanwhile the warlords lost all trust in the Sovari. In secret, the intelligence services were given orders to obtain any additional information they could. The Sovari had not shared their secret of telepathy with the Council. This aided the Sovari in gently thwarting the intelligence services' efforts to gain further information from them.

The quarantine zone around Origin served as a flash point for wars against the quants, evulta, and nakori. So, too, would the planet become a central factor at the beginning of the Hourglass War.

# APPENDIX 6
# THE INTERSTELLAR COMBINE

## PREFACE

SOME BELIEVE THAT THE state exists to serve its citizens. Some believe the citizens exist to observe the state. When observing Vaar society, one could conclude that they favored the latter ideal. The state was central to Vaar society. There was no free market in the Combine. The state owned all resources, all means of production, and all trade goods. There was no free enterprise. The state was the only employer and determined all wages, standards, and practices. There was no organized religion; the state was the only source of both moral and legal authority. There was no nuclear family; the state was parent and provider. There were few personal liberties, and the state had broad discretion in how it treated its citizens. There was no privacy in the Combine. Citizens had no secrets from the state.

Indeed the state touched nearly every aspect of life in some way, but even the state answered to the military.

# 6A

# BREADTH

AT THE START OF the Hourglass War, the Interstellar Combine had undisputed control over five galaxies. Majority control was exerted over seven more. Presences ranging from space stations to small colony clusters existed in over a thousand more. The rate at which the Vaar expanded over the eras was inconsistent. Sometimes they hungered to put their hands on as much territory as possible. Others, they acted lethargically and focused on consolidating their present holdings. How one defined a galaxy came into play here as well. The Vaar typically considered satellite galaxies a part of the galaxy they orbited. If one operated by their definition, the number of galaxies they visited diminished considerably. Nonetheless, the Vaar visited more individual galaxies than any known species. In turn they left their mark on each of them.

Some of this incredible reach was due to simple availability. The more galaxies that were concentrated in one region, the easier it was to hop from one to the next via transpatial drive. The Virgo Cluster held thousands of galaxies, compared to the less than a hundred in the Solar Group. But one should not see this as taking anything away from the Vaar. They had interacted with more sapient species than any other, humanity included. The Vaar never gave up their lust for exploration. This often motivated them to continue reaching for new galaxies and establishing token presences even when major colonization was not a priority.

While their reach was vast, the heart of the Combine lay in its five main galaxies, which the Empire referred to as the core galaxies. These included the Vaar's native galaxy, the Deep Sea, as well as the Proximity Sea, Disorder Sea, Vortex Sea, and Ink Sea. While they touched many more galaxies, 98 percent of all Vaar lived in these five, through modernity.

**The Deep Sea:** The Vaar's native galaxy, the Deep Sea, was a lenticular galaxy that took its name from its thick galactic disc. The Deep Sea was a relatively small galaxy at under thirty thousand light-years in diameter. The galaxy was notable for its thick, dark halo of interstellar dust. The Vaar were the only sapient species native to this galaxy, which hosted Prithone, the Vaar home world, thirty-five of the Combine's one hundred most populous planets, and roughly half of all star hives the civilization had built. The Deep Sea was considered a fortress galaxy for the sheer number of battle stations and battery worlds within it.

**The Proximity Sea:** The Proximity Sea was the first galaxy discovered by Vaar astronomers beyond their own, and the Proximity Sea's discovery helped the Vaar to understand the concept of galaxies in general. Its name was derived from the fact that it was the galaxy closest to the Deep Sea. The Proximity Sea was the native home of the quorim species. The Proximity Sea was sometimes known as the Fleet Sea in the Combine War Forces because the majority of the Combine's shipyards were located in this galaxy. Like the Deep Sea, the Proximity Sea was a lenticular galaxy and remained on the smaller side of the spectrum at just under seventy thousand light-years in diameter.

**The Disorder Sea:** The second galaxy visited by the Vaar beyond their own, the Disorder Sea, was named for its nature as an irregular galaxy. The galaxy was classified as an irregular dwarf and was an extremely small galaxy measuring less than eleven thousand light-years across. The Disorder Sea was the smallest galaxy the Vaar possessed that was not a direct satellite of another.

**The Vortex Sea:** The Vaar described spiral galaxies as *yeble* or *vortex* galaxies. This galaxy was the first of its kind identified by Vaar astronomers and formerly hosted the Rethan Republic. The Vortex Sea was the largest of the core galaxies with a breadth of just over 117,000 light-years.

**The Ink Sea:** The Ink Sea was the last added to the Vaar's central galaxies. An irregular galaxy, it took its name from its large quantities of dark dust and interstellar gas that obscured much of its starlight as viewed from Prithone. It, too, was a relatively small galaxy at fifty thousand light-years across at its widest point. The Ink Sea was believed to have once been a spiral galaxy that was distorted into its present form as the result of a near collision with a larger galaxy.

# Border Galaxies

THE VAAR HAD A significant presence in the border galaxies, but for one reason or another, they did not have complete control over them. In many cases, this was simply because the Combine had not initiated an effort to fully incorporate them. In a handful of other cases, it was due to the presence of alien powers that the Combine had not seen fit to conquer. While there were some civilizations in these galaxies that could prove militarily inconvenient for the Vaar, none could defeat them if the Combine decided that it wanted their territory. Only the most notable of the border galaxies are listed.

**The Elder Sea:** The Elder Sea was a small lenticular galaxy spanning fifty-two thousand light-years. The galaxy had a large number of old, dim stars yielding its name. The galaxy had few naturally habitable planets and numerous tiny satellite galaxies. Because most of the naturally habitable planets in the region were located in these satellites, the bulk of Vaar colonization went there.

**The Spectacular Sea:** The largest galaxy in which the Vaar had an appreciable presence, and one of the largest in the Virgo Cluster, the Spectacular Sea was a supergiant elliptical galaxy numbering more than a trillion stars with a diameter of over 240,000 light-years. It was populated primarily by ancient stars, and while it once boasted many habitable worlds, this number dwindled considerably long before the Vaar arrived. Due to its distance from the core galaxies and lack of easily colonized worlds, it was not subjected to great colonization efforts.

**The Time-Lost Sea:** Known as the Hourglass Galaxy to the Solar Empire, the Time-Lost Sea took its name for the unusual temporal phenomenon that occurred within its borders. The Combine controlled more than half of this galaxy by volume but possessed more than 90 percent of its naturally habitable planets. This would prove a constant source of discord between the Combine and the galaxy's native powers as they sought to expand but found no room to do so.

# 6B
# TECHNOLOGY

AT THE START OF the Hourglass War, the Combine lagged well behind the Empire in most technological realms. Despite this, the Vaar were more technologically progressed for a civilization so much younger than the Empire. While it was true that the Vaar received outside help, the situation was much more complex than that. The Vaar had been receiving outside help for a long time.

Modern revisionism of history in the Combine went to great lengths to scrub the historical record of just how much of the Vaar's development was thanks to the Sovari. Through much of the Combine's history, they were regarded as wise counselors, borderline seers who advised those holding the reins of power. But what so many forgot was that the Sovari restored Prithone after an apocalypse. The Sovari drew the Vaar out of the resulting dark age by teaching their people studies such as math and science, among other things.

When scientists in the Combine could not solve a problem, they entreated the Sovari for aid. More than once, the Vaar skipped centuries, or even thousands, of years of research by learning details of the universe such as physical constants from the Sovari. The Sovari were careful about how much information they gave to scientists. Careful to ensure they did not gain knowledge they were not ready for. Careful to govern the outgrowth of technology and regulate it to a pace the species could handle. The Sovari rarely took credit for these developments, usually pointing scientists in the right direction rather than giving them the correct answers in black and white.

The true understanding of the Vaar's scientific and technological mastery was often hidden by other factors. A central component of the misconception that made the Vaar appear more primitive was in how they lived. The consumer culture other developed species shared was largely absent in the Combine. Whereas many others clamored for status symbols, obvious displays of wealth, and the latest techno-gadget trinkets, the Vaar generally did not. Status symbols were bestowed, not purchased. Technology was a drug that could enhance but could also cause dependence and weakness. Displays of wealth were often no more than conspicuous waste.

Many jobs that had been eliminated by AI and automation in the Empire were alive and well within the Combine. Every citizen had a duty to work, and the state had an obligation to ensure each citizen had work to perform. While it was true that automation often created jobs, the stark reality was that it usually destroyed far more. Were this not the case, automation would generally be far less appealing—one of its primary draws was the gained profit, which was lost by paying wages. Every job lost to automation was one a Combine citizen could no longer perform. Every job replaced by AI was likewise one unavailable to a citizen. This created a strong cultural anathema toward automation and AI.

A cultural hallmark of the Vaar was the need for a citizen to work. A citizen needed work to perform to have a sense of purpose in society and a sense of personal accomplishment for their spent days. The Vaar used both automation and AI but under much tighter restrictions. Automation was used when it was necessary. AI was often restricted to jobs that a citizen could not perform efficiently. The massive surveillance network used by State Security, for example, made extensive use of AI. Quadrillions of beings couldn't be monitored by a few workers. Even so, all violations found were elevated to organic agents for review.

The attitude regarding the importance of work even extended into the civilians' private lives. The average Solar would happily take their meals from a food printer and never give it a second thought. The average Vaar, by contrast, would put work into the meal by cooking it. The idea that the process could be more important than the result was often strong with the Vaar.

The most significant technological gaps were those that related directly to military capability. This again was a case where the Vaar was behind, but not so far behind as perceived. The ability to miniaturize disrupters to infantry scale was what kept these weapons out of the hands of most ground forces. What the Empire did not realize was that the Vaar had developed infantry-scale disrupters before the two civilizations ever met. The Combine War Forces did not see the need to undergo the arduous process of replacing their infantry's small arms with new weapons; what they already possessed was effective against all known foes. It was only after contact with the Empire that the Combine realized its infantry needed disrupters. Once this decision was made, the Vaar could rapidly prototype, tool-up production, and distribute disrupters to their infantry—an effort they could accomplish without help.

The Combine's disrupters were weaker than Imperial weapons. The Type II disrupter rifle used by the average Deep Marine was only marginally more powerful than an RA-117 despite the former weapon being many times the latter's mass. But it was still a functional disrupter that the Vaar developed on their own.

Where the Combine would receive the most technological aid was in relation to sensor, communications, and locomotive systems for their forces. The earliest encounters with the Empire demonstrated how badly the Combine was outclassed in sensor technology, particularly with jamming and counter-jamming these systems. It was difficult to hit a target they couldn't see.

Not all species progressed their technology at the same rate. Therefore it was difficult to compare the Combine's capabilities directly to the Empire at any given point in the latter's history. However if one were to be forced to make such a comparison, then the Combine's military technology was roughly on par with what the Empire possessed one or two millennia before the Solar Eclipse. The Empire had reached a point where large technological jumps were rare and often separated by thousands of years. One of the things that made the *Prince of Mars* so significant was that it was the first ship built in thousands of years that could be considered technologically revolutionary, rather than evolutionary.

Perhaps the area where the Combine was furthest behind the Empire was in AI. This should come as no surprise given the species' disdain for it. But this severe weakness proved problematic for the Combine throughout the war. The Vaar adopted extremely strict access protocols for their networks to keep Imperial AIs out. Protocols so strict that they were often stifling to the people using them.

In a handful of areas, the Combine was ahead of the Empire. The most significant of these, with military applications, was the Deep Fleet's ability to identify and track the warp-wake of star ships. In the years leading up to the war, the Combine went to enormous efforts to push the leading edge with these systems out of fear that Armadas' jamming systems would nullify the former's ship-to-ship weapons.

The Council of Warlords did not mind and even hoped that they were seen as drastically more primitive by the Empire. Faced with such a powerful opponent, the Combine sought every possible advantage, including being underestimated by the enemy.

# 6C
# POPULATION

EVENTUALLY EVERY STAR-FARING CIVILIZATION had to face the realities and necessities of population control. Although this was not a universal rule, the larger a population grew, the faster it could continue growing. If left unchecked, fertility could result in runaway growth that outstripped any ability to expand to new homes or provide resources for the numbers trying to reach infinity.

Entire species had bred themselves to extinction with this problem. One positive aspect of the state's totalitarian control in the Combine was its ability to regulate the issue closely. The Vaar often exploited this control to slow growth it was not ready for or exploited short-term population explosions to rapidly fill newly acquired territory.

The Combine went to extraordinary efforts to hide the true size of its population. The Council of Warlords had long considered population figures to be a military secret. Only the Council of Warlords had access to the most complete numbers. The intelligence services went to equally extraordinary efforts to confuse efforts by foreign intelligence agencies to divine this number. Even after Commando Corps agents obtained the exact figures, they were discarded by the intelligence services as a counterintelligence ruse.

At the start of the Hourglass War, the total population of the Combine stood at 519 quintillion. As the most numerous species in the Combine, the Vaar accounted for 74 percent of this total. The second most numerous species was the quorim, which accounted for 22 percent of the total. The remaining species in the Combine accounted for the 4 percent remainder.

The Combine government practiced strict population controls. It was illegal for anyone to procreate without a state license. Violation of these regulations resulted in forced sterilization and state confiscation of the child to be raised as an orphan. Procreation wasn't difficult, however. The Combine mandated reproduction by each citizen. Exactly how many children a citizen was required to have varied. In years of low expansion, the number was often set to ensure replacement rate and prevent contraction. In years of large-scale expansion, the numbers increased.

Eugenics was never a difficult subject among the Vaar, and the licensing policies also played into this. The Vaar's eugenic ideals focused on limiting the reproduction of those carrying significant or impairing genetic defects. Those with heritable defects were restricted from breeding unless genetic modification could prevent those defects from passing to their children.

Disqualifying defects included mental handicaps, immune disorders, and similar issues that could result in a child becoming a burden on the state. The Combine's policies enabled the Vaar to have a constant, but controlled, growth throughout most of their history. The only periods of real population decline came about as a result of major conflicts such as the Rethan War.

The majority of children were raised first by one parent and then by the state. The Vaar discouraged pair-bonding, so reproduction tended to be a procedural affair. Whenever a Vaar or Viss desired—or was mandated—to reproduce, they asked for a contribution from a partner. This was generally considered a compliment, though the request was not always honored. In any case, it was the sole responsibility of the initiating parent to raise the child until the age of six.

An illegal sex market in the Combine was particularly sought after, where Vaar and Viss were known to seek payment from initiating partners. This was illegal, and as all transactions were tracked, this often took the form of gifts. This was difficult for the state to prosecute because the motivation behind the gift couldn't be determined with proof.

It was also notable that most Vaar and Viss fell into the natural or artificial category—determined by whether they were gestated in an artificial womb. When the male was the initiating partner, the female transferred the fetus to an artificial womb to be kept by the male until the child was ready to be born. Some Viss did so even when they were the initiating partner, while some chose to carry the child naturally. In any case, the state enforced strict requirements that the gestating and infant child receive routine checkups to correct any developmental disorders.

A special exception to these rules existed for warlords of all types. This concept known as *warlord's privilege* granted a warlord sexual rights to any opposite-sex citizen of breeding age. This tied into the Vaar's eugenic preferences and was one of the few areas where they actively pursued controlled breeding for a positive effect. Warlords were considered the pillars of Combine civilization and thus were given broad discretion to spread their genes throughout the population.

Warlord's privilege was robust, and not even another warlord may refuse to honor it unless it would interfere with their duties. For the majority of Vaar and Viss, being approached by a warlord for this purpose was considered a great honor.

At the age of six, all children became wards of the state and attended a state-run boarding school. The exception was those who chose to attend a warrior academy instead. The parent's custody was effectively severed at this point. The parent could only visit or take the child out of school at approved times such as holidays, while the state had no obligation to send a child to a school convenient to the parent. In these schools, the young Vaar and Viss were subjected to a constant battery of aptitude testing throughout their education. The results of these tests determined their adult vocation. By age twelve, the child began training for their adult profession.

New adults did not immediately enter the workforce. Every Vaar and Viss between the ages of sixteen and eighteen gave a mandatory two-year term to the State Service Regiments. The SSR was a general labor group that performed tasks such as city beautification, construction projects, and other similar tasks. After their term, the young adult began the profession they trained for. Candidates who applied and were accepted as soldiers skipped this step and began military school, which lasted another two to ten years depending on the military vocation chosen for the individual.

The Combine's alien population was much more heavily controlled. The Vaar never liked having aliens in their territory, but they had moral compunctions against exterminating an entire species. This attitude grew in strength, at least among the Council of Warlords, after the discovery of Origin. The Combine still exerted strict population controls over its non-Vaar citizens who were generally held to reproduction rates meant to sustain them. An exception to this was the quorim who, having proven useful in scientific and engineering fields, were allowed far more latitude.

Multiple species did not regularly cohabitate on the same worlds within the Combine. Again, the exception was made for the quorim. Other non-Vaar generally lived on planets reserved for them with new worlds granted only if the Council of Warlords saw fit to allow it. This policy became increasingly stricter after the proliferation of the alchemic printer, and off-world trade became far less critical for a population to survive. Some of the only spaceships routinely operated by non-Vaar were large hydrogen barges, which collected the substance from sources in space before returning to their home planets to supply printing systems there. The ships remained the property of the Combine state.

As the majority of aliens lived on worlds populated by aliens, the Combine left them to their own devices in many ways but monitored them closely as well.

# 6D
# SAPIENCE AND DEGREES OF CITIZENSHIP

Vaar and aliens lived different realities within the Interstellar Combine. The Vaar approach to sapient alien life in several ways mirrored that of the Praetheen Unity. The Vaar did not relish the idea of exterminating sapient species, nor did they desire to integrate aliens into their civilization.

Of the species under the Combine's dominion—not including Vaar— only six were capable of interstellar travel before the Vaar encountered them.

The current Combine model of citizenship was created to address the status of aliens within their civilization. There were five degrees of citizenship, each with particular rights and privileges.

**First Degree citizenship:** No sapient in the Combine was born with First Degree citizenship. Citizenship in the First Degree must be earned through military service. Any Combine citizen could volunteer for military service, but Vaar and Viss were generally selected for it because it was based upon aptitude testing during their school years. Exceptions were made in the event of major wars where volunteers would not only be accepted, but conscription could be employed.

First Degree citizenship meant membership in the Combine military for life and at all times, being subject to military jurisdiction. First Degree citizens were held to higher standards of behavior under the law, faced harsher penalties for criminal behavior, and were tried by military courts. Citizens in the First Degree were eligible to vote in any election occurring where they resided. The rights and privileges of First Degree citizens were nearly identical to those of Second Degree, but if a First Degree citizen who retired from active military service wished to enter politics, they could bypass the many years of service in the bureaucracy mandated for Second Degree citizens.

**Second Degree citizenship:** This degree of citizenship was the one to which all Vaar and Viss were born. They would remain so provided they were not accepted into the military and did not commit violent offenses. As such the majority of Vaar and Viss were citizens in the Second Degree.

Aliens could occasionally rise to Second Degree citizenship through great feats of public service, though this was rare. Prior to the Hourglass War, the Council of Warlords realized it would have to lean on segments of its alien population to help prepare for the conflict. The quorim were the species most affected. While many quorim already worked for the military, they did so purely as civilian workers. With the need to further integrate them, the Council of Warlords authorized any quorim who voluntarily joined—and were accepted to—the Combine War Forces to be promoted to Second Degree citizenship.

Second Degree citizens had the right to challenge guilty verdicts rendered against them, as well as the right to compensation for any property seized from them by the state. They had the right to vote in local elections and to enter the government bureaucracy where they may one day be able to run for election themselves. Second Degree citizens had an expansive right to life and could not be executed by the state for any crime but treason.

**Third Degree citizenship:** This degree was reserved for alien species who made notable and significant contributions to Combine society as a whole. To an observer, this could be seen as a reward to species who had accepted their Vaar overlords and worked to their benefit. The Combine would argue that this distinction was given to species who successfully integrated into Combine society as contributing members rather than as burdens to the state. The most prolific Third Degree citizens were the quorim, who were greatly valued for their technical expertise. As a species, they had authored many technological advances and made many contributions to Combine society.

A species could be elevated to birthright Third Degree citizenship at the behest of the Collective Committee and with the consent of the Council of Warlords. The latter was the real obstacle as the Council of Warlords blocked most efforts to elevate member species to this level. The degree of contribution required to Combine society as mandated by the warlords often trended toward unrealistic.

Third Degree citizens had most of the civil rights of Second Degree citizens but may not vote in elections or run for office despite many serving in the state bureaucracy. Additionally Third Degree citizens could be executed for treason or murder of any First, Second, or Third Degree citizen.

**Fourth Degree citizenship:** It was into this degree of citizenship that most of the Combine's alien population was born. Even the primitive species in Combine territory were regarded as Fourth Degree Citizens—they simply were not aware of their citizenship. Most species with Fourth Degree citizenship were primitive, were not independently capable of interstellar travel, and as such were often easy to ignore.

The Combine government regarded Fourth Degree citizens with a sort of neglect, rarely paying attention to them unless they collectively created problems. In general the Combine government cared little for these species, which were seen as poorly or noncontributing members of society. This could be somewhat of a mixed blessing as they received little in social services but suffered relatively little in terms of scrutiny. However, the Combine aided these citizens in natural disasters or similar calamities. In at least one example with a species known as the lo'keth, the species became aware of the existence of alien life and their citizenship status when the Vaar made first contact to help them cope with a natural disaster that would have otherwise been an extinction event.

The batul was one of the few Fourth Degree species capable of interstellar travel prior to conquest by the Combine. The species was most well-known among the Vaar as traveling merchants. However as the state owned all star ships, most batul booked passage on Vaar ships to ply their trade. When the quorim were offered Second Degree citizenship for joining the military, many batul lobbied for the same. The Council of Warlords refused. Ever the traders, the batul then asked for Third Degree citizenship instead for any who joined the War Forces. Their offer was accepted.

**Fifth Degree citizenship:** Ostensibly this rank of citizenship was the one to which perpetrators of violent crimes were demoted. Fifth Degree citizens effectively had no rights under the law and became state property. While most Vaar and aliens could only fall to this rank through criminal wrongdoing, all Rethan in the Combine were born into this degree. It wasn't a stretch to say Fifth Degree citizens had few rights, if any. To kill a Fifth Degree citizen was generally considered destruction of government property than murder.

# 6E
# GOVERNMENT

THE COMBINE GOVERNMENT WAS a colossal beast composed of a mountain range of bureaucracy. The Combine explained its government as a limited, meritocratic democracy. This description was, in short, garbage. For the civilian population, at least, the Combine was the result where bureaucracy grew to the point that instead of becoming an unavoidable part of government, it instead defined the government. One positive thing that could be said about the bureaucracy was that, for its size, it was surprisingly quick and efficient. Bureaucrats had work quotas, too.

Some of the young Vaar and Viss would be selected for a position in the government bureaucracy in their youth. These eager citizens entered the government as low-level functionaries attempting to manage the government that tried to be all things to all citizens. Many young citizens were overjoyed to learn they were chosen to work in government. This exuberance died quickly as they realized the incredible workloads they needed to shoulder to climb the mountain. Ostensibly one's ability to ascend the bureaucracy depended on faithful execution of their duties. That only carried one to a supervisory position. The ability was based on currying political favor from senior bureaucrats as well as personal politics among coworkers. All while managing workloads that made mental health easily the largest health expenditure for young bureaucrats.

Only those who spent two hundred years or more in the bureaucracy were eligible to run for an elected office. This could only be done with the approval of those further up in the bureaucracy. Such positions included planetary governors or membership on the government's many, many councils. Only individuals who came from a military background could bypass the otherwise mandatory terms of service in the bureaucracy. The state was careful to ensure that there were never more than two candidates up for election to the same position. Any vote not cast by an eligible citizen was automatically counted as a vote for the incumbent.

The top of the mountain for the civilian government was made up of the Collective Committee. This was the supreme *civilian* lawmaking body in the Combine. Membership on this council was a full-time job, much of which was spent overseeing the subcouncils that answered to the Committee. The chairperson of the Committee was the First Councilor, assisted by the Second and Third Councilors.

The First Councilor was primarily responsible for setting the agenda of the Collective Committee and determining what would be voted on, on any given day. The Second Councilor was second in the line of succession in the event of the First Councilor's death or incapacitation. In council, the Second Councilor was primarily responsible for moderating debate. The Third Councilor served as a sergeant-at-arms, helping to ensure the Collective stuck to the agenda set for it on any given day.

Most legislation required approval from a majority before it became law. The high councilors had limited veto power. If a measure passed without the First Councilor's vote, he could veto the provision, citing specific reasons, and force the legislation to be voted on a second time. If the measure passed a second time, the First and Second Councilors could together veto the legislation on the same criteria. This veto could be repeated once more if the Third Councilor agreed with the previous two. However, this was the extent of their ability to block legislation, and if passed a fourth time, it became law despite their objections.

The veto power of the high councilors was meant as an opportunity for these senior politicians to note any flaws they found in the legislation and offer a chance to address them. This power was rarely exercised because only a simple majority was needed each time to overcome their veto. Historically this veto power was exercised most often when the high councilors believed that a law would be rejected by the Council of Warlords.

The high councilors were all elected to eight-year terms, and there was no active term limit. Given the ageism and value placed on seniority in Combine society, it was not uncommon for the high councilors to be the longest, second-longest, and third-longest sitting members of the Collective. As of the Hourglass War, only Vaar and Viss were permitted to sit on the high collective. Combine citizens voted for neither the high councilors, nor the other councilors on the Collective Committee. Council members were elected by the subcouncils they represented, and these councilors in turn elected the high councilors.

Beneath the Collective Committee were more than six hundred subcouncils tasked with areas of government responsibility. These included planetary agriculture, citizen health and wellness, and shipyard workers. Each subcouncil was made up of bureaucrats advised by an assembly of professionals from relevant fields. Every world had its own governor who worked with the subcouncils to meet state guidelines on productivity and implementation of law.

The state was at the center of Combine society, but the state answered to the military. The Council of Warlords was the ultimate authority over the Combine. All laws and regulations passed by the Collective Committee were subject to review, or even unassailable veto by the Council. The Council of Warlords had full authority to pass law on its own. It reserved some aspects of government to itself and did not permit the Collective Committee to influence it.

The Council of Warlords was the only body that could make decisions for the military or foreign policy. The Council decided how much of the national budget was reserved for the military and how much was available for the rest of government.

The military was an active part of civilian society. On most worlds, the same police handled both the military and the public. Military engineers designed warships and battle stations but also deep space habitats, dams, and civilian power plants. The Combine military was the public works for a great deal of the nation's infrastructure.

Four distinct grades of warlords served on the Council: junior warlords, elevated warlords, rank warlords, and senior warlords. Junior warlords made up the bulk of the Council by numbers. As of the Hourglass War, the War Forces recognized 4,217 distinct military vocations. Soldiers and warriors were subjected to quarterly evaluations of their performance. Individuals who scored highest became junior warlords for the following calendar year. Seniority was used to break any ties.

Junior warlords attended the meetings of the Council and served primarily in an advisory role to the senior warlords. They did little actual voting, but this was an opportunity for the most accomplished members of the military to speak directly to its leadership. Junior warlords served a one-year term, but if the candidate continued worthy performance upon returning to their regular duties, they could be nominated again. Junior warlords were generally addressed as *warlord* only in council. At other times they were addressed by their military rank.

Rank warlords consisted of military personnel who attained the rank of warlord in their service. These warlords did not have voting power in most situations. Instead they served as advisers to the senior warlords. In general, becoming a rank warlord would be a stepping-stone to becoming a senior warlord. Like junior and elevated warlords, they voted when the senior warlords were deadlocked.

When rank warlords were encountered in the field, it was often because they were assigned a specific duty. This came either from the grand warlord or the senior warlords as a group. In this position, they had broad discretionary power to exercise their assigned duties.

Elevated warlords were individuals who performed great acts of loyalty, selflessness, and courage in the face of the enemy. This included all, but was not limited to, warriors decorated with the Star of Prithone, the highest commendation for valor in the War Forces. These individuals were deemed by their courage and dedication as being worthy to attend Council meetings. This position was a lifetime appointment, and the elevated warlord could choose to attend Council meetings at will. The rules of order for the Council mandated that any elevated warlord who requested to speak be allowed to do so.

The senior warlords were the real power in the Council and performed the majority of the voting that occurred within it. The eligibility requirements to join the high warlords were strict, and even among those who spent their entire lives in the War Forces, few ever qualified. To become a high warlord, one must be nominated by at least two other senior warlords and be confirmed to the Council by a simple majority of the remaining senior warlords.

To be eligible for nomination, a Vaar or Viss must be a flag officer. They must have served at least one term as a junior or elevated warlord. They must have consistently maintained the respect of their subordinates throughout their career. They must be combat veterans if they were warriors and if a war was fought in their lifetime. Last they must be deemed to be of such character that they may be entrusted both with the safeguarding of society and the leadership of the military.

Senior warlords were technically appointed to a lifetime term, however, most would retire well before their lifespan expired. This opened room for other worthy candidates and ensured that a warlord did not remain beyond the point when his mental faculties began to decline. A senior warlord could be removed from the Council by two-thirds of the vote of other senior warlords in the event of criminal behavior, cognitive decline, or dereliction of duty.

As of the Hourglass War, there were three hundred senior warlords, most serving as the heads of particular military and joint-service departments. The warlord of the Deep was the chief of staff for the Deep Fleet, the Warlord of the Clandestine was the head of State Security, and so on. Senior warlords had broad and highly discretionary power over what lay within their purview. If two or more senior warlords claimed authority over the same issue, the one with the longer term of service on the Council generally took priority. This made it difficult for one senior warlord to interfere directly in the activities of another. If one warlord took issue with how another was managing his responsibilities and the two could not resolve the dispute, it had to be brought to the Council as a whole.

The grand warlord was the true head of state for the Interstellar Combine and the chairperson for the Council. He was the Combine's chief executive officer, commander-in-chief of the military, and its chief diplomat. The exact authority of the grand warlord could be difficult for an outsider to divine. He was not an autocrat, but there were areas of responsibility where he wielded near dictator-level authority.

The Council, specifically the senior warlords, collectively set the Combine's foreign policy. The grand warlord could hold great influence in determining that policy, but ultimately he was compelled to follow it, even if he did not agree with it. He was the primary spokesperson for the Council, regardless of how he felt about the message. He commanded the military but could not unilaterally declare war. He could veto any piece of civilian legislation he pleased, but only the Council may pass legislation that directly affected the public. He was the only person who could initiate proceedings to remove a sitting warlord from the Council, but he was the only exception, as any senior warlord could call for a vote to relieve him of his position as a result of death, retirement, or criminal behavior, mental incapacitation, or dereliction of duty. Upon voting, three-fourths of the majority had to agree.

The Council of Warlords was meant to be a sort of roundtable environment, where the most accomplished and experienced minds in the military could work together to craft solutions. He wielded great executive power, particularly when the Council was out of session, but he must answer to it. As the head of the Combine War Forces, he was the only one who could summarily issue direct orders to another senior warlord—but only within his executive purview. The grand warlord was there to guide the Council, not order it about.

Ideally the grand warlord best represented the ideals of the War Forces, and they were most capable of guiding it in times of moral crisis. In practice, this position was generally held by the best politician among the senior warlords.

How much power the grand warlord possessed often hinged upon the strength and charisma of the individual holding the office. Some grand warlords were little more than figureheads, while others wielded near-autocratic control.

Another noteworthy position was the warlord of aspiration. The warlord of aspiration was only chosen if the candidate had been both a junior and elevated warlord in the past. The warlord of aspiration's official responsibility was the military education system. He was the only individual on the Council who could unilaterally make changes to the core curriculum taught to military students. But he was more than simply the head of the education department. He was accorded this position because he was considered an exemplar of conduct and valor that all soldiers and warriors should emulate. In the absence of a holder to this office, a committee made up of other warlords managed the curriculum for military students.

Long periods passed without a warlord of aspiration. Even after meeting the criteria, the warlord must be chosen. In the eyes of the Council, it was better to have no exemplar than a substandard one.

In practice, the warlord of aspiration spent relatively little time on his official duties. Beyond minor tweaks individuals made, the core curriculum for military students remained largely the same for many years. It was common for the Council to assign warlords to oversee special matters personally. When there was a Warlord of Aspiration, he was often one of the Council's favorite picks to show just how much attention they were paying, and how serious they were about results.

The Council voted on few things. Each warlord had clearly defined responsibilities and broad authority to manage them. Most of the voting that occurred, did so when two or more senior warlords were in dispute or when the Council needed to act on policies affecting the public. Because senior warlords could not directly issue orders to other senior warlords, voting also occurred when the Council wished to grant a senior warlord a specific task.

Senior warlords had the unique privilege of exercising Lo'taam. This word did not translate well. It embodied an ancient concept pertaining to generals being judged by those they led. This concept tied into the idea that even the greatest warrior was worth less than a general, for a single warrior could be in only one place at a time and fight one battle at a time. A general could lead legions, motivating his troops to feats none could achieve alone. A general's men didn't need to like him, but it was paramount that they respected him. Lo'taam was the ancient practice of a general calling upon his troops to demonstrate their respect for and faith in him, or their lack thereof.

In lieu of accepting the other senior warlords' judgment, a senior warlord may invoke Lo'taam. Most were reluctant to invoke this privilege without a compelling reason, lest it inspire disobedience in the lower ranks. If invoked, the challenger must ask another senior warlord to plead his case. Any other warlord could be asked, the grand warlord included. If none accepted, then the challenge was defeated. If a senior warlord accepted, then a short trial began. The warlord who had agreed to plea the case proceeded to do so before the assembled Council. After this, a vote was cast to decide whether to release the warlord from the protested obligation. Only the junior and elevated warlords could vote in Lo'taam.

Beyond the rare Lo'taam, the junior and elevated warlords generally voted only to break a tie among the senior warlords. This was uncommon, and in the rare event that a tie remained, the rank warlords would vote. If somehow, there was still a tie, the grand warlord would be compelled to cast the deciding vote.

# 6F
# ECONOMY AND TREASURY

THERE WAS NO FREE enterprise in the Combine, only the state. All resources, production, and goods were produced by the state and sold by the state. The state was the only employer and paid all wages. The state set the price for all goods and services. These prices were often determined primarily by political factors. Often, the cost of a given thing depended less on the difficulty and time to produce it, and more on the state's desire, or lack thereof, for citizens to possess it.

The base unit of currency in the Combine was the *dokun*. This word translated poorly, but *finance ration* was a close approximation. The dokun's existence served as an internal accounting tool for the state rather than a simple trade tool. Due to how the Combine economy functioned, the dokun was not a very fungible currency. Beyond the Combine's borders, the dokun was close to worthless. It was illegal for citizens to send dokuns out of the nation. Those who traveled beyond the Combine's borders were required to carry no more than an amount approved by the state when travel was authorized. A citizen who returned with more or less than they departed with would need a good explanation.

The Combine conducted precious little trade with outsiders. More often than not, if a foreign power had something the Combine wanted, the Council of Warlords asked for it. If it was not surrendered to the Combine, it was taken by force of arms. In the rare situation that the Combine chose to trade, it bartered rather than used dokuns.

The majority of dokuns existed as digital currency to better enable the state to monitor all transactions. Physical dokuns were minted in the form of coins produced from aluminum. These physical dokuns were generally held by banks for emergencies. If a world lost its access to the central network, physical dokuns were dispersed to the citizens to pay for their needs until the network was restored. At this point, the citizens were required to turn in any remaining dokuns they had to be digitized.

One should be careful not to misunderstand how the wealth of the Combine was distributed or how wages were paid. A general laborer working in a foundry was never paid the same wages as the director overseeing that foundry. Every general laborer in that foundry and others were paid the same base wage, as was every director of the various foundries. One of the things that made the military so prestigious was that the starting pay for soldiers was much higher than that for most laborers and only went up according to rank.

The wages of any occupation were set by the state, ostensibly according to how valuable each occupation was to society. Educators were—like the military—some of the better-compensated professionals as the state relied heavily on them to indoctrinate each generation.

For virtually every profession, there were state-mandated productivity quotas. Workers who overproduced may be compensated extra, but the state was under no obligation to do so. Often it did not except in times of war or shortage. On the opposite side, the state had no qualms about docking the pay of employees who failed to meet their quotas. Repeated failure could be considered criminal.

All property, such as real estate, belonged to the state. A citizen owned neither the house nor the land it was built on. The best the citizen could do was to engage in an indefinite lease with the state on the property, but this lease could not be inherited.

Vaar and Viss lived in common tenements, and generally only high-ranking government or military officials ever had something like their own house. If a Vaar had his own house and died, and one of his children desired the home, they had to enter their own lease with the state, supposing that the state was willing to do so, rather than tender the property to someone else.

The Solar Empire under Emperor Mason Mandrake made a concerted effort to weaken the Combine's ability to wage war by undermining its economy prior to the Hourglass War. One of the most well-known aspects of this campaign was the opening of numerous black markets in Combine territory to distribute Imperial goods. These black markets offered almost everything, including weapons, in hopes of sparking an armed rebellion in the Combine's borders.

These efforts caused enormous trouble for the Combine and tied up many of the State Security's resources. Directly under the purview of Imperial intelligence services, these black marketeers proved extremely elusive to the authorities working night and day to catch them. The Combine's greatest concern was the number of weapons being smuggled into the nation and sold to private citizens. While the actual number was quite small, State Security's inability to determine the actual number resulted in tying up resources far out of proportion to the actual threat.

The black market for consumer goods and luxury items would prove even more problematic to the state. The state feared that the ability to purchase these items would not only weaken demand for local products, but it would positively predispose Combine citizens toward the Empire and perhaps even result in the Vaar adopting their own consumer culture. As with the efforts to control illicit weapons, the amount of state resources expended to combat this threat was well out of proportion to the threat's actual magnitude.

Black markets would not be the only means the Empire employed to undermine Combine society. Even though they were worthless, black marketeers often accepted dokuns as payment but only in physical form. This created a native black market to feed physical dokuns to civilians so that they could purchase Imperial goods. The dokuns received by Imperial agents were generally disposed of, as they had no value outside the Combine. Those operating the black markets were paid in troys by the Imperial government.

The Empire would also create vast fortunes of counterfeit, physical dokuns and spread them among Combine citizens as payment for their assistance or information. Anti-counterfeiting technology was an area where the Empire was light-years ahead of the Combine. The latter was unable to identify counterfeits from its own currency. Yet more resources were tied up as the state tried to develop the means to detect these counterfeits. More resources were then devoted to stomping out the organized criminals who popped up to help citizens launder their illicit dokuns.

In the end, the Hourglass War began before the Empire could inflict any long-lasting damage on the Combine economy, but the resources tied up in combating these efforts would have a measurable effect, diminishing the Combine's ability to combat other and more serious efforts by Imperial intelligence.

# 6G
# THE COMBINE WAR FORCES

THE COMBINE WAR FORCES, the Interstellar Combine's military, was a massive organization made up of four branches—the Deep Fleet, Deep Marines, Planetary Defense Force, and the State Security Services. At the start of the Hourglass War, it was eclipsed only by the Solar Armed Forces.

Ever since the Interstellar Combine replaced the Deep Republic, the War Forces prized versatility. This value began due to the enormous burdens the military carried to keep civilian society functioning. Soldiers needed to have many skills and were often transferred between services based on need. Into modernity the War Forces strongly encouraged personnel to continue training in new skills and to serve at least once in a different service from the one they originally joined. While it was not a strict requirement, nearly every senior warlord served in at least two of the services. All services shared the same lieutenant ranks, so many warriors and soldiers started exploring other services around this time.

While this policy came at a degree of cost in specialization, it resulted in a versatile force. Many of the Deep Fleet's personnel were capable of acting as infantry in the vein of the Deep Marines or the Planetary Defense Force. At the same time, members of both services were often capable of performing crew functions on a Deep Fleet warship. This made it easy for one service to "donate" personnel to another if it had a numbers problem.

## Warriors and Soldiers

THERE WERE TWO DISTINCT types of personnel in the Combine War Forces: warriors and soldiers. The clean distinction between warriors and soldiers grew out of the era of the Deep Republic and the Combine's formational days. In those days the military was often forced to take over civilian duties. The numbers required to maintain huge infrastructure, in turn, mandated civilian workers. This resulted in military personnel often being placed in direct supervision of civilian workers. The Council of Warlords later determined that it was easier to simply conscript civilians in these work sectors into the military. Since that time, *warrior* has referred to the elite military quasi-caste, as opposed to regular enlisted and conscripted soldiers.

Many in the Empire mistakenly believed that *kal* (*warrior*) referred to combat personnel, and *zon* (*soldier*) referred to non-combat military personnel. While all warriors were combat troops, not all combat personnel were warriors. Warriors were over-represented in the most critical areas of battle, yielding the impression that they were more numerous than they were. In most years, the Deep Fleet was composed of 10 percent warriors, the Deep Marines 21 percent, the Planetary Defense Force fewer than 1 percent, and the Security Services around 12 percent. The remainder in each service was made up of soldiers, enlisted or conscripted.

Warriors were chosen from an early age to be the elite of the War Forces. Those who were trained to become warriors were chosen at age six, when they and their peers began state boarding school. Warrior candidates were chosen based on size, project growth, intelligence, aggressiveness, and overall health. Those with the highest marks were pulled out of the state boarding school system and sent to military academies instead. While this was considered a great honor, the childhood of a warrior was a difficult one. The mental and physical demands were tremendous, and warrior trainees were considered as having the highest suicide rate among Vaar youth.

Warrior trainees were monitored closely, and those who could not handle it were generally transferred back to the state school system but remained monitored for suicide. No shame was levied on those who washed out, and many ended up joining the War Forces as soldiers later in life.

Given the War Forces' love of versatility, warrior trainees trained for the Deep Fleet, Deep Marines, and Planetary Defense Force. Every warrior was expected to serve in any of these three forces, though State Security only recruited experienced personnel from the active-duty services with few exceptions.

Warriors were exclusively male. There was no specific prohibition on Viss membership, but there was a de facto prohibition. The physical standards for warriors were meant to bar all but the strongest and most fit. Vaar warrior trainees trained constantly to meet these standards, and still many failed. There simply were no Viss who could meet these standards. Cyberization only increased the gap as males had much more body to augment.

The Solar Legionnaires were trained that an easy way to spot warriors on the battlefield was their possession of a melee weapon in addition to anything that was part of a soldier's combat kit. A warrior may carry most any melee weapon with which he had trained, but he must carry one. His melee weapon was both part of his uniform and a reminder. Warriors did not surrender, and if all other weapons failed, he was expected to die with his melee weapon in his hand. In addition to their combat weapon, warriors often received highly ornamental, ceremonial weapons as commendations.

A warrior's armor was extremely important as well. Vaar did not bother with clothing; their body was already protected by their carapace of plates. Clothing was seen as feminine by the majority of Vaar. A Vaar's identifying marks, rank insignia, and commendations were often carved directly onto their plates. Armor was armor, however, not clothing. Whereas most soldiers only wore their armor in combat or to ceremonial functions, warriors were typically expected to be in their armor when they faced the public. All warriors were permitted to customize their armor—in particular, its helmet—so long as the design bore no vulgarity. Most warriors did this only for ceremonial or "dress" armor. Modification of combat armor tended to make one stand out on the battlefield. This was generally bad practice as standing out tended to attract fire and annoy one's coworkers.

Warriors did not graduate from their academy until the age of twenty, with the training program only shortened in times of war. Whether they were selected for officer or enlisted positions, they began at the same ranks as soldiers but advanced the chain quicker. Warriors were extremely over-represented in the special forces. The honor of serving in these forces was considered more important than rank, and many warriors declined promotion or even accepted rank reductions to serve in them.

If warriors were the elite, soldiers were the rank and file. Soldiers were made up of Vaar and Viss who met one of three categories. The first was that they did not qualify for a warrior academy but were selected for soldiers school in the state system. The second category included those who completed their state school, volunteered for the military, were selected, and then were sent to training. The third consisted of those conscripted in times of war. Warrior washouts were considered part of the first category.

There was a degree of acrimony between warriors and soldiers in some units. To be fair, this usually did not come from the warriors. The academies impressed heavily on the warrior cadets that soldiers fought and died alongside them, entitling them to respect soldiers. Most of the acrimony came either from soldiers who went through state school after failing to qualify for a warrior academy, or those who mistook the eagerness of warriors to enter combat as a lack of concern for the lives of those they served alongside. All in all, warriors were promoted more quickly but had the most difficult assignments. Warriors were also held to higher standards of discipline and received harsher penalties for breaking them.

A unique privilege extended to warriors was the ability to join a warrior's lodge. Membership to a lodge was by invitation only, though most were multi-service. Lodges provided a roundtable environment where members spoke freely. They were intended as a place where every warrior had a voice and offered his ideas or concerns about the operation of the War Forces. Soldiers were generally not permitted to join these lodges, barring a few exceptions. Any soldier who became an elevated warlord due to valor shown in action gained the status of warrior for the rest of his life. These individuals almost certainly received an invitation from one lodge, if not many.

# Rank Structure

THE WAR FORCES HAD many ranks. The Solar Armed Forces still relied on a rank structure created before humanity was an interstellar power. But there was a big difference between a military with trillions of personnel and a single-planet military that had one or two million. The Solar Armed Forces responded to the growth by increasing the size of units in the existing system, and with it the total number of personnel beneath a particular rank. The sheer number of ranks served a secondary purpose. Though not quite so long as Solars, the Vaar were a long-lived species. The number of ranks was meant to provide soldiers and warriors a tangible sense of career advancement, even though the magnitude of their responsibilities may not grow considerably within the same time frame.

Beyond the degrees of rank shown below, every officer rank had three sub-ranks called points. More points were senior to fewer points. Points were based solely on time in service and could be skipped. A Sixth Degree Lieutenant—two points—for example, could be promoted to Fifth Degree Lieutenant—one point—for battlefield performance.

| Flag Officers | | | | | |
|---|---|---|---|---|---|
| Deep Fleet | | Deep Marines | | Planetary Defense Force | |
| Kalo'taa (Grand Warlord) | | | | | |
| Rank | Contextual Translation | Rank | Contextual Translation | Rank | Contextual Translation |
| Kalo'fona | Warlord of the Deep | Ka-lo'ujran | Warlord of the Marines | lo'thone' naga | Warlord of the PDF |
| Kalo'kal | Fleet Warlord | Kalo'ujra | Marine Warlord | Kalo'na-ga | PDF Warlord |
| Shon'terr | Admiral 1st Degree | Hon'terr | Marshal 1st Degree | Ul'terr | General 1st Degree |
| Shon'din | Admiral 2nd Degree | Hon'din | Marshal 2nd Degree | Ul'din | General 2nd Degree |
| Shon'zet | Admiral 3rd Degree | Hon'zet | Marshal 3rd Degree | Ul'zet | General 3rd Degree |

| Flag Officers | | | | | |
|---|---|---|---|---|---|
| **Deep Fleet** | | **Deep Marines** | | **Planetary Defense Force** | |
| **Shon'met** | Admiral 4th Degree | **Hon'met** | Marshal 4th Degree | **Ul'met** | General 4th Degree |
| **Shon'tas** | Admiral 5th Degree | **Hon'tas** | Marshal 5th Degree | **Ul'tas** | General 5th Degree |
| **Shon'va-set** | Admiral 6th Degree | **Hon'va-set** | Marshal 6th Degree | **Ul'vaset** | General 6th Degree |
| **Shon'ja-set** | Admiral 7th Degree | **Hon'jaset** | Marshal 7th Degree | **Ul'jaset** | General 7th Degree |
| **Shon'in-go** | Admiral 8th Degree | **Hon'ingo** | Marshal 8th Degree | **Ul'ingo** | General 8th Degree |
| **Shon'na-dul** | Admiral 9th Degree | **Hon'na-dul** | Marshal 9th Degree | **Ul'nadul** | General 9th Degree |
| **Shon'vul** | Admiral 10th Degree | **Hon'vul** | Marshal 10th Degree | **Ul'vul** | General 10th Degree |

The ranks of Fleet, Marine, and Planetary Defense Forces warlord were both political and military. The Council of Warlords determined how many of each rank each service was entitled to. These individuals were senior warlords for as long as they retained the rank, and they answered to the chief of staff of their service in the military chain of command.

| Line Officers | | | | | |
|---|---|---|---|---|---|
| **Deep Fleet** | | **Deep Marines** | | **Planetary Defense Force** | |
| **Rank** | Contextual Translation | **Rank** | Contextual Translation | **Rank** | Contextual Translation |
| **Shako** | Captain | **Tanho'taa** | Grand Colonel | **Zanho'taa** | Grand Colonel (PDF) |
| **Sha-ko'nep** | Under-Captain | **Tahno** | Colonel | **Zanho** | Colonel (PDF) |
| **Tos-no'laan** | Senior Commander | Tahno'laan | Sub-Colonel | **Zan-ho'laan** | Sub-Colonel (PDF) |
| **Qu** | Commander | **Gon'terr** | Army Leader 1st Degree | **Qoro'terr** | Lieutenant Colonel 1st Degree |
| **Qu'tah** | Under-Commander | **Gon'din** | Army Leader 2nd Degree | **Qoro'din** | Lieutenant Colonel 2nd Degree |
| **Reen'terr** | Lieutenant 1st Degree | | | | |
| **Reen'din** | Lieutenant 2nd Degree | | | | |
| **Reen'zet** | Lieutenant 3rd Degree | | | | |
| **Reen'met** | Lieutenant 4th Degree | | | | |
| **Reen'tas** | Lieutenant 5th Degree | | | | |
| **Reen'va-set** | Lieutenant 6th Degree | | | | |
| **Reen'ja-set** | Lieutenant 7th Degree | | | | |
| **Reen'ingo** | Lieutenant 8th Degree | | | | |
| **Reen'na-dul** | Lieutenant 9th Degree | | | | |
| **Reen'vul** | Lieutenant 10th Degree | | | | |

| Non-Commissioned Officers | | | | | |
|---|---|---|---|---|---|
| Deep Fleet | | Deep Marines | | Planetary Defense Force | |
| **Bon' ten'terr** | Senior Crew Leader 1st Degree | **Lu- gen'terr** | Group Leader 1st Degree | **Sopen' terr** | Gate Guardian 1st Degree |
| **Bon' ten'din** | Senior Crew Leader 2nd Degree | **Lu- gen'din** | Group Leader 2nd Degree | **Sopen'din** | Gate Guardian 2nd Degree |
| **Bon' ten'zet** | Senior Crew Leader 3rd Degree | **Lugen'zet** | Group Leader 3rd Degree | **Sopen'zet** | Gate Guardian 3rd Degree |
| **Bon' ten'met** | Senior Crew Leader 4th Degree | **Lu- gen'met** | Group Leader 4th Degree | **So- pen'met** | Gate Guardian 4th Degree |
| **Bon' ten'en'tas** | Senior Crew Leader 5th Degree | **Lugen'tas** | Group Leader 5th Degree | **Sopen'tas** | Gate Guardian 5th Degree |
| **Bon'ten' en'terr** | Crew Leader 1st Degree | **Vu- gen'terr** | Phalanx Leader 1st Degree | **Vel- gen'terr** | Wall Leader 1st Degree |
| **Bon'ten' en'din** | Crew Leader 2nd Degree | **Vu- gen'din** | Phalanx Leader 2nd Degree | **Vel- gen'din** | Wall Leader 2nd Degree |
| **Bon'ten' en'zet** | Crew Leader 3rd Degree | **Vugen'zet** | Phalanx Leader 3rd Degree | **Vel- gen'zet** | Wall Leader 3rd Degree |
| **Bon'ten' en'met** | Crew Leader 4th Degree | **Vu- gen'met** | Phalanx Leader 4th Degree | **Vel- gen'met** | Wall Leader 4th Degree |

| Bon'ten' en'tas | Crew Leader 5th Degree | Vugen'tas | Phalanx Leader 5th Degree | Velgen'tas | Wall Leader 5th Degree |
|---|---|---|---|---|---|
| Bon'ten' en'vaset | Crew Leader 6th Degree | Vugen'va-set | Phalanx Leader 6th Degree | Vel-gen'vaset | Wall Leader 6th Degree |
| Bon'ten' en'jaset | Crew Leader 7th Degree | Vugen'ja-set | Phalanx Leader 7th Degree | Velgen'ja-set | Wall Leader 7th Degree |
| **Enlisted** | | | | | |
| Bon'terr | Crewman 1st Degree | Ohn'terr | Hammer-man 1st Degree | Jeer'terr | Shieldman 1st Degree |
| Bon'din | Crewman 2nd De-gree | Ohn'din | Hammer-man 2nd De-gree | Jeer'din | Shieldman 2nd De-gree |
| Bon'zet | Crewman 3rd De-gree | Ohn'zet | Hammer-man 3rd De-gree | Jeer'zet | Shieldman 3rd De-gree |
| Bon'met | Crewman 4th Degree | Ohn'met | Hammer-man 4th Degree | Jeer'met | Shieldman 4th Degree |
| Bon'tas | Crewman 5th Degree | Ohn'tas | Hammer-man 5th Degree | Jeer'tas | Shieldman 5th Degree |
| Bon'vaset | Crewman 6th Degree | Ohn'vaset | Hammer-man 6th Degree | Jeer'vaset | Shieldman 6th Degree |
| Bon'jaset | Crewman 7th Degree | Ohn'jaset | Hammer-man 7th Degree | Jeer'jaset | Shieldman 7th Degree |
| Bon'ingo | Crewman 8th Degree | Ohn'ingo | Hammer-man 8th Degree | Jeer'ingo | Shieldman 8th Degree |
| Bon'na-dul | Crewman 9th Degree | Ohn'na-dul | Hammer-man 9th Degree | Jeer'nadul | Shieldman 9th Degree |

| Bon'vul | Crewman 10th Degree | Ohn'vul | Hammer-man 10th Degree | Jeer'vul | Shieldman 10th Degree |
|---------|---------------------|---------|------------------------|----------|-----------------------|
| Zhorja | Field Trainee | | | | |

The rank of *field trainee* was reserved for soldiers who were conscripted into service. This was effectively a probationary grade, and a conscript must participate in at least one operation before leaving probation. Those who performed unsatisfactorily as field trainees were sent back to repeat their basic training.

The War Forces had no equivalent to the senior-most enlisted ranks of the Imperial services. While the functions were performed by senior enlisted personnel, they were appointed to the position and did not receive a specific grade for the position.

First and Second Degree flag officers rarely held field commands. In general they were administrative personnel. In part, this ensured that any flag officer who made it to warlord was personally familiar with the administrative side of operating the force. Similarly the qu, gon, and qoro ranks tended to be on the staff of higher-ranking officers rather than holding field commands of their own.

## The Deep Fleet

THE KAL'FONA OR *DEEP Fleet* was the portion of the Combine War Forces responsible for the control of space in war and peace. At the beginning of the Hourglass War, the Deep Fleet was second in size to the Solar Armadas among known fleets. Deep Fleet ships were typically much lighter than Imperial equivalents. When counted by number of ships, the Deep Fleet was the largest. The Solar Armadas, however, was larger by total tonnage of warships.

The War Reserve Fleet boosted the size of the Deep Fleet. The Combine maintained a massive inventory of warships and relied on an attrition-based policy of replacing old ships with new models. The Deep Fleet replaced older ships as they wore out. Rather than scrapping them, they were refurbished and transferred to the War Reserve, where they were kept for as long as the force believed they could be sufficiently upgraded with modern technology. If a major war broke out, these ships were brought into service as second-line and supplementary forces.

The core of the Deep Fleet was in its large force of destroyers, of which it had fifteen classes at the start of the Hourglass War. The Armadas had one. This diversity was twofold. The first reason was a result of the attrition-based replacement policy. Combine technology advanced considerably in the years prior to the Hourglass War, and improved designs came along before the new design had replaced the old. The other reason was one of specialization. Because the Deep Fleet was so reliant on destroyers, it required them to perform many duties. The Deep Fleet was much more willing to design specialist classes that would serve alongside general-purpose vessels.

When compared to the Empire, the Deep Fleet was slower to give up a carrier-based battle doctrine. Part of this was attributable to the cultural presence held by carrier-based bombers due to their decisive efforts in the Gray Fleet Crises and the Rethan War. One of the biggest problems in modern warfare with a fighter or bomber-centric doctrine was that it became difficult to build such a craft that could carry weapons large enough to threaten a peer or near-peer adversary's warships. If too large they not only presented easy targets for ship-based weapons but grew to a point that they became warships rather than bombers or fighters. When first contact was made with the Empire, the War Reserve included thousands of carriers. The Deep Fleet scrapped many of these ships, realizing their bombers could not carry enough firepower to harm Imperial warships but were easy prey for both an Armadas ship's interceptors and its anti-ship weapons. Like the Empire, the Deep Fleet used fighters almost exclusively for scouting duties. The primary difference was that Deep Fleet fighters remained crewed, versus the AI-controlled fighters of the Armadas.

The Deep Fleet had few capital ships in comparison to the Armadas. Cruisers were primarily used by admirals as command ships. Battleships were rarer. Despite being larger than cruisers, they were rarely used as command ships. Often, their design lacked the necessary facilities to prevent their becoming admiral's yachts. Similar to the Armadas, the Deep Fleet's battleships were assigned based on need rather than being part of the general organizational structure.

The Deep Fleet saw an enormous modernization program after contact with the Empire. The most visible fruits of this were the *Reverie*-class supercruisers, *Hunter*-class destroyers, and the new Tasvo-II missile. The *Reverie*-class supercruisers were directly inspired by the *Hurricane*-class of the Solar Armadas. The Deep Fleet not only enjoyed the idea of what amounted to a mobile star base, but many in the Council of Warlords wished for a showpiece. Many of the Combine's civilians had become enthralled, even intimidated, by the sight of Imperial ships. The Council wished to show the public that it could build ships just as impressive. Because of technical issues and construction delays, the first ship, *Caustic Reverie,* was rushed through its final construction. It was later rushed through its star trials, a move that risked leaving design flaws or technical bugs unexposed.

The *Hunter*-class was a more practical design. When drafted, it was intended to become the new standard destroyer for the Deep Fleet. This destroyer was built specifically to fight the Solar Armadas. To aid it in this task, it carried the most cutting-edge systems the Combine could provide. The ship was also the test bed for a new stealth system designed to creep up on the enemy and reach engagement range before being detected. This was meant to offset the superior range of Armadas weapons. This system proved *far* more effective than the Empire anticipated, carrying with it a reminder about the potential cost of underestimating an enemy.

The Tasvo-II missile was designed to be the anti-ship weapon the Deep Fleet carried into battle against the Armadas. The word *tasvo* came from a pre-Ivex language and referenced a creature from Vaar mythology. Tasvo were oceanic monsters, effectively colossal eels said to be capable of swallowing entire ships in the Vaar's age of sail. Despite its name, the Tasvo-II was not an upgrade of the earlier Tasvo-I. The Deep Fleet employed the same trick humanity had many times before, as recently as the development of the *Prince of Mars*. To help hide the new weapon's nature from Imperial spies, it was dubbed Tasvo-II to give the impression that it was a modification of an old weapon rather than a new design. The Tasvo-II was a multistage weapon, including a booster stage with its own MID, a primary stage, and a submunitions dispenser. The booster stage could be removed when not needed, reducing the size of the weapon by half and allowing for a higher rate of fire. In terms of destructive power, it was roughly on par with the Arc-5. This, too, was a surprise for the Empire, who did not believe the Combine could make powerful inflation charges so compact.

The Tasvo-II experienced many developmental complications. By the start of the Hourglass War, only the *Caustic Reverie* and the small number of *Hunter*-class destroyers were armed with this weapon. In the case of the *Hunter*-class, it carried a mix of Tasvo-I and II, as the Combine had not yet built enough to fully outfit these vessels with them. They could not manufacture their own, either, like the far larger supercruiser.

Unlike the Solar Armadas, the majority of the Deep Fleet's ships did not have their own logistics capacity beyond the ability to synthesize additional fuel for themselves. This was not an option for the automation-spurning Vaar; they could not fit a worthwhile capacity into one of their ships and still have the volume for the tactical systems a warship needed. The *Reverie*-class was meant to change this but was ultimately a failure in this regard. While the ship did have an appreciable logistics capacity, too much was sacrificed for it. This resulted in an under-armed ship for its size. Due to the lack of logistics capability on their warships, the Combine maintained a vast fleet of support vessels to aid in deployments.

One of the Deep Fleet's primary weaknesses, when compared to the Armadas, was in power generation. The Combine was unable to build anything comparable to Imperial MAS reactors. While the technology of the MAS reactor was not new to the Vaar, they were too far behind to catch up. Despite having fewer systems to manage, the *Caustic Reverie* had around one-quarter the power-to-mass ratio as did *H.M.S. Hurricane*. This was the primary motivator to assault Avalon and thus steal one of its reactors. This deficiency in power systems received serious alleviation from the Combine's new ally as the Hourglass War continued.

Another weakness of the Deep Fleet compared to the Armadas was in inferior interceptor systems. To hit a target at warp was a difficult task, particularly when the target was small and moving at extreme speed. This proved a significant weakness for Deep Fleet ships early in the war, often forcing them to expend offensive ordnance in a defensive role. This weakness was greatly ameliorated with aid from a new ally.

The Deep Fleet possessed two significant advantages over the Solar Armadas. The first was in the force's wake-homing technology. Most Vaar destroyers carried wake-homing systems as part of their standard sensor package. This provided a situational advantage that could enable Combine warships to detect Imperial warships from greater distances using passive-only systems, assuming the Armadas ship was in the right direction for its wake to be detected. This was the only circumstance where Deep Fleet ships could out-detect their Armadas nemesis. The Tasvo-I carried an option for a wake-homing sensor, while it was included as default equipment in the Tasvo-II.

The second advantage of the Deep Fleet when the war began was in crew training. Unlike the Empire, the Combine was expecting a war. Deep Fleet crews drilled relentlessly in the years leading up to the conflict. When the war began, the average Deep Fleet crewman had more than 50 percent more training hours than his Imperial rival. Deep Fleet officers had as much as 80 percent more training hours than their Armadas opponents.

When compared to the Solar Armadas, the Deep Fleet was somewhat of a top-heavy force. The Armadas often treated its ships like infantry in space, and individual warships rarely operated alone. While a captain may command a single large vessel, captains and commanders often captained one ship while having operational authority over others. By contrast the Combine operated more like ancient "wet" navies. Deep Fleet ships often operated alone. Though multiple ships could operate together without an admiral and with the senior captain being in command, this was rare. In general, any multi-ship formation was commanded by an admiral, particularly in times of war. This led to the Deep Fleet having more admirals than the Solar Armadas.

The Deep Fleet, with the aid of the State Security, went to enormous efforts to hide its activities from Imperial intelligence in preparation for the attack on the Hourglass. This included listing upgrades to front-line ships as refits of War Reserve vessels, relisting warships as transports to hide their deployments, and many other actions. The Deep Fleet did not deploy any of its battleships to the Hourglass Galaxy as the BMI did not believe they could be deployed without alerting the Empire.

| Deep Fleet Organization Structure | | |
|---|---|---|
| **Unit Name** | **Contextual Translation** | **Constitution** |
| **Kal'fona** | The Deep Fleet | 24 Kal'zet, commanded by the warlord of the deep |
| **Kal'zet** | Combined Fleet | 7 Putt'la, commanded by a warlord |
| **Putt'la** | Galaxy Patrol | 7 Putt'narr, commanded by an admiral in the third degree |
| **Putt'nar** | Quadrant Patrol | 7 Putt'orr, commanded by an admiral in the fourth degree |
| **Putt'orr** | Sector Patrol | 7 La'reen'gee-terr, commanded by an admiral in the fifth degree |
| **La'reen'gee-terr** | Star Cluster First Degree | 7 La'reen'gee-din, commanded by an admiral in the sixth or seventh degree |
| **La'reen'gee-din** | Star Cluster Second Degree | 7 La'reen, commanded by an admiral in the eighth or ninth degree |
| **La'reen** | Star | 4–7 ships, commanded by an admiral in the tenth degree |

Note: War Reserve Fleet not counted. The War Reserve included approximately 60 million ships in 100,016 capable of returning to service.

## The Deep Marines

THE TUMA'FONA OR DEEP Marines—marines of the Deep—were the primary ground combat force of the Combine War Forces. The Deep Marines were responsible for planetary assault, all marine functions on Combine warships, and all related duties. Though they shared the same function for their nation as the Solar Legionnaires, key differences distinguished the constitution and doctrine of each force. The Deep Marines did not utilize an organic force structure like the Legionnaires. Deep Marine units were highly specialized, partly from necessity.

Nearly all ground vehicles operated by the Deep Marines had an operational crew made up of Viss. Due to their smaller size, one could design a compact space for them. Generally the only ground vehicles designed with a Vaar crew in mind were command vehicles so that the leader could occupy it, whether male or female.

Similarly there was a division between assault forces and clearing forces. Assault forces were the front-line units that led attacks on enemy holdings. Clearing forces followed and were primarily Viss. The clearing forces handled many urban warfare tasks, such as clearing buildings, while the assault force fought battles in the streets. In open terrain, the assault force generally led, while the clearing force served as a second line, responding to any counterattack that punctured the main line of assault. Last of those performing traditional marine functions on Deep Fleet ships, Viss accounted for roughly two-thirds of their numbers. A Viss was more likely to fit on ships and corridors built by smaller species.

This gender division created complex logistical issues for the service. The size disparity between the average Vaar and Viss was simply too big, making it difficult for them to share equipment. This was particularly an issue with most handheld devices; a Viss's hand was not large enough to wield a Vaar's weapon or tool.

On the ground, the Deep Marines remained an infantry-centric force when compared to the Solar Legionnaires or Solar Army. Vehicles moved infantry to the front, then provided support. What the Deep Marines lacked in vehicular combat capability, they made up for with artillery. In some respects, it was fair to call the Deep Marines an artillery-centric force. Much of their combat doctrine was based on strategizing the position of their artillery to soften the enemy before infantry moved in. Point defenses existed on the ground, too. An artillery piece could fire on a target on the opposite side of a planet via ballistic trajectory. That didn't do much good if the shell was intercepted on its way down.

The Deep Marines began migrating to an armor-centric force after war games showed that such a need was required against Imperial forces, but the war began before the Deep Marines could complete the transition. The high concentration of this armor on the front lines was prone to making it seem more prevalent than it was. One such fruit of these efforts was the unit that came to be known as the *colossus* by Imperial forces. The Vaar name for this machine was the *relget*, a name given to a large predator native to Prithone. Like the machine, the relget required eight legs to properly handle its great mass.

The *colossus* was originally designed to liberate Origin from Imperial control. The Deep Marines knew that the Empire had installed an elevating wall around their colony. Unsure how difficult it was to bring this wall down, the colossus was designed to climb over it if necessary. The Deep Marines ordered many more for similar conditions on other worlds after realizing its potential.

The Deep Marines were not nearly as concerned about avoiding collateral or environmental damage to the planet they were fighting over. This made the force more willing to employ indiscriminate weapons. The Deep Marines were more likely to use nuclear weapons and others with similar long-term effects.

The Empire went out of its way to avoid the unnecessary deaths of civilians, but the Deep Marines believed civilians should leave if they wanted safety. Some warlords tried to reform this attitude based on what Solars called "humanitarian" grounds, but these efforts were met with little success.

The word *ohn* in Ivex could be translated as *he who fights with a hammer* or, more simply, *hammerman*. This rank was a nod to ancient tradition. Given a Vaar's plates, early combat looked different than it did for humans. Metallurgy had to advance significantly before a Vaar could manufacture a blade capable of cutting or piercing another Vaar's plates. Thus hammers and other blunt weapons were the primary weapons of war until the development of sufficiently powerful firearms. Even the Ivex word for *rifle* (*ohn'venne*) meant *reach hammer*.

The Deep Marines was sometimes considered the most prestigious of the War Forces and the most requested branch by new warriors. Warriors saw it as the service where they were most likely to see personal combat. Personal combat (that being with the enemy in visual range) was perceived to bring greater glory, proving the courage of those who served in it. Many marines still transferred to the Deep Fleet, and the difference in prestige seen between the two was small. Even warriors who planned to spend most of their career in the Deep Fleet often served in the Deep Marines first.

| Deep Marines Organization Structure | | |
|---|---|---|
| **Unit Name** | **Contextual Translation** | **Constitution** |
| **Tuma'fona** | The Deep Marines | Commanded by the warlord of the marines |
| **Tel'foma** | Deep Legion | 14 Tel'terr, commanded by a warlord |
| **Tel'terr** | Legion First Degree | 14 Tel'din, commanded by a marshal in the Third or Fourth Degree. |
| **Tel'din** | Legion First Degree | 7–14 Tel'zet, commanded by a marshal in the Fifth or Sixth Degree. |

| Deep Marines Organization Structure | | |
|---|---|---|
| **Tel'zet** | Legion Third Degree | 7–14 Ohn'wa, commanded by a marshal in the Seventh or Eighth Degree |
| **Ohn'wa** | Hammer Army | 7–14 Ohn'phun, commanded by a marshal in the Ninth or Tenth Degree |
| **Ohn'phun** | Hammer Tsunami | 7–14 Ohn'exl, commanded by a sub-colonel, colonel, or grand colonel |
| **Ohn'exl** | Hammer Flood | 7–14 Ohn'rass, commanded by a lieutenant in the First or Second Degree |
| **Ohn'raas** | Hammer Storm | 7–14 Ohn'teel, commanded by a lieutenant in the Third to Fifth Degrees |
| **Ohn'teel** | Hammer Wave | 7–14 Ohn'bree, commanded by a lieutenant in the Fourth to Sixth Degrees |
| **Ohn'bree** | Hammer Group | 7–14 Tagen, commanded by a lieutenant of the Seventh to Tenth Degrees |
| **Tagen** | Column | 7–14 Vu, commanded by a phalanx leader in the Fourth or Fifth Degree |
| **Vu** | Phalanx (from a pre-Ivex language, relating to a primitive formation similar to a Greek *phalanx*) | 21 marines, commanded by a phalanx leader in the Sixth or Seventh Degree |

# The Planetary Defense Force (PDF)

THE PLANETARY DEFENSE FORCE was established by Grand Warlord Von'tu following the Rethan War. The PDF was created specifically to defend the Combine's worlds from assault, be it bombardment or invasion. The PDF served a similar function in this regard to the Solar Army but with a different doctrine. Like the Solar Army, the PDF suffered a stigma of being less prestigious than the other services. This lower prestige stemmed from the fact that few warriors chose to join the PDF. Not since the Rethan War have the Vaar had to defend their planets in any meaningful way. As a result, the PDF was seen as the branch least likely to yield battlefield experience.

This issue was further compounded by the PDF's narrow focus. Unlike the Solar Army, which could and would be used offensively when needed, the PDF was primarily a defensive force, lowering the odds of any warriors finding combat. Not blind to how rarely the PDF had been used, the state school system usually sent its best soldier candidates into the Deep Fleet or the Deep Marines.

The PDF had a different doctrine for doing its job. The Solar Army maintained networks of planetary defenses such as planetary and theater shielding and surface-to-space weapons. The Army was fully equipped with tanks, artillery, and other assets to contest a landing on a world if an enemy breached defenses. The PDF focused on stopping a threat before it reached ground, using shielding and surface-to-space weaponry. If an enemy managed to enter the planet's atmosphere, through these defenses, the PDF was not equipped to fight a ground war. PDF troops were trained to evade the enemy and conduct guerrilla operations against them.

The PDF spent more of its time as a garrison force, stationed on each world to keep the population in line. When first created by Von'tu, the PDF often tried to station soldiers on the world of their birth, the logic being that these soldiers would fight hardest to protect their home. In modernity, no PDF soldier served on their planet of birth, nor any one planet for too long. Soldiers may be reluctant to do their duty against a rebelling world if they were emotionally attached to its population. The PDF's relatively low numbers and lack of heavy equipment meant that it was likely to rely on aid from the other services if a planet rebelled.

The chief of staff for the PDF was the Kalo'thone'naga (warlord world defense). Due to the scarcity of warriors in the PDF, this was one of the only warlord positions routinely filled by a soldier. As a result the PDF was the only branch that never had a member ascend to the rank of grand warlord. While it was not a requirement for the office, only warriors were ever appointed to the position.

| Planetary Defense Force—Organizational Structure | | |
|---|---|---|
| Unit Name | Contextual Translation | Constitution |
| Tep'thone'jer | Planetary Defense Force | 7 Jer'la, commanded by the warlord of the PDF |
| Jer'la | Galaxy Shield | 14 Nar'jer, commanded by a general in the Third or Fourth Degree |
| Nar'jer | Quadrant Shield | 7–14 La'reen'gee-jer, commanded by a general in the Fifth or Sixth Degree |
| La'reen'gee-jer | Cluster Shield | 7–14 Tone'nolon, commanded by a general in the Seventh to Tenth Degrees |
| Thone'nolon | Planetary Collective | 7–14 Thone'tass, commanded by a colonel or grand colonel |
| Thone'tass | Planetary Wall | 7–14 Thone'upt, commanded by a lieutenant colonel in the Second Degree |
| Thone'upt | Planetary Moat | 7–14 Thone'jer, commanded by a lieutenant in the First or Second Degree |
| Thone'jer | Planetary Shield | 7–14 Jer'nolon, commanded by a lieutenant in the Third or Fourth Degree |
| Jer'nolon | Shield Collective | 7–14 Jer'zellon, commanded by a lieutenant in the Fifth or Sixth Degree |
| Jer'zellon | Shield Formation | 7–14 Jer'tass, commanded by a lieutenant in the Sixth or Seventh Degree |

| Planetary Defense Force—Organizational Structure | | |
|---|---|---|
| **Jer'tass** | Shield Wall | 7–14 Jer'beck, commanded by a lieutenant in the Eight to Tenth Degrees |
| **Jer'beck** | Shield Trench | 7–14 Jer'un, commanded by a wall leader in the First to Fifth Degrees |
| **Jer'un** | Shield Team | 14 personnel, commanded by a wall leader in the Fifth to Seventh Degrees |

## The State Security Service

THE STATE SECURITY SERVICE of the Combine was made up of two primary bodies. There were many smaller groups as is appropriate to a nation that often thought the quality of government was determined by the size of its bureaucracy. The smaller organizations answered to one of the larger two. These were the Bureau of Military Intelligence and the Bureau of Domestic Tranquility.

The Bureau of Domestic Tranquility was the domestic intelligence service, or in other words, the secret police. The BDT, as it shall be further referred, was tasked with the detection, suppression, and apprehension of dissidents. Even the ISA, the secret police of Yuangi, the largest such service in human history ultimately pales in comparison to the BDT. Agents of the BDT were found in all ports of call, media stations, schools, and more. Many BDT agents were covert, working full-time civilian jobs as their cover.

The Council of Warlords did not allow the BDT unlimited discretion, but the discretion they possessed was still broad. BDT agents could detain citizens with minimal suspicion and could hold them for extended periods regardless of whether charges were laid. The BDT also had broad discretion to freeze or confiscate assets. Fortunately for Combine citizens, the warlords took a *very* dim view of the bureau using this power for any reasons but counterintelligence or handling organized crime. More than once, the Council made public examples of BDT agents who used this power in prosecuting personal disputes.

The BDT was one of the most prolific users of AI in the entire Combine. With such a massive population, AI was essential to monitor the countless communications that occurred daily. Even so, suspicious communiqués were elevated for review by organic agents.

The Bureau of Military Intelligence was the primary agency responsible for intelligence conduct in relation to foreign nations, persons, and military forces. The BMI oversaw and ensured the coordination of the intelligence branches of each of the War Forces' branches, while conducting extensive intelligence on its own. The BMI excelled at intelligence aspects such as reconnaissance, communications monitoring, and other technical realms. The agency was less capable in terms of what the Empire would consider sapient intelligence—intelligence gained through personal interactions with relevant personnel. It was not so much that the BMI was bad at this task, only that it was better at the others.

Where both bureaus truly excelled was in the realm of counterintelligence and counterespionage. Both operated together in this role, dividing up their efforts based on whether foreign intelligence was targeting civilian or military interests. The full measure of their skill was demonstrated leading up to the Hourglass War.

Imperial intelligence services—the Commando Corps in particular— went to enormous efforts to tap Combine communications. The Corps alone tapped tens of thousands of deep space repeaters, communication satellites, and elements of the Wide Range Network's backbone. The BDT and BMI identified more than 60 percent of the planted bugs and used them to spread misinformation to the Imperials. The BMI accurately guessed when the *Polarized Aggression* was destroyed that the ship's PACKET machine had been compromised. Rather than change the communications codes, the BMI flooded the military channels with misleading info.

The two services neutralized most of the silent agents created by the Commando Corps. After learning about the threat from an outside source, the agencies kept a careful eye on personnel with access to the most sensitive information. The personality profiles the agencies had on these individuals were so complete that even minor changes were noticed. With the carefully controlled sharing of less valuable secrets and monitoring the Empire's reaction, the services built a list that alerted them to the presence of silent agents. Most of those identified were either transferred to less sensitive projects or carefully fed misinformation. Only in the most sensitive cases such as the *Hunter*-class destroyers were these agents placed into indefinite containment.

These efforts and many more were crucial in the successful surprise achieved by the War Forces in their initial assault on the Hourglass Galaxy. It was only by the massive misinformation campaign that the Combine masked the deployment and movement of so many forces into position.

Despite the names of their services making them sound as though they were part of the civilian government, both the BDT and the BMI were military organizations. They were considered joint services operating under the authority of the warlord of the clandestine. The majority of their personnel was drawn from the military police with a few soldiers recruited directly out of military school for their positions. The organization, however, used the

Deep Fleet's rank structure below the level of warlord.

The State Security Service had a complicated relationship with the warriors of the military. Warriors traditionally spurned serving in the BDT or the BMI, both of which offered little opportunity for combat. On the rare occasions warriors joined the State Security Service, they generally served in the field units of the BMI.

The BMI maintained its ground forces and a limited number of warships. Its ground forces were drawn primarily from the Deep Marines and were often deployed on contested worlds to maintain discipline among the marines, PDF, or civilian work brigades there. The handful of warships operated by the BMI drew their personnel from the Deep Fleet. This small force was meant to aid State Security in deploying its forces without heavy reliance on the Deep Fleet's assets.

The War Forces were required to turn over all prisoners of war to the BMI, which handled interrogations and long-term incarceration. The BMI generally kept specialized experts close to the front line of battle to interrogate military prisoners as quickly as possible after their capture.

# 6H
# THE WIDE NETWORK

THE WIDE NETWORK WAS the Combine's closest analog to the astranet, but it was an *vastly* inferior system technologically. Similar to the troubles in developing infantry disrupters, miniaturizing transpatial gateway technology was a feat most civilizations were unable to perform. Unlike disrupters, the Combine could not perform this task on a massive scale. The few routers that existed in the Combine were intended for use only by the military. The majority of people and goods that engaged in interstellar travel did so on ships, and travel was rare in the Combine. Not only was it far less convenient, but a citizen required state permission to leave their world.

Interstellar communication was the primary function of the Wide Network, and while it was adequate for government functions, it became the butt of many jokes for civilians. The portions of the network meant for civilians typically received notoriously poor maintenance and support. Meanwhile, those portions dedicated to military and government functions often received more maintenance than necessary.

The Wide Network included a layer similar to the astranet's railroad. Unlike the routers, these were open to authorized civilians. The Wide Network's railroad was less robust and efficient than the Empire's. Most of the conduction lines led to areas of economic importance or to transpatial gateways to access other galaxies.

With the help of an outside force, the Vaar made significant strides in improving the Wide Network's technologies. This included advances in router technology and its implementation on the *Reverie*-class supercruisers. Prior to this, miniaturizing routers to fit into warships was too difficult to be worth the effort. Though the Deep Fleet aspired to install such routers on all ships, it did not have the industry to do so. As a result, only command ships generally received authorization.

The Combine invaded Avalon to seize one of the station's MAS reactors, with a secondary mission to seize relevant technology because Avalon was meant to be the Hourglass Galaxy's central astranet hub. The legionnaires on Avalon demolished devices the Combine might have studied or reverse engineered before the mission could succeed.

# 61
# THE VAAR LANGUAGE

THE PRIMARY LANGUAGE SPOKEN by nearly all Vaar was Ivex. Little was known about the history of this language, but Ivex was created by the first Sovari and taught to those who followed them. Ivex was constructed to be a difficult language to learn. The Sovari did this to ensure young Vaar and Viss were mentally stimulated in the process of learning to communicate.

Due to the sheer complexity of the language, this entry provides only a summary of it, rather than an attempt to educate on its dynamics. One of the confusing elements of Ivex was that it was a language with few true adjectives. Ivex relied on noun modifiers, which were placed at the beginning or end of the word. The same modifier could change the meaning depending on where it was placed.

In written form Ivex was a logographic language similar to Ancient Mandarin. Every word in the language was represented by a character. There were tens of thousands of individual logograms, and how many an individual knew was often an indicator of their education. The average citizen knew around twenty thousand of the more than two hundred thousand found within the language, with more educated individuals knowing as many as seventy thousand. A minimum of six thousand was considered mandatory for basic literacy.

Ivex was a mix of Voltim, the language of Aka'lona, and Ruken, the language of the Eastern Coalition, both coming before the Vaar were an interstellar species. The use of these two languages from different regions to create Ivex was meant to represent the unity of the Vaar as one people.

One frustrating element of Ivex, particularly for foreigners, was its dependence on idioms. Many of these idioms were necessary to speak the language at a conversational level.

| Ivex Sample Idioms | |
|---|---|
| **Idiom (translated to Ancient English)** | **Meaning** |
| Aklonese bargain | A deal or pact with an untrustworthy partner |
| Break the tooth/broken tooth | An act or event that causes inconsequential injury |
| Defecate in the neighbor's door | To take a complaint far beyond the point of reasonable behavior |
| Dismiss the schematic | To reject credible information due to personal bias |
| Drink the river | To hoard resources to the point of actively harming others |
| Eat the plants | To engage in a pointless activity |
| Choke the enspa | To punish a person who was innocent of a crime or misdeed because they probably committed others |
| Do the Von'tu | To engage in sexual intercourse (used almost exclusively by males) |
| Don't ask a goza for math | Do not have unrealistic expectations of someone's performance |
| Don't jump off the ship | Don't do something self-destructive because you're upset |
| Drink the blood | Let nothing go to waste (used primarily in times of shortage) |
| Eat the ugo'sat | To engage in something extremely unpleasant but necessary |
| Follow the Fourteenth example | To sacrifice oneself |
| Feed the children to the goza | To have one's priorities out of order |
| Fornicate the enspa | To make a very serious, and likely embarrassing, mistake |
| Give a Rethan mercy | To show unwarranted kindness |
| Go swimming | Go away and don't come back. Stems from the fact that Vaar and Viss were generally too dense to swim in water |

| Ivex Sample Idioms | |
| --- | --- |
| **Idiom (translated to Ancient English)** | **Meaning** |
| Grow some plates | An insult, specifically to males accusing them of feminine or childish behavior |
| Perform the inevitable | To pay taxes |
| Please the state | Similar to "Do the Von'tu" but used primarily by females |
| Practice for the Void | To sleep |
| Sing with skeletons | To attempt a task with inadequate resources |
| Set fire to the neighbor's cattle | To destroy something belonging to another out of envy |
| Slay one enspa to kill millions | Deal with a problem now before it begets others (refers to the asexual reproduction of the enspa) |
| Slay the goza | The final act in a chain of abuses that provokes a (often violent) reaction |
| Smoke the rinds | To intentionally fail at a task in the hope of being relieved of the responsibility |
| Speak the jungle | To perform a seemingly impossible task |
| Speak to the Sovari | I don't care; go talk to someone who does |
| Suffer Von'tu's boredom | To no longer take pleasure in a task one once enjoyed |
| Take the free meat | To walk into an obvious trap |
| Would you ask the Sovari? | Do you want an honest answer? |

# APPENDIX 7
# TECHNOLOGY—II

## 7A
## BRAIN BOTTLE

BRAIN BOTTLES WERE A collection of devices that were designed to contain and sustain an organic brain. The primary purpose of a brain bottle was to allow a sapient being to transfer their brain between host bodies. The form-fitting casings, usually metallic, contained the brain in a specialized seal. Most brain bottles incorporated subsystems designed to supply the brain with oxygen and nutrients over a limited term so that it remained safely alive while outside of the host body.

Brain bottles were often designed to use a type of synthetic blood commonly referred to as *oxycereb*. This artificial blood was capable of holding a higher concentration of oxygen than normal blood while regulating its delivery to the brain.

When brain bottles were first introduced, they could leave hosts vulnerable to many problems. The brain was constantly forming new neural connections while altering existing ones to adapt to change. So, those who routinely switched between bodies could develop neurological disorders as their brain attempted to adapt to its switching hosts. Those who spent too much time in a different body risked the brain forgetting how to properly control the original.

Modern brain bottles were designed to work with the brain to help avoid these issues. These brain bottles were capable of affecting the changes in neuron structure to a degree and could help to stave off many potential issues. But this process was not perfect. Those who used autobodies couldn't spend too much time in them if they intended to return to an organic body. Standards for safe practice limited how often one switched bodies.

Brain bottle technology grew to encompass many other functions, eventually leading to the differentiation between transferable and non-transferable brain bottles. Non-transferable brain bottles were designed primarily to preserve the brain. They protected the brain from trauma and worked with medical devices to heal an injured brain. These bottles kept detailed maps of the brain's neurological structure that devices such as medical nanites could use when reconstructing damaged parts. This reduced the recovery time for those who suffered brain trauma and increased the likelihood that a person could be restored to—or close to—their pre-injury condition.

When a Solar was mortally wounded, their nanites initiated a preservation protocol. In this state, the rest of the body was effectively sacrificed in favor of preserving the brain for as long as possible. With technology such as deep-fryers available, everything that was not the brain was expendable in such a critical situation. Brain bottles were capable of duplicating many of these features for non-Solars and added a level of redundancy for Solars.

Transferable brain bottles incorporated the features of non-transferable units while allowing movement between bodies. These brain bottles could also be used to keep the host brain alive independent of the body for an extended period with the help of external resources. Transferable brain bottles required numerous cybernetic upgrades. Brains weren't meant to be removed, so cybernetic upgrades typically included a skull that opened to make a transfer possible.

The process of installing a brain in a brain bottle was a complex procedure and required the device to be calibrated to the specific user. These devices required routine systems checks and maintenance to ensure they operated correctly. One of the biggest downsides to brain-bottling was that the procedure was tough on the patient and entailed a long recovery time. A brain bottle created a bridge between the brain and body that didn't exist naturally. Then, the brain needed time to adapt to the bottle and exert normal control over the body.

Though there were pushes for it, the Solar Armed Forces never adopted brain bottles as a standard upgrade for all soldiers, though the reason why is inconsistent. A soldier's skull was a cybernetic made primarily of bond-forged titanium incorporating shock absorbers, temperature controls, and many other defensive measures. The position that opposed making the bottles standard equipment claimed that anything that could penetrate the defenses a soldier already had was unlikely to leave any brain left to save.

In another claim, military personnel were known to hype up the importance of brain bottles for special forces who often faced some of the most intense combat. This had more to do with giving these soldiers the option to switch to new bodies than it did to preserve their brains.

The actual truth was a bit more complicated. First, requiring every soldier to be upgraded with a brain bottle would extend their training period by months for recovery. Additionally some brains reacted poorly to the process and couldn't be bottled, and said process must then be aborted. It was not always simple to determine ahead of time how well or poorly an individual's brain would react, and the groups that pushed for all soldiers to be brain-bottled were often the same groups that favored all soldiers being furnished with autobodies. This posed a significant logistics issue, wherein a soldier's original body must either be preserved or a new one provided when a soldier wished to return to their flesh. All of these and several others imposed costs and burdens that the military could not justify.

The Vaar had the technology for brain-bottling for many centuries, and as a species, the process was somewhat simpler. The natural regenerative properties of the Vaar brain made complications both more rare and less severe. At the same time, the regenerative capacities of the average Vaar made the entire concept less desirable.

It was a semantics issue whether Vaar had two brains or a single brain broken up into a pair of sub-brains. The upper brain engulfed the smaller, lower brain, which was responsible for respiration, thermal regulation, and digestion. The upper brain was the seat of reason and conscious thought and handled all voluntary motor control. It could also pick up several autonomic functions from the lower brain if the lower brain should be damaged. In general, a Vaar needed to experience severe trauma to both brains to die. Because of this, brain-bottling was often utilized only in transferable form. This was also rare due, in part to Vaar attitudes toward cybernetics.

The most visible brain bottles among the Vaar were in the Deep Marines' juggernauts. All juggernauts were made up of convicted criminals who were guilty of crimes ranging from murder to cowardice. These individuals were involuntarily brain-bottled to be placed in their juggernaut autobodies. If a juggernaut's autobody was destroyed but their brain survived, it would be transferred to a new autobody so the individual may continue serving their sentence. Brain bottles could also be used in the rare case of warriors granted vek'thim, so they could be transplanted to a body built to avenge their dishonor. Unlike the brain bottles of juggernauts, those of a warrior receiving vek'thim did not include behavioral limiters meant to help control the subject.

# 7B
# FIELD STABILIZERS

FIELD STABILIZERS WERE ONE of the most important defenses on an Imperial warship. These systems functioned much like armor. Because they required constant power, they were considered active systems. Field stabilizers employed the Hyams Effect to "stiffen" the space-time within their influence, making it far more resistant to manipulation by a disrupter pulse or inflation wave. The idea that Imperial warships were "solid kilosteel" was a matter of perspective. It was true that there were no open voids outside of the ship's citadel, but the outer hull of a warship was not simply a giant kilosteel plate.

Field stabilizers were arrayed throughout a ship's hull, forming concentric layers. These shells of field stabilizers were generally referred to as *waveheads*, a compound of wave-stabilizing bulkhead. These waveheads were separated from each other by the layers of kilosteel that formed the bulk of the hull. The innermost wavehead generally defined the borders of the ship's citadel. Within the citadel lay the propulsion systems, power generation, crew accommodations, and control systems. Additionally, retractable field stabilizers were used to selectively plug maintenance shafts, ammunition chutes, and other things that would otherwise present a weakening void in the hull.

To fully understand the function of field stabilizers, one must understand warp weaponry and how to defend against it. Long before mankind had achieved faster-than-light travel, he had learned that warps in space-time would bow around massive objects. This behavior was first observed in the phenomenon known as *gravitational lensing*. Given this and the fact that space-time generally behaved as a fluid, it was often easiest to use water as an analogy.

If a wave of water met an object, one of two things would happen. If the wave was stronger, the object would be swept up or even torn apart by the wave. If the object was stronger, the water would flow around it. The extremely massive and dense body of a ship already provided some protection, encouraging such a wave to flow around it. However, this was not enough against modern weaponry. Even a kilosteel hull could be torn apart by the inflation charges of a warship's missiles or torpedoes. Field stabilizers were the equivalent of shoring up and anchoring an object so that it may survive being stuck by such powerful waves.

The warp field that allowed a ship to travel at FTL provided some protection. Shield systems provided a great deal more. However, given how

hyams fields interacted, weapons typically had the advantage as it was easier for them to reach the higher and more concentrated intensity needed
to penetrate shield systems. Warships were often destroyed when attacks
leached through their shields and wiped out interceptors and shield-projec-
tors, which by necessity, were located on the outer hull. As these systems
degraded, incoming attacks would inflict increasing and eventually overwhelming amounts of damage. Field stabilizers were often the last defense
a warship had in this situation.

Though it was a less common scenario, field stabilizers and the waveheads they formed were generally a warship's best defense against the ordnance guns of another warship. Given the intensity of the warp field produced by an ordnance shell, even a relatively small ship's guns could often
penetrate the shields of a much larger warship. The outcome was dependent
on how the waveheads and shells stacked up against one another. If the
waveheads were strong enough, they could collapse the warp field of the
incoming shell by making space-time too difficult for the shell's MID to
manipulate. This left the shell with only its momentum and kinetic energy,
though this should not be underestimated. A large mass traveling a fraction
of $c$ was prone to make a violent impression. The presence of $c$ powerful
field stabilizers in the form of waveheads could easily make the difference
between a ship damaged by such a hit and one outright destroyed by it.

Waveheads also protected against the kinetic impact of a shell as it was
difficult for matter to move when the space-time it occupied was inhibit-
ing that movement. In the best-case scenario, a shell may even deflect or
ricochet, gaining precious distance before it detonated. It was more likely
that the shell would embed itself in the hull and detonate. The waveheads
worked to contain this otherwise catastrophic damage, forcing the expanding wave to flow out and around the ship rather than through it. This generally resulted in heavy damage and stripped away layers of the hull, but it was
vastly preferable to allowing the destructive wave to flow through the ship.

How well waveheads could resist incoming shells was a largely relative
thing. A battleship hit by a destroyer's shells was certain to suffer damage
but could survive a considerable number before it was at risk of being destroyed. A destroyer had little chance of surviving even a single direct hit
from a battleship's guns.

The ability to form field stabilizers into waveheads was a relatively new
feat of engineering for the Interstellar Combine when the Hourglass War
began. While most species who had harnessed the Hyams Effect postulated
the technology, implementation required a great deal of engineering excel-
lence. A field stabilizer's job was the precise opposite of a massless impulse
drive. One attempted to prevent changes in local space-time, while the other
existed to create them. The Solar Empire was one of the few civilizations
with the scientific and engineering expertise to make these two pieces of
technology play nice with each other.

The *Reverie*-class of supercruisers were the first Vaar warship design
with waveheads, followed closely by the *Hunter*-class of destroyers. This

resulted in ships that were markedly more resilient against Imperial weapons than those they fought alongside. In both cases, the unexpectedly good design of these classes' waveheads made them far tougher than the Armadas anticipated they would be.

# 7C
# INSTRUMENTS OF DESTRUCTION

## Missiles, Rockets, Torpedoes, Shells, and Star Bombs

IT WAS NOT UNCOMMON for military technologies, weapons in particular, to bear more similarities than differences in terms of the actual science and engineering. How a weapon was employed and its specific job had as much bearing, if not more, on what it was called. The Solar Armadas and the various fleets in the Empire used a variety of weapons that could be difficult to tell apart at a glance.

An initial note on these technologies was in how their accuracy and destructive power were rated. Due to the special nature of disrupter-type weapons, raw energy figures were often less helpful at deriving their potential. It was a difficult task to hit a target at warp. Both the accuracy and the destructive potential of these weapons were generally defined as a radius, which was usually measured in light-seconds or roughly 300,000-kilometer increments. Any target not designed to endure the attention of warp weaponry was apt to suffer catastrophic damage if within this radius. The degree of damage increased the closer the target was to the center. If a weapon's accuracy was a smaller radius than its destructive radius, it was considered sufficiently accurate for military use. As the inflation wave—also known as a rip field—produced by an inflation charge traveled at FTL, often getting close to a warp-driven target was enough. As an example, the Arc-5 missile's submunitions had a destructive radius of 0.45 light-seconds and an accuracy of 0.22.

Much to the annoyance of the Armadas, the Solar Army and Solar Legionnaires did not agree on the definition of what constituted a missile. Both ground services used the term broadly. The Armadas defined a missile as a self-propelled, self-guided warhead-type weapon utilizing a Multiple Independence Guidance warhead. MIG referred to the submunitions that missiles distributed to destroy their targets.

The Solar Armadas had long regarded missiles as its primary weapon. They could be easily produced in massive quantities, they could handle a variety of targets, and swarms of submunitions were effective counters to point defenses. If a large target could survive one missile, the obvious solution was, of course, more missiles.

The primary missile used by Imperial forces at the start of the Hourglass

War was the 5 anti-ship missile designed by Galaxy Staryards Corporation. The Dominion developed two replacements for the Arc-5 prior to the war's onset. The first was the Radian-1 meant as the next-generation weapon carried aboard the *Prince of Mars*. Due to its greater size, however, the Radian could not be adapted to the launch equipment of existing ships. This led to a further evolution of the Arc series, specifically the 7 developed for legacy ships. The Solar Armadas transitioned to the Arc-7 over the course of the conflict but would not adopt the Radian-1 in significant numbers despite its superior capabilities. This was because many Armadas ships, particularly those designed in Del Tierr, could not accommodate the Radian's larger launch equipment without significant and time-consuming modifications to their hulls. Unwilling to break standardization across its ships, the Armadas relied on the Arc-7, which it would just after the Battle of the Hourglass.

Torpedoes were missiles and came in three primary subtypes. These were light torpedoes, heavy torpedoes, and micro-torpedoes. Light torpedoes were designed to share the same external dimensions as whatever missile system was currently in service. Light torpedoes were often built from the same hull, simply trading out internal systems to accommodate a single, more powerful warhead. Light torpedoes were generally used by warships as a close-range weapon. They were generally slower than missiles and lacked submunitions. However they were much more powerful, and being used at a shorter range gave interceptors less time to react to them. The primary light torpedo of the Armadas was the Torc. This Tirrish weapon was used by the Armadas, the forces of Del Tierr, and other noble and royal guard fleets. The Dominion's Grand Fleet and those forces that shared its equipment relied on the more powerful, but more difficult to produce, Sine-5. Because they shared the same dimensions, light torpedoes and missiles could share launch equipment.

The Armadas did not use heavy torpedoes on their warships but used them as mines and in similar applications. Heavy torpedoes were a doctrinal alternative to missiles. Heavy torpedoes were much larger than missiles, rivaling them in speed and range while being much more powerful. Rather than submunitions, heavy torpedoes relied on hardening by things like enhanced shielding to survive the attention of interceptors. The decision to use missiles or heavy torpedoes was to choose between hitting more often and hitting harder. While the Armadas and many guard forces relied on missiles, the fleets of Del Tierr and several others relied on heavy torpedoes. The Dominion's Grand Fleet was the only force that used both. In application, the missiles functioned much like decoys to the torpedoes for point defenses, but unlike true decoys, they could cause significant harm if not neutralized.

Micro-torpedoes were used primarily by monitors, sloops, and other such small ships particularly when they were placed in the unenviable position of fighting an enemy warship. Such weapons were also useful when these smaller platforms had to engage other ships in their own weight class. The current micro-torpedo used by small Imperial vessels was the M/Torc-9. This weapon was in effect a single submunition from an Arc-5 warhead designed to be fired independently rather than as part of a missile's MIG warhead.

The term *rocket* was defined by the Solar Army as a missile or torpedo designed specifically for surface-to-space combat. These weapons were primarily used to set up planet- or asteroid-bound launch batteries and defended nearby worlds from warships. Most rockets were based on modified missile or torpedo designs. This modification generally took the form of a specially designed booster stage meant to propel the munition safely away from the planet before the weapon's primary MID engaged. Often this booster stage consisted of a separate, low-power MID designed to move through an atmosphere without having destructive effects on the local environment, an effect achieved by minimizing their wake. These environmental MIDs were exclusively sub-light while carrying the weapon into space.

Star bombs were munitions designed for space-to-surface combat and were used to bombard inhabited worlds. It wasn't possible to turn a weapon like an Arc-5 or a Torc-7 on an inhabited world. Not if one wished for any population or usable planet to remain. Weapons intended for use against space targets generally employed inflation charges, and those meant for bombarding ground targets often relied on vortex charges. This allowed the destructive potential to remain precise and confined.

Star bombs were generally tiny in comparison to space weapons, and rather than being fired by a ship's primary warhead projectors, they were typically launched by a ship's interceptor batteries. This could create a difficult situation because it did not take a very powerful planetary shield to block these comparatively weak weapons. This forced warships into mass bombardments to break such shield systems or attempt precise hits with a ship's pulse cannons. Armadas often described the situation as attempting to pry a raw egg out of an enemy's hand without breaking it. The preference for avoiding civilian casualties was a principle of the Mandrake Dynasty for as long as that dynasty had existed.

Beyond vortex charges, star bombs had a variety of specialty munitions. The sheer number of them was beyond the scope of this entry but left ship captains with options when that ship must handle planetary business.

# 7D
# ORDNANCE GUNS II: FLEET GUNS

SIZE MATTERS, PARTICULARLY IN engineering. Ordnance guns are generally the largest and heaviest weapons a warship carries. These weapons are enormous, and they have to be. It would make little sense to put a small gun on a warship and ask it to perform a job that a missile or torpedo can already do—likely better.

The reason for these weapons' existence can be summarized in two factors: wake and linear speed. All objects utilizing a massless impulse drive to travel will distort space-time to do it. When distorted in this manner, space-time does not immediately return to its previous state. Much as an ocean-going vessel leaves a wake of disturbed water behind it, an object traveling via MID will leave a warp-wake. If sufficiently intense, this wake can be dangerous to anything that enters it.

When a warship fires a munition, that munition must pass through the ship's warp field. To do this, the munition requires its own sufficiently intense warp field to punch or phase-cancel through the mothership's field. If the munition lacks this, it will likely be destroyed by the field of the ship that fires it. As a consequence of this reality, a warship is exposed to the warp-wake of any munition it launches.

This factor creates a limit on the size of a missile or torpedo. Ground units typically need not worry about the wake of their munitions; at that scale, the effect simply is not strong enough. Warships do not have this luxury. In normal operation, a warship's field stabilizers will protect it from being damaged by its own munitions. For most weapons, this works well enough that any damage can be written off as ordinary wear and tear, easily dealt with during routine maintenance. But to use an appreciably larger munition, one has entered the realm of the fleet ordnance gun. While these weapons bear some similarities to their groundside cousins, they are a very different animal.

The shells of fleet guns do not have disposable cases or sabots; they are fully integrated units. Nor do these munitions utilize fusion power packs, as nuclear fusion simply isn't up to the job. These weapons rely on xenomatter for fuel, with bombshells powered by a substance known detonation complex. Xenomatter typically cannot power a weapon like an inflation charge as it undergoes pair-decay too slowly. If one attempted to use xenomatter in this manner, the munition would self-destruct before most of the xenomatter decayed, thus wasting it entirely. Detonation complex undergoes pair-decay like xenomatter but thousands of times faster.

Fleet ordnance guns are multi-piece designs that are highly-complex. Most warships will use artificial gravity systems to move the shells to the gun for loading. Anti-gravity systems are often more energy-efficient when one must move particularly massive objects than would be pure electromagnetics in their place. The firing chamber of the barrel is a gauss magnatron much like those used in groundside guns. Acceleration through the weapon's bore is handled via a combination of electromagnetics and artificial gravity. As with groundside guns, these are frictionless systems where the projectile never makes physical contact with the bore of the weapon.

The bulkiest part of the system is the recoil track, which forms the second layer of the gun. This consists of rows of high-resistance gears. When the gun fires, the recoil's momentum is transferred to these gears, which spin to burn off the momentum. This greatly reduces the amount of recoil that must be absorbed by the ship. The gears of the recoil track, in turn, are covered by the stabilizer assembly, which is effectively a tubular wavehead inserted between the recoil track and the barrel's armored housing.

The most important part of the ordnance gun is the field projector, mounted on the muzzle of the gun. This device is a giant warp field generator, somewhat similar to a shield projector. The purpose of this device is to create a warp field 180 degrees out of phase to the wake of the shell fired by the gun. This results in incomplete phase-cancellation of the shell's wake. This process is not perfect, nor is it desirable for it to be so. Nullifying the shell's wake would not only require a great deal of power, but it would also hinder the shell's attempts to move at warp. The process *is* enough to severely weaken the resultant wake to the point that it will not damage or inflict unacceptable wear on the hull of the ship firing it. Due to the importance of this component, a fleet gun will not fire if the field generator has been damaged.

Another issue addressed by ordnance guns is one of linear speed. Linear speed is a term used by the Armadas to refer to an object's velocity *within* its own warp field. It is always a sub-light figure. In most applications, an object's linear speed is irrelevant. With munitions, however, linear speed can be very important. Imperial ships and those of a peer adversary will travel and do battle at warp. A situation where a ship overtakes and rams into a munition it has fired is obviously unacceptable. Linear speed is the solution, as its contribution to final velocity may be irrelevant, but a ship or object with a high linear speed will accelerate much more rapidly under the power of an MID than will one with a low linear speed.

The situation with linear speed can be roughly compared to a man standing on a moving walkway. If the walkway begins moving and the man simultaneously takes off running, he will accelerate more quickly than if he stands still. However if the walkway continues to accelerate, eventually it will reach a point where its movement renders the man's to be irrelevant.

Ordnance shells use multiple methods to gain a high linear speed. The first is the combination of electromagnetics and artificial gravity used to eject the round from the barrel. The second comes in the form of a device known as an amp. The word *amp* descends from the acronym AMP or Antimatter Propulsor. This device is an evolutionary descendant of the antimatter rocket concept and uses xenomatter as fuel. The amp will fire while the shell is still in the barrel and continue for some time after helping to steer the projectile during the early stages of flight.

In general, an ordnance shell will require a linear velocity of 3–5 percent of *c* to ensure that when its drive activates upon leaving the barrel, it will accelerate rapidly enough that the launching ship cannot overtake it. Missiles and torpedoes have similar concerns, but their smaller size allows simpler electromagnetic launch from warhead projectors.

A final contribution of linear speed happens when the shell finds its target. Ideally, the shell will penetrate the target's warp field, penetrate the target, then detonate. In a less ideal situation, a shell could penetrate the target's warp field but have its own field stripped in the process. The combination of sheer mass and high linear speed would still allow the shell to deliver a menacingly powerful impact.

Due to the use of electromagnetics and artificial gravity, the larger a shell's caliber, the longer its barrel will be proportionally. A longer barrel translates to a longer acceleration curve, which reduces the intensity of recoil. A heavy cruiser's guns, for example, are typically 50 calibers in length, or 50x as long as their projectile is wide. Those of battleships and supercruisers tend to be 55–65 calibers. The guns of the *Prince of Mars* were 72 calibers.

It is important to remember that any gun is simply a launch platform for the projectile. This is true of black powder muskets, it is true of rail guns, and it is true of ordnance guns. The shell does all the actual work. The shells of groundside guns are generally stripped down and miniaturized rotary MIDs. Fleet shells, by contrast, are larger hyper-velocity torpedoes manufactured from kilosteel hulls. They will always equip a bombshell, usually in the form of an inflation charge. They include their own sensors, jamming systems, counter-jamming systems, interceptors, counter-interceptors, and more.

For all their power, fleet guns have some disadvantages. Some have questioned the Armadas' limited use of ordnance guns and whether or not the service is as serious about peer adversaries as it claims to be. The disadvantages of these guns see that service reluctant to form a dependence on them.

Once in flight, ordnance shells are typically considered the fastest objects in the known universe that have positive mass. Only the fields of warp sensors and communications are known to be faster. Such sensor and communications waves are so fast that, in most practical scenarios, they are treated as being instantaneous.

Fleet shells are huge and make attractive targets for point defenses. The magnitude of their threat means that it is easy for an adversary to justify using offensive weapons to intercept them. A combination of hardening and extreme speed helps these weapons avoid interception.

All of this speed vastly limits a shell's maneuverability. The sheer size of their drives and the speed at which they are operating means that their MIDs have difficulty performing the polarity shifts needed for rapid changes in direction. A missile or torpedo that misses its target can usually circle back and try again, multiple times if necessary. An ordnance shell generally cannot. If it misses, it will either try to select a new target ahead of it or simply self-destruct.

Ordnance shells are vastly larger than missiles or torpedoes. They take far greater amounts of time and power to produce. When possible, it is often more time efficient for a warship to receive delivery of shells from a stockpile rather than manufacture its own. A ship may not even have the facilities to manufacture shells for other ships. A battlecruiser can make shells for itself and for any smaller ship. A heavy cruiser could make its own shells but would be unable to produce the larger shells for a battlecruiser or battleship.

For the Armadas, it is somewhat of a recursive issue. Because the service does not see fleet guns as ideal ship-to-ship weapons, it does not employ them in a way conducive to that use. On Armadas ships, ordnance guns are typically mounted in the hull—specifically in the roots of the wings—and can only fire forward. This forces the ship to point itself at an intercept course to the target to minimize the maneuvers the shells must make—and raise the odds of a hit. The Dominion's Grand Fleet and Tirrish King's Navy, by contrast, are more keen to use these weapons for ship-to-ship and thus turret-mount them.

In any case, these weapons are best used in their point-blank range. That is the range at which the target is close enough that its speed and maneuvers will not have time to effect the likelihood of a hit. While this range varies by gun and shell, it will almost always be inferior to the effective range of missiles or heavy torpedoes. This is in direct opposition to the Armadas' preferred doctrine of keeping its distance and drowning the enemy in missiles. Against stationary targets, however, there are few weapons that will compete with an ordnance shell's range.

Shells can typically detonate in one of two ways: contact or proximity. As their terms imply, proximity shells will detonate upon coming within range of the target. Shells set for contact detonation will attempt to penetrate the target before detonating. The shell's onboard systems will often determine which of the two is chosen.

The Armadas typically reserve ordnance guns for stationary, and particularly well-fortified, targets. This could be a well-hardened space station or a hostile star hive in need of bombardment. In fleet combat, the guns will usually be reserved either for finishing off large targets, or as a secondary weapon to be used if a ship needs time to manufacture new ammo for its warhead projectors.

The biggest weapon is not always the correct one for the job. Fleet guns are technically autocannons that will continue to reload and fire until ordered to stop, but these weapons employ massive shells that take time to move. Smaller guns like those on cruisers often tandem-load their shells.

Three to five will be inserted in the barrel, one behind the other, and then fired sequentially. The process of loading more can take many seconds or even minutes. Given this, enough rapid-firing warhead projectors can potentially put a greater volume of ordnance on the target in the same period of time. Thus the Armadas tend to reserve these weapons for when the strength of an individual shot is more important than the total volume on target.

The Dominion's Grand Fleet and the noble guard forces that mirror it make the heaviest use of ordnance guns for ship-to-ship combat. The Dominion, however, has a much more aggressive battle doctrine that focuses on pushing the enemy and denying them zones of importance. In these scenarios, it is beneficial to have a weapon that can kill in one or two hits what might take dozens or even hundreds of missiles to achieve. Del Tierr's King's Navy also makes heavy use of ordnance guns, often using them to destroy targets that survive being softened by heavy torpedoes.

The advent of the *Prince of Mars*-class that debuted in the Hourglass War would turn the assumptions about ordnance guns on their heads. This ship carried the new TO-N-8800 guns, which eclipsed the TO-N-6000— and its 6600 upgrade for the title of largest in service. The guns were particularly notable, being the first to use what were known as longwave shells.

Longwave was a development code name used to hide the nature of these weapons from both military and industrial espionage while they were in development. By the time the weapons reached the deployment stage, the name had stuck. Longwave shells brought two important developments. The first was the phase cap, and the second was the composite MID.

Phase caps were specialized nose cones placed on the shell designed specifically to defeat the waveheads of a hostile target. Waveheads are often the best defense against ordnance shells as they can both collapse the shell's warp field and hinder the shell's ability to penetrate by deforming the target's hull. Phase caps were designed to concentrate and intensify the shell's warp field, enhancing its ability to cope with such defenses. A backward compatible technology, the Dominion would immediately begin retrofitting its existing stockpiles of shells with phase caps and upgrading the logistics facilities on their warships to produce them. By the time of the Battle of the Hourglass, all ships in the First Order were using phase-capped shells for their ordnance guns.

The more important development of longwave shells was the composite MID. The use of a composite MID brought a dramatic increase to a shell's acceleration and maximum speed. This had the secondary effect of greatly expanding the shells' point-blank range and, with it, their ability to reliably hit enemy warships. This was an emergent property rather than a design goal, but one the Dominion happily seized. The shells of all ships were replaced with versions propelled by composite MIDs, but this work was just beginning when the Battle of the Hourglass took place.

The guns of the *Prince of Mars* were designed to defeat the unified matrix shielding of a hostile star hive and destroy their generator platforms. This job normally required prolonged bombardment by an entire fleet. The *Prince of Mars* was expected to accomplish the task in only one or two salvos.

| Example Ordnance Guns by Shell Size | | |
|---|---|---|
| Gun Category | Projectile Caliber | Example Gun / Platform |
| Arc-5 Missile | 22x222m | Complete missile assembly, given for relative scale |
| Ultra-Light | 75x375m | RG-GW-190 / *Beneo*-class frigate RG-GW-300 / *Rogue*-class frigate |
| Light | 100x515m | RF-GW-202 / *Deimos*-class destroyer |
| Medium | 250x1,250m | TO-N-6200 / *Indefatigable*-class cruiser |
| Medium+ | 280x1,400m | TO-N-6800 / *Loredai*-class heavy cruiser |
| Heavy | 451x1,952m | Combine Type-1 / *Reverie*-class super-cruiser* |
| Heavy | 508x2,200m | TO-N-6000–6666 / *Hurricane*-class supercruiser, *Scarborough*-class battleship, *Legacy*-class battlecruiser |
| Super-Heavy | 800x10,400m | TO-N-8800 / *Prince of Mars*-class heavy battleship |

* Prior to the Hourglass War, the Interstellar Combine had prototyped its own fleet ordnance guns but had never deployed them. No need for such a weapon was seen until contact with the Solar Empire. The *Caustic Reverie* was meant to be the Combine's first ship to field such a weapon. This design consideration was responsible for the ship's vertical hammerhead. The war, however, began before the ship's guns were ready, leading the vessel to be deployed without them. Her sister ships would incorporate these weapons from the start of their service.

# 7E

# KILOSTEEL

THE WORD *KILOSTEEL* REFERRED to a family of materials known for their highly resilient properties and great density that equaled or exceeded one kilogram per cubic centimeter. The Solar Empire used kilosteel to manufacture its warships, space stations, and similar structures since as early as the Praetheen War. While kilosteel had changed a great deal since then, it was still kilosteel. Kilosteel was valued, as its great density could provide defense against warp-based weapons—inflation charges in particular. Unlike some denser, synthesized materials, kilosteel was chemically and radioactively stable over a wide range of conditions. Perhaps most important was that kilosteel could be viably produced in massive quantities.

Even in the era of the alchemic printer, cost was a factor. The two most common costs that factored into the production of goods were the power spent producing it and the time required to do so. Time, in many cases, was the most important factor given the enormous power-generation capabilities of a nation like the Empire. Every hour spent producing a good for one product was time that same machinery was not producing it for another. A premium existed for any item requiring skilled labor to manufacture. While kilosteel was time-consuming to produce, it was far less so than any of the viable alternatives.

Kilosteel generally began its life in a stellar forge, where matter in the form of hydrogen was drawn from a star and then subjected to alchemic manipulation via the Hyams Effect. When first synthesized, kilosteel existed as a liquid. To construct a warship, this liquid kilosteel was pumped into a reusable, multi-piece mold, where the bond-forging process for the material took place, and it solidified into its finished form. Afterward phase resonators, along with drills and blades of astranium or R-steel, were cut and drilled into the hull to form compartments.

Kilosteel was differentiated by type number, which was simply a chronological progression. Type-1 was the first kilosteel to be produced, with each successive formulation approved for general use assigned a later number. At the time of the Hourglass War, there were three types of kilosteel mentioned and used most: type-41, type-42, and type-44.

Type-41 kilosteel, also known as *ship kilosteel,* was the version used most often for constructing the hulls of warships and military space stations. This material had a density of 1,000.02 grams per cubic centimeter, a melting point of 11.21 GK, a tensile strength of 77.1 PPa, and a compressive strength of 84.4 PPa. To put some perspective to these numbers, kilosteel's melting point of 11.21 GK was approximately 718 times the temperature at the core of Earth's sun. With a heat capacity of 21.1 joules per gram, it not only had a high melting point but also extreme resistance to having its temperature raised. The material's compressive strength was 84.4 PPa, higher than the pressures used to achieve fission in the nuclear weapons of most species. Its tensile strength of 77.1 PPa made it more than 20 million times more resistant to shearing than pure tungsten.

Type-42 kilosteel was denser at 1,207 grams per cubic centimeter, with material properties ranging from 27 to 38 percent higher than that of type-41. Type-42 kilosteel was often referred to as armor-grade kilosteel because it primarily reinforced critical areas of a ship. This includes included the ship's citadel and reactors. Type-42 was more than twice as expensive to produce as type-41. The only power to make warship hulls out of type-42 was the Dominion's Grand Fleet, which built its ships primarily from this grade of kilosteel. Only the Grand Fleet and Solar Armadas could afford such an expense for a single ship, and of the two, only the former was willing.

Type-44 was originally synthesized as part of a project to produce a new kilosteel with properties that mirrored type-42 but at a lower expense. It resulted in a tougher, but also more expensive, product. Up to the Hourglass War, type-44 was used almost exclusively in the construction of ordnance shells for warship guns. Type-44 was easily the densest form of usable kilosteel with a density of 4,400 grams per cubic centimeter and material properties 36 67 percent higher than type-41. Beyond its use in ordnance shells, type-44 was also a component of the field stabilizer arrays used to construct the waveheads of large warships such as battleships and battlecruisers. The only warships to be built from type-44 hulls were the *Prince of Mars* and its sister ships, which came online during the Hourglass War.

No other ships were constructed in this way; even the Dominion could not justify such opulence on further vessels. The benefits were still significant as it allowed *Prince of Mars* ships to have the toughest hulls of any ships in service while having much greater useable volume than its contemporaries. Whereas *H.M.S. Hurricane* was 57 percent kilosteel by volume, *Prince of Mars* was only 25 percent, yet it had the stronger hull.

Kilosteel was rarely used in terrestrial applications due to its weight and density, which could often prove problematic, but there were notable applications, particularly for military purposes. One of the most common ground-based applications was in the form of microkil. Microkil was a microscopically thin layer of kilosteel, often only a few atoms thick, applied as a coating on existing armor, usually bond-forged titanium. In these applications, the kilosteel helped protect against threats such as kinetic weapons, lasers, and the like by virtue of its material properties.

The Solar Empire was the only known power to utilize kilosteel in manufacturing its warships. While the Vaar had successfully synthesized kilosteel in laboratories long before contact with the Empire, it never successfully developed the means to mass produce it. The Combine instead focused on illstas. Illstas, which was used in most Combine warships, was only about one-tenth the density of kilosteel, and while still quite durable, it was brittle in direct comparison.

Illstas had one advantage over kilosteel, that being that on a kilo-for-kilo basis, it required approximately half the energy to manufacture. For a civilization like the Combine with inferior energy harvesting and production capabilities, this benefit greatly aided the Combine's efforts to bring additional ships to battle during the Hourglass War.

# 7F
# NEXT GENERATION PROPULSION

## The Compound and Composite Drives

IN 99,919 AN, THE DOMINION'S Galaxy Staryards Corporation succeeded in building the first prototype ship powered by multiple massless impulse drives operating in parallel. This was a major feat of engineering that GSC and other enterprises had tried countless times before without success. The Solar Armadas was so enamored with the concept that it demanded a functioning craft incorporating this development without delay. A few years later, this prototype manifested in the *Rook*-class reconnaissance sloop. This was easily the fastest true ship ever made. But a much bigger development was on the horizon.

The *Rook* was developed as part of a secret project known as Wingbow. This project hinted at much greater possibilities than the final product. The *Rook* operated with two synchronized rotary drives, which were slaved to each other and to two uni-operation compression drives. This arrangement of two rotaries and two compression drives was known as the 2-in-2 System. While this system worked, it carried many weaknesses. The four linked drives had to be held to an incredible level of synchronicity to function and avoid potentially disastrous results. The precision and complexity of this system made it suitable only for niche applications. Its fragility made it wholly unsuited to something like a true warship which had to be capable of sustaining significant damage while continuing to function.

The next logical step after the 2-in-2 System was to combine the unidirectional compression drives and a rotary drive into a single, unified system. This compound drive, as it came to be known, was not a minor feat of engineering. But modeling of the concept hinted at enormous rewards. The *Rook* and Project Wingbow behind it were Armadas initiatives.

GSC asked its customer if it was willing to wait while the compound drive's potential was explored. But when GSC could not determine how long it would take, the Armadas answered in the negative. Thus the *Rook* went forward with the 2-in-2 System. As the project wrapped up, GSC continued to explore the potential of the compound drive on its own.

In a rare event for such projects, progress came at a much faster rate than anticipated. Further testing by GSC showed that if the compound drive could work, it had the potential to be far faster than the 2-in-2 System the

*Rook* ultimately took to service. As prototypes were tested, the development team realized there was even more potential than they had anticipated.

The compound drive brought two significant developments. The first of these was a dramatic drop in complexity. If two or more drives were placed at the correct distance from each other and activated in the proper sequence, they would self-synchronize. The compression of space-time by the first drive could be co-opted by the second, and any more in the sequence. This forced the additional drives to operate with the same degree of warp as the first drive in the chain. This behavior was not possible with the *Rook*'s 2-in-2 System. Nor was this achievable simply by using multiple compression or rotary drives. The inherent simplicity of this method carried with it great benefit, being orders of magnitude simpler than the 2-in-2 System. With this simplicity came a dramatic drop in complexity and, along with it, fragility.

The second and equally significant development was the production of a warp superwave. Wave forms could merge with and manipulate each other. Once the multiple drives were operating in self-synchronicity, they had a multiplicative effect on the warping of space-time around the ship. This effect had long been predicted but had never been scientifically tested until this point. Due to the highly secret nature of this project, this result was not shared with academia for many years.

The result was a simpler, tougher, and higher-performing means of warp travel. The super field created by the multiple drives had tactical benefits beyond speed. The intensity of warped space-time was as powerful a defense as many shield systems. With working prototypes to show for their work, the development team sent their notes up the chain of command.

The entire development team was swimming in cash and benefits once High King Jonas IV was briefed on the potential. The painfully long development process of the *Prince of Mars* was finally seeing light at the end of the tunnel. But the ship lacked a next-generation propulsion system to round out its arsenal of cutting-edge technology. The compound drive offered a solution to that problem. GSC's development team had never anticipated applying their work to a ship of *that* size, but none involved were about to turn away from the potential rewards of contributing to such a prestigious project. The development of the compound MID and its successful implementation on the *Prince of Mars* marked the beginning of the end for the era of single-MID warships. The *Prince of Mars* left the Valhalla Shipyards in 100,016 propelled by four compound drives.

Though the *Prince of Mars* ended its star trials before the propulsion system could be run to its limits, by that point several new records had been set. The ship was slated to test the unofficial records held by the *Rook* when it was called away to the Battle of the Hourglass. In his messages home to update his father, High Prince Heinz von Rhinegrave made a simple statement that if the raw speed the *Prince of Mars* achieved with its new compound drives did not prove its status as a true technological leap, then nothing would.

The compound drive sounded like a simple evolution of existing systems, but it was much more than that. The appetite for a multi-MID ship had existed as long as the MID itself. That appetite had only been whetted by the *Rook*. But with the successful development of the compound drive, that appetite was fed. Only the immense and gold-plated research infrastructure of Galaxy Staryards Corporation could have taken the idea from genesis to operation so quickly. The first compound MID was an effort involving more than 700,000 scientists and engineers. Thousands of prototypes were built, tested, and blown up in only a few years. Entirely new exotic materials were developed for the drive. New chemicals were developed for lubricants. All in all, more than two thousand new patents were created as byproducts of this effort.

No sooner did GSC have a functioning compound drive than eyes turned toward using it in weaponry. Engineers developed the composite drive out of the compound drive. This involved stripping the drive of everything it did not need if it would only be used once. All avenues for raw performance were maximized as again, the device only had to work once. With most of the work already done in developing the compound drive, work on the composite drive went off simply. The composite drive was incorporated into new weapons that were already in development at the time: the new longwave ordnance shell and the next-generation missile and torpedo systems such as the Arc-7, Radian-1, and Vertex-1.

# 7G
# POWER GENERATION

THE DEMAND FOR POWER was unceasing. For advanced civilizations such as the Solar Empire, these demands could be astronomical in scale. The Empire and few comparable powers used many methods of power generation depending on their needs and applications. To list every single method of power generation used by the Empire, and the various implementations, would be its own encyclopedia. This entry covers a collection of the most common methods.

## Fission Bottle

THE FISSION BOTTLE WAS an extremely common method of power sourcing due to its inherent simplicity. The fission bottle was little more than a core of fissile material contained inside of a Teller or, more likely, Messer-type thermoelectric converter. The Messer converter was a modern evolution of the ancient Teller converter constructed with extensive use of bond-forged materials. Bond-forged materials were excellent insulators of heat and near-perfect electrical insulators. Combined with their strength, they were safe for applications such as these. The density of the material provided radiation shielding while the extreme melting points of such materials made it impossible for the fissile core to melt its way out. The fissile core emitted radiation that heated the inner walls of the converter, and the converter, in turn, produced electricity.

One of the most important elements of the Messer converter, relevant to many forms of power, was the fact that it could perform neutrino capture. This greatly increased the efficiency of these systems by allowing them to tap the energy of neutrinos rather than allowing them to escape the reactor and take energy with them.

Fission bottles were often used as batteries or as primers for larger power devices such as the fission-primed fusion reactor.

# Fission-Primed Fusion Reactor

THE FISSION-PRIMED FUSION reactor (FPF) was one of the simpler and more common methods used by the Empire for generating electrical power. Such devices were ubiquitous and could be found in ground vehicles, providing supplemental power on ships, driving the MID systems of civilian ships, and in a wide host of other applications. These systems were prized for their sustainability and simplicity.

The FPF relied on a first stage composed of a fission bottle. This provided the seed power for the second stage wherein the Hyams Effect was used to compress hydrogen for the generation of power via nuclear fusion. In general the fusion chamber took the form of its own Messer-type reactor. The bulk of the power harvested from the reactor for external use was drawn from the reactor's fusion stage.

FPFs were one of the more ubiquitous forms of power as they were safe, easy to operate, and resistant to damage. There was no worry of an FPF exploding because nuclear fusion required considerable effort to sustain, and any damage to the device resulted in shutdown. Radiation leakage was the only real danger of an FPF, and while not an irrelevant danger, it was generally easy to contend with for any society with the technology to build such a device. The use of dense, bond-forged material was often sufficient.

FPFs could be found in applications ranging from power armor, to ground vehicles, to supplemental power on star ships and stations. On most warships, FPFs served as an emergency power source, ensuring power to systems such as artificial gravity, life support, and thermal regulation.

# MAS Reactor

THE DEMANDS FOR POWER were unyielding and, in many cases, staggering in scale. At the scales of the largest Imperial warships and objects requiring similar power, even xenomatter lost value as a viable fuel source. The volume needed to store it became problematic. In these situations, one entered the domain of the Multiple Active Singularity reactor. This type of system provided the majority of power on Imperial warships, battle stations, and battery worlds, and supplied the immense demands of the unified matrix shielding in fortified stat hives. As its name implied, it relied on artificially created singularities to provide power.

When the public contemplated a singularity—a black hole—the image conjured was one of a behemoth many times the mass of a star. Black holes were a diverse lot and could range from massive to minuscule. It was the *density* of matter, not its quantity, that determined a singularity.

The most critical component of an MAS reactor was what was known as a singularity cell. This device was used to house one or more artificial singularities within as a containment vessel. The Hyams Effect was used to create opposing high- and low-pressure zones of space-time within the cell to keep the imprisoned singularities from contacting the walls of their container or each other. After an initial charge initiated the bottling, the singularities provided the power used to contain them. So long as the singularity cell remained undamaged, containment was as safe as it would ever be. A complete MAS reactor could involve microscopic singularities stacked in their cells to serve as the main source of power.

All ships and stations utilizing MAS reactors incorporated fail-safes designed to detect damaged or defective cells and either re-bottle the singularities or eject them. While there were situations where these systems could fail, such as battle damage, if a ship was so damaged that these systems were offline, there was probably no ship left to save.

MAS reactors used many sizes of singularities ranging from hundreds of thousands to millions of tons. Although even the largest remained microscopic in volume, both their radiation and their angular momentum could be tapped. The amount of the latter could be adjusted based on demand. In both cases, the singularities depleted over time. They could be recharged by feeding them more matter.

By manipulating the space-time around the singularities via the Hyams Effect, the rate at which they decayed, and with it the power they produced, could be raised. This came at the cost of more frequent feeding or replacement of singularities. In many cases a damaged singularity cell was set to overdrive, with the ship storing as much of the power as it could and venting the rest. This provided an option to deal with damaged cells beyond simply ejecting them.

Not every ship had an MAS reactor. Civilian ships with far lower power demands operated on fusion systems. Pickets and smaller ships, which outnumbered true warships, ran on xenomatter. On these ships the MID was a literal engine, annihilating xenomatter to power itself and the rest of the ship. It was only in the warships that the ravenous hunger for power justified the installation of an MAS reactor, or many. The *Hurricane*-class supercruisers operated with sixteen MAS reactors divided among their various systems. The even larger *Prince of Mars* employed thirty-two reactors. All warships with MAS reactors included at least two to provide some redundancy in their power capacity.

Many ships powered their massless impulse drive separately from any MAS reactor on the ship. In these cases, the drive systems were powered by xenomatter reactors during normal operation. This enabled the primary propulsion system and the main power grid to exist isolated from one another, protecting them from each other in case of damage or malfunction. The ship's MAS reactor provided the power the ship required to synthesize additional xenomatter for its warp drive. In other ships, the drive system operated with power supplied from the MAS reactor, and the drive system maintained xenomatter auxiliary generators for emergency use.

MAS reactors had their share of drawbacks and limitations. These devices of enormous technological sophistication were maintenance-intensive, difficult, costly, and time-consuming to build. While Imperial warships could fabricate and replace most of their own onboard systems, repairing or replacing a damaged MAS drive was complicated, compounded by the fact that the ship would be without its main source of power in such a scenario.

If a ship or station utilizing an MAS reactor was destroyed, it could result in the creation of a rogue singularity as those kept in containment escaped and began to merge. It was more inconvenient than insurmountable. The resultant singularities could be moved via gravitational attraction, transpatial relocation, or other methods. The Solar Armadas maintained units dedicated to the task of removing rogue singularities from the sites of space battles. The preferred remedy in this situation was to direct the rogue singularities into an existing black hole.

The MAS was a well-used and understood technology, but fear and ignorance often saw their use limited in certain fields. It was generally forbidden for an MAS reactor to be installed on any planet with a civilian population. The idea of an MAS reactor failing was such a well-worn trope in Imperial fiction that it bordered on cliché. The closest MAS reactor to a civilian population was on the generator platforms of star hives.

The unified matrix shielding that protected hives from hostile warships required far more power than could be tapped from a local star. MAS reactors enabled a hive more power for defense. If a hive platform was destroyed, the imprisoned singularities could consume the remnants of the platform, and they would continue orbiting the local star as would any other object of appropriate mass. Remaining satellites could easily be steered away from it but were generally separated by sufficient distance for this to be unnecessary. Hives using such systems incorporated numerous contingency mechanisms on the off chance that the resultant singularity fell toward the star rather than orbit it.

MAS reactors were also incredibly heavy. In most cases, a fully stocked MAS reactor exceeded the hull mass of the ship carrying it, making them difficult to build, install, and otherwise manipulate when necessary.

The Interstellar Combine possessed the technology for MAS reactors but struggled to manipulate the decay of singularities. Nor could the Combine confine fuel singularities as efficiently. This forced their ships to make extensive use of their primitive form of xenomatter for supplementary power. The *Caustic Reverie* was similar in volume to *H.M.S. Hurricane*, though significantly lighter. Despite having fewer systems to power, at peak output, the ship generally had significantly less power available to its systems than did *Hurricane*.

# Microfusion Cell

MICROFUSION CELLS WERE COMMON sources of power in infantry-grade weapons, power armor, and other applications where a disposable battery was a useful source of power. Microfusion cells were tiny, expendable fusion reactors meant for a finite number of uses. These systems utilized a simple chemical battery to provide the initial electric charge for hyams compression of hydrogen fuel. The thermal converter in which the hydrogen resided converted the resulting heat to electricity, and any waste heat was shunted to a heat sink within the unit.

Most microfusion cells utilized a synthetic form of hydrogen, the most common being 209-octium. This variation on hydrogen contained a single proton, seven neutrons, and synthetic 209 particles in lieu of electrons. The 209 particles were used to stabilize the atom and prevent it from immediately decaying. This variation on hydrogen was used because an atomic nucleus with eight particles had a larger volume than base hydrogen, deuterium, or tritium. This higher volume allowed for more reliable atomic collisions. Similar motivations guided the use of deuterium and tritium in thermonuclear weapons long before humanity was an interstellar power.

Microfusion cells were known for their use in infantry disrupter weapons. A prime example of such a cell was the 12x30mm fusion cell used to power the RA-119 assault rifle. This cell issued five hundred grams of compressed 209-octium, which provided the weapon with enough power for fifty rounds at the RA-117's standard discharge rate.

Under most circumstances, 209-octium and similar fuels were safe. In this state, it burned poorly as it slowly sublimated. If it were exposed to extreme shock, enough to atomize the 209-octium brick, it could become explosively flammable. Such situations were not common but posed enough of a risk for microfusion cells to be kept in shock- and blast-resistant storage.

# 7H

# WARBODIES

THE TERM *WARBODY* WAS bound to cause some argument. There was no agreed-upon definition of what constituted a warbody. The term referred to an individual with an above-average number of cybernetic implants geared toward combat. The threshold where a person moved beyond simply being cyberized had never been codified in law, nor by the regulations of the Empire's military services.

When most people thought of a warbody, they thought of an individual inhabiting a robotic body with little more of their organic tissue than their brain. Such a body was often known as an autobody. This was a condition also known as becoming a total-conversion cyborg. Others defined a warbody as a person whose cybernetics by mass exceeded the mass of biologic matter.

Because there was no true definition of a warbody, this entry will give common examples of entities commonly considered warbodies.

The majority of the Solar Commando Corps' officers utilized the HM-9 autobody when anticipating heavy combat. This was a bipedal robot designed to be operated by an implanted brain rather than an automatech core. The head, torso, and bulk of the limbs were composed of bond-forged titanium with a microkil coating. Critical areas were protected by astranium plates, and the entire unit equipped heavy barrier shielding. The body was equipped with several mounting points for weapons, as well as additional armor and shield systems. The hands and feet were composed of relatively simple limbs sheathed in programmable matter, allowing the hands to morph into simple weapons or tools, while allowing the feet to adopt different configurations depending on the terrain and desired speed of travel. Most commando officers and many of their auxiliaries preferred this autobody when expecting heavy combat, and when they need not worry about compromising disguise.

The Vorhan Tohl, who defended the high king, were an example of "sleeper" warbodies. The best example was found in the kurai members of that organization. The bulk of these kurai were more cybernetics than flesh by mass. Their iron skeletons were bond-forged to greatly enhance their durability. Artificial musculature, ligaments, and tendons were also installed. Most of these kurai incorporated cybereyes rather than biological eyes so that they were never without the sensor capabilities normally found in a combat helmet.

These kurai were also routinely equipped with R-steel dermal armor, providing incredible resistance to penetrating injury whether it be from blade or projectile. All major organs save the brain were replaced with artificial versions capable of operating despite extreme trauma. The most important upgrade was known as the neural magnetic array.

Last these kurai had their skulls replaced with R-steel to provide maximum protection to their brain. These individuals were considered "sleeper" warbodies because, from a visual standpoint, they appeared to be primarily organic.

Unlike the example warbody given prior, the kurai of the Vorhan Tohl also equipped power armor to further enhance their capabilities, and it was where the majority of their 4CM defense was found. The simians and kodaz in the Vorhan Tohl also received extensive augmentation, though it was often less. The bodies of simians and kodaz were less tolerant of cybernetics before it led to neurological problems.

Imperial soldiers could be considered warbodies depending on how far one wished to stretch the definition. Nebulous definitions could be applied to things that should not qualify. However most soldiers considered upgrading beyond the standards mandated by the services to be a prerequisite for a warbody.

Warbodies were not without their disadvantages and special concerns. In the example of transfer to an autobody, most species' bodies did not react well to the absence of their brain. It forced one who wished to return to their body to utilize sophisticated life-support systems in the brain's absence. Or to use means such as a deep-fryer to synthesize a new body each time. Lack of desire to take on such a burden was one reason why the Imperial forces preferred to cyberize living soldiers rather than brain-bottle them all into autobodies.

Cyberization was an issue with many medical concerns. The brain and the body were designed for interoperation with one another. The replacement of biological tissue with cybernetics could have long-standing neurological and psychological effects. Small changes in body chemistry could even affect mood in the short-term and personality in the long-term. Lack of pain denied a person feedback that not only warned them of injury, but it was easy to take risks they otherwise would not with the presence of pain. Sloppy cybernetic design could result in neurological changes, many of which could have marked negative effects.

Cybernetics must be designed with all of these factors in mind and often calibrated to their host to avoid negative effects. Over the eras, the Solar Empire became experts at designing cybernetics so that they did not have negative physical or mental effects on their host.

Cybernetics were a shade easier for the Vaar, as their bodies self-repair repaired and moderation capabilities made the kind of negative effects mentioned above much less of an issue. However the Vaar had many cultural biases related to cybernetic augmentation. The Combine tended to limit cybernetics both in the military and among civilians to those who had an actual need for them. Cybernetics with military applications were limited to military personnel. Juggernauts were a clear case of a Combine warbody.

*Meet author Bryan G. Shewmaker*
*and get updates for forthcoming books*
*in the Solar Winds series!*

www.TheEncephalon.com
www.Facebook.com/SolarWindsSeries